CONTENTS

Principal Characters   *vii*

A World in Ruins   1

Notes   285

Glossary   289

The Translator

Principal Characters

Abayan: Swarna's son with Uthayan.

Anil: an older Sinhala Leftist journalist who befriends Thiravi.

Chella: an elderly widow related to Arasi's late husband Velautham.

Gunananda (named Punchibanda at birth): a fundamentalist Bhuddhist monk obsessed with Swarna, and possibly responsible for her first husband Uthayan's death.

Gunarathnam (Gunam): Velupillai's older son.

Indran: Thambirasa's younger son, whom he now depends on to reverse the family's misfortune.

Kalan: (lit. Time), who is the attendant to the Yaman, the god of death.

Kanaka: a friend of Raji's in the refugee camp in Tamil Nadu.

Kanthsamy Nadaraja: also known as squint-eyed Nadaraja, the 'scarecrow' who betrays Rakini to the military.

Kathirgesu: a teacher and master storyteller from a village in Jaffna, and the father of Prabu. He becomes a member of the executive council of the Tamil Cultural Assembly.

Kulasekaram: the husband of Thavamani, father of Siva, Vasanthi and Param, father-in-law of Mala.

Latchumidevi (Laxo): Pumani's daughter who joins the Movement and is killed.

Leela, Sheila, Mala: Saraswathi's older daughters.

Lek: Nesamalar's neighbour in Bangkok, and a sex worker. Traditionally, Lek is a masculine name.

Mahesh: Thambirasa's older son, who joins the Tigers as a sharpshooter.

Maheswari: a woman from Nainativu, who had moved there with her husband, the late Ponnusamy. She's the mother of Raji, Rajendran and Viji.

Manickavasagar: a social worker in Germany, who helps form the Tamil Cultural Assembly.

Manimekalai: the daughter of Swarna and Thiravi. She is named after the Tamil epic heroine from the Sangam period.

Mathavan: a young man from Trincomalee.

Mathi: an expert forger who works on the stolen or bought passports to smuggle people overseas.

Nagamma: Sankarapillai's wife and mother of Thiravi, Suganthi, Vaani and Nesan.

Nesamalar: a schoolteacher who is left stranded in India by a people trafficker.

Nimal Perera: a friend of Thiravi's, and a former JVP member who was forcibly disappeared by the military.

Ponnusamy: the late sub-postmaster in Nainativu, he was the husband of Maheswari.

Prabu: the son of Karthigesu, an educated young man who becomes a thug during his long separation from his family as he journeys West.

Pumani: Rajanayagam's daughter.

Puvanendran: Rakini's younger brother.

Rajakaruna: runs the pharmacy in the refugee camp in India, and helps train Raji to run the clinic.

Rajalakshmi (Raji): Maheswari's older daughter.

Rajanayagam: a retired Supreme Court Judge who seeks refuge in India after his home and family are ruined by the war.

Rajendran (Rajan): Maheswari's son, now an 'agent' who helps smuggle Tamil people abroad with the help of his crew of forgers and thieves.

Rakini: a friend of Arasi's, and an experimental poet writing about the political situation.

Sankarananda Thero: the senior Buddhist monk at the Nagadipa Vihara.

Sankarapillai: Thiravi's father, a former teacher and politician.

Santhi: Thiravi's sister, who is disappeared and believed to be buried in Semmani.

Saraswathi: Viswalingam's wife, and mother of seven children.

Sellakili: a friend of Rakini's.

Sellathambu: a friend of Ponnusamy's.

Singaravelan/Singari: a thief who steals passports for the people smuggling crew led by Rajendran.

Sinthamani: a young woman who died when the boat she was in capsized in the sea.

Siva: a friend of Suthan and Thiravi's, colludes with the army and unsavoury rebel factions to transport goods into Jaffna.

Siva: a young man with a heart condition who had joined the Movement and been taken out of it by his father Kulasekaram. This Siva is married to Mala.

Sivanthan: Pumani's son who had killed himself following abuse in prison.

Sivasamy: also known as Sivasamithamilan (Tamil Sivasamy), an Indian Tamil self-respect activist who becomes sympathetic to the Movement.

Suntharalingam (Suntharam): a Tamil political activist.

Suthanthiran (Suthan): Suntharam's son.

Swarna: a Sinhala woman married to Uthayan.

Thambirasa: managed the lease on Maheswari's paddyfields, he is desperate for one of his sons to go overseas and return their family to a wealthy position.

Thamilarasi (Arasi): Suntharam's daughter.

Thangamma: the late Ponnusamy's sister.

Thavamani: wife of Kulasekaram and mother of Siva, mother-in-law of Mala.

Thayalan: Suthan's friend in Germany, married to Buvana.

Thiraviyam (Thiravi): Sankarapillai's older son, owner of the cooperative store.

Thisayan (Thisai): a former student of Thiravi's, an activist for the rights of hill country Tamils.

Thiyagu: a man with developmental disabilities, who was betrothed to Sinthamani.

Velayutham: Arasi's husband, a farmer. Killed by the army.

Valambikai: Suntharalingam's wife.

Velupillai: Maheswari's brother.

Vijayalakshmi (Viji): Maheswari's younger daughter, now married and settled in Canada.

Viswalingam: Saraswathi's husband, a man from Nainativu who has a gift for languages.

Vithuran: the child of Nesamalar and Malli, a thug who was expelled from the Movement.

Yogeswaran: Velupillai's younger son, who falls in love with Raji and joins the rebels with her encouragement.

Batch **120536** (North)

From **2-01-01-4-35**

To **4-50-90-1-01**

ISBN **978-1-774151-21-1**

WORLD IN RUINS, A

Ord#	Carton Qty	Move Qty	Move Ctns	Move Units	# of Ords	Pick Qty
	25	2		2	1	2

10/30/2024

1995

1

Kachai, Sri Lanka

THOSE WERE DAYS WHEN all traces of time's passing were lost. If the sun rose, it struggled to set. If the moon appeared, it was too tired to disappear, too lazy to dissolve, even as the night grew darker. The torpor of these markers of time were a sure sign of life's pleasures being eroded away.

In that coastal village the wind shifted, danced, or beat as it always did. Its briny scent was unchanged. The usual, gentle sounds on the northern shore. How loudly the ocean and the strait could roar! Even greater tremors rose beyond. But they were not constant.

For Arasi, day and night had become indistinguishable, apart from the presence or absence of light. She had gone back to Colombo twice for different reasons after sending her mother to India. The journeys had yielded nothing but demanded much effort. The national women's organization for democracy, the Freedom Koels, repeatedly indicated that they could do no more to ease her tormented mind than try and comfort her. The investigation into Rakini's disappearance had caused only a minor stir in the women's groups, smaller political parties, and magazines. The political establishment did not budge.

Her days passed in fatigue and frustration. It seemed the same for everyone around her at the time. Whenever she picked up Rakini's poem, "The Dark Cloud," she became tearful and determined to do something, but then her mind would soon be overcome by exhaustion and grief, hardening into a sense of futility. Rakini's disappearance wasn't her only concern. Their problems were like a field of thorns. Everyday sustenance was just one of these prickly thorns. As early as daybreak some difficulty or other would manifest itself and hover before them.

Just moments after dawn, the day's first problem arose. It wasn't an immediate problem, but merely a sign. Encountering a friend after a long time did not lift her spirits the way it ought to have. That unbroken silence concealed something fearful. "Puvanendi . . . !" Arasi had called out and felt crushed by his silence. "Puvanendi . . . Puvanendi . . . Puvanendran . . . isn't it . . . ?"

He nodded yes. Had he tried to smile? There was no outward sign of it. It was only she who had been excited and chattered. He had stood immobile. He'd turned gaunt but looked hardened. His appearance gave away his training. She was seeing him after five years. She had guessed what might have happened to him. When she considered the fate of his sister Rakini, there was no doubt he would have made the choice he had. She knew they were moving towards an endless horizon. Her happiness at seeing him tore through the amazement and fearful tremor she had felt initially.

"If you keep standing like this . . . ? Come sit here, will you?" she said. She took him by the hand and made him sit on the verandah. It was only then that she noticed two others standing in the lane beyond the fence.

There was no more need for explanations. He had come to inquire about her Colombo trips and her poems. She almost smiled. "Ask them to come inside and sit down too," she said, quelling her apprehension.

He refused. "We . . . we'll go now, akka. We just need some explanation from you on one or two matters."

"Ask."

He told her that her poems were becoming stronger in their opposition to Tamil Eelam: "Akka, we have entered into a continuing war against majoritarianism to win us a homeland for Tamils. In times of war individual rights may suffer much. We can enjoy the full rights of freedom after we gain Tamil Eelam and establish peace. But your poems argue for individual rights even as you stand on revolutionary soil . . . "

"And all this time I had thought they were just ordinary poems . . . "

He tried to smile then and failed. But the attempt brought a tender pleading into his voice. He chose his words carefully as he began to explain: "That's true to some extent, akka. I read your poems myself. Apart from a few, most of your poems don't have a tone of protest. Even those few poems had to be considered only because of your background. Turn this space, darkness, silence into poetry, then no one will ask any questions. But don't write any more poems like 'Told to a Friend.' They raise suspicions against you; it will become necessary to take action."

Was it a warning? Some protestations stirred within her. But she set them aside. She asked another question instead: "Thambi . . . what do you mean my 'background,' that brought these poems to your attention . . . ?"

He said: "You know the World Tamil Cultural Assembly—have you heard of it?"

"Mm. I've seen something in the papers. People who left here and went abroad have started something and are running it . . . "

"Some of our people started it in Germany. There's a branch

in France. Your brother who lives there has an active role in it. The Assembly's political leanings are not clear yet. But it's clear from the outset that they won't align with us. In this situation, the allusions in your poems . . . the silences . . . these aren't going to escape attention, akka . . . "

How beautifully he called her akka. It felt sweet to her heart. But he was here to cripple the wings of her poems. Her husband was dead. Her father, mother, brother, all had left her behind. Her friend and relative Raji had been carried away by a wave somehow and was stranded somewhere. Another friend Rakini . . . she was lost. In this state, only her poems gave meaning to her life. And he was telling her to stop writing them. She could not ignore the fact that he had framed his inquiry as a conversation with someone who knew her and appreciated her. Though he had used a few words of warning, she thought he had still behaved gently. She saw it clearly in his not bringing in the two boys who had come along as his armed guard.

There was nothing more for him to say and he stood up. "Do you understand us clearly, akka?" he asked.

As she nodded her head, smiling, he turned to leave.

He had only taken two steps before he turned back to her and asked: "Akka, have you had any news from amma . . . since she left for India to find aiyya?"

"No," she replied.

It pleased her that he had asked.

He walked away.

2

Kachai, Sri Lanka

PUVANENDI'S VISIT THAT MORNING left her feeling listless the rest of the day. Though she had much to get done, she found herself unable to move.

She had sent him away with an answer that wouldn't aggravate the problem. But it was only a small fraction of what she felt. Not even a tenth of the emotions that erupted and swirled within her found their way into poetry. And of those, she only sent a few to the magazines. Even when they were published, she thought no more of it than that her feelings had been documented some-where. But now she understood that they stirred a few people. That was the higher aim of creativity. It was a good thing.

Grandmother Chella arrived then.

"Come in, aacchi."

The old woman sat on the verandah. "I kept thinking you'd come. No sign of you. So, I thought I'll come see you, and I set out this morning," she said. "Never mind, have there been any letters from amma? Has she found Suntharam? Why the delay? Is she planning to stay there?"

"I don't know anything myself, aacchi. I worry about it from sunrise to sunset. It's been a year and a half since amma left . . . not even one letter. Did she find aiyya . . . or not . . . did she got to Mr Viswalingam's place . . . or did she lose the address and is wandering around? Or did she send a letter and it has just not reached here? What am I to think, aacchi?" Arasi unburdened all her fears.

Hearing the kettle whistle, she hurried inside to make the tea. As they sat drinking it, they continued their conversation. "Everyone agrees that the letter must have not reached here, just as you said," Chella went on. "There's a way to get your mail without losing it now."

"What is that?"

"If you tell them to send letters to someone you know in Colombo, you won't have any trouble. The only problem is that you have to get them through people who travel back and forth to Colombo."

Arasi thought that sounded like a good plan.

"People who have families abroad are getting money sent to them this way," Chella continued. "I asked Mr Sivakoluntham for the address of some people he knows, and I've brought it with me. The problem is . . . how will I get the money. Why, child, you yourself have gone to Colombo two or three times. Will you need to go again sometime in the next few months?"

"Why would I need to go to Colombo, aacchi?"

"Why, your brother is abroad, isn't he? He must be sending you some money here and there?"

"No one sends me anything. If I eat, it's by my own hand . . . " Arasi laughed.

"So what? If you want to inquire about your mother you have to go to Colombo, don't you? What will you accomplish sitting around here?"

"You're right. But do you just go and come for free? The trip costs a lot of money."

Chella knew about her life. She thought her strange and unreasonable. Why else would she still be here when her in-laws had left the place, why had she turned down their offer to take her? They had left saying they couldn't bear being reminded of their son over and over. She had stayed back so she could keep remembering.

The old woman was easily overcome by pity. She understood the sorrow in a widow's life. "I know a few people who go back and forth to Colombo. But . . . it's a money matter, isn't it? Who knows what's in people's hearts? I have to think twice. If it was you, I wouldn't be afraid. Mm. If we don't have the means, what can we do?"

Arasi's heart melted. "Okay, aacchi. If there's any reason for me to go to Colombo in a hurry, I won't leave without telling you."

Chella was content with that.

She stood up. "All right, I'll see you again, child. If you get hold of a bicycle, come by and visit me. I'll give you a Colombo address."

Arasi had a few addresses herself, but she agreed all the same.

Later that night, in her distress Arasi found herself unable to sleep. It was close to ten o'clock and the lack of human activity had left the place in utter silence. The breeze blew gently. The summer heat pervaded everything. Her skin felt clammy. It was too late to go wash. She looked for a place in the front yard where she could sit in the sand beside the fence. She felt for a box of matches in the pocket of her dressing gown, and her fingers closed around it. There was an unlit lantern along the inner wall of the verandah.

She could see the flicker of a lamp beyond the barbed wire of her neighbour's fence. Then it went out.

She recalled Chella aacchi. She didn't even think about Puvanendi, whom she had seen after five years, and who had grown so fierce.

Chella had caused a crack that let some light into her heart. Arasi had not thought in that direction at all. She had stayed immobile all this time, staring at one spot, feeling like she had lost everything by a curse. And she had made no attempt at all to try to get word from her mother . . . Mala . . . her mother-in-law . . . anyone.

Chella was a sign of the times. At one time everyone complained that people were running, fleeing the country. Now it seemed to Arasi that the complaint had eased off. Many of the families she knew had fled. Some had failed in the attempt and had lost their money in Colombo or failed to get their money when they returned. She knew how they had suffered after their frenzied attempts. It had all quietened down now. But Arasi knew the frenzy had changed shape and turned into something else.

She couldn't get all worked up over it as she had done in the past. One way or another, she had become used to the clamour of a few people in the community. Hadn't they all become used to the war?

Suddenly, there was a flash, like lightning towards the north. It looked like moonlight on fire. Then she saw that it was neither moonlight nor fire. The Elephant Pass Army Camp was in that direction. The Tigers had attempted many times to capture the military camp that held such strategic advantage in the north. Their operations had names like Frog Leap*. Whether with small or large losses, they had always ended up escaping. Was this yet another attempt? Was the army firing flare rockets overhead to reveal the hiding places of their enemy?

Her thoughts returned to her mother.

What had happened to her? What had happened to aiyya? What could she do, where she was? She didn't have a husband to help her. There was no urgent need for such protection where she lived. The man wearing black who had roamed around menacing the Paranthan, Kilinochchi, Elephant Pass, and Mirusuvil areas had been shot and killed the previous year, or the year before. She heard that he had been tied to an electrical pole and shot. Now they had no fears of that kind. But a woman without her husband was still half a woman.

Amma had lived a sheltered life. The expanse of Nainativu had been the full extent of her travels. If she hadn't met with aiyya in India . . . Arasi began to shiver thinking in what state amma might be.

Arasi decided she must write a letter quickly.

3

Kachai, Sri Lanka

ONE DAY, SOON AFTER Arasi had sent off the letter, she thought, why not visit Nainativu. There were lots of people there to whom she could speak about her parents, and even Suthan. She might find it hard to answer their questions. What of it? There was no use hiding from them. Her experiences had taught her that it was better to face things than to hide from them.

The next Friday morning she set off for the island. At a time of such uncertainty, it was best to seize the opportunity to do any traveling she needed to get things done. They had all grown accustomed to this pragmatic approach. By the time she had traveled by van from Kodikamam to Jaffna, got on another van to Kurikadduwan, and boarded the ferry for Nainativu, the sun was submerging in the western sea. It used to be a three- or four-hour journey. Had the hundreds upon hundreds of the dead who had fallen between these places become the obstacles slowing down what once was a quick journey?

When she stepped out onto the Temple jetty, her heart cried out, "Ammale!" The agitation and fear locked up in her heart flew through the entrance of the tower and toward the inner sanctum.

Death was nothing new. How many deaths had she seen in the past few years! They weren't merely deaths, they were murders. Bombed, shattered by mines . . . so many young people dead. Her heart pounded even as the sea water splashed on her during the short ferry trip. Even as she told herself she could get used to anything, the panic she felt now told her that she was not used to it yet.

She knelt at the Amman shrine and worshipped with her forehead touching the ground. Her eyes closed, she stood by the closed door of the inner sanctum and prayed. How to understand the cruelties of a time when it became difficult to tell the difference between kunkumam and splattered blood? It was because he understood what was happening that aiyya had kept murmuring about pacifism in spite of their losses and distrust. Time blown apart! Relatives lost . . . separated . . . when would it ever return to normal?

When she turned around, having taken time with her prayers, she saw the priest in the front yard. There was still time before they opened the doors for the evening worship. She took some kunkumam and holy ash from a hollow in one of the inner pillars, smeared it on her forehead and prepared to leave.

She hadn't met this priest before. But something about him struck her as familiar.

"Where's the priest who used to be here?" She approached him and asked.

"It's been about two years since . . . he passed away."

"Oh . . . !"

That meant it had been at least two years since she had come to the island or the temple.

"I'm his son," the young priest explained. "I was serving at the Mari Amman Kovil in Kotahena. After appa died, they asked me to come here, so I came."

She smiled faintly and appeared to listen. She understood why his appearance had drawn her attention. The green-edged verty above his ankles was perhaps six feet long. He had a red silk sash tied at the hip. They both looked two or three years old. Who knew what the priest's livelihood would be, here? His poosai offerings seemed a great sacrifice in her mind. He could have received all kinds of donations in Kotahena. The devotees crowded into Mari Amman Kovil, even now. But Naina's Nagammaal lives under the cloud of war. The island was becoming deserted. The devotees rarely gathered here. Yet somehow, she felt that Amman would take care of her priest, and it reassured her.

It was Nainativu. And yet it was not. At one time she had known every face here. Now not one seemed familiar. She thought that she must go and see the condition of Raji's house, even if only from the outside.

Arasi had heard that life on this island would never turn to ash and fold, even under the kind of hardship that forced you to avert your gaze. Raji had even said so. That claim seemed to need some proof to sustain it now.

The birds flew on overhead. The coconut and palm rustled and danced. The waves threw up their screens of foam and danced on the shores. An old dugout that had been dragged ashore ages ago, had decayed even further. It didn't seem that the people up and about here had any faith in their future. More importantly, she couldn't see any consciousness of a future in them. The primary aim of the human species was to survive. Labour was a different matter. But somehow its primary aim had gone astray. Loss of faith in the future was the biggest tragedy in human history.

She passed the teacher Sankarapillai's house along the way. The entrance was chained and padlocked. The rooftiles of the cooperative store by the fence were cracked and some had fallen off. The teacher's front porch used to gleam in the mornings. It was now covered in dry fallen leaves. It was only then that she fully grasped what destruction was. The teacher could have died. Or he could have been united with his wife and children in Ariyaalai.

She had met him when she had come back more than two years ago. He had told her about Thiyagu going missing. It was he who had told her about the tragedy that had befallen Thiravi's family, as tears streamed down his face. The man who gave her news about the island was not there anymore. Who could she go to for news about him? What had happened to Thiravi?

She did not tarry near Raji's house. One of the frangipani trees in the front yard had bent over in a long-ago storm and now leaned on the wall. There was no other sign of damage.

She walked briskly through the paddy fields behind the houses and reached her neighbourhood as dusk was falling. Kanthasamy appa had been stretching his legs in a leisurely stroll down the street. She walked along with him. She could see her house even from where they stood. The fence was destroyed, but the house looked fine, and the roof seemed to have held up. Even the kitchen seemed to have withstood the destruction of time.

She had planned to stay there that night. If she found something, she would eat, or she would fill her stomach with the cool of the well water and go to sleep. She had come expecting all this. No one thought of heading anywhere and returning home the same day anymore.

Kanthasamy shared his dinner with her. But not before wringing half the life out of her with his questions about Suntharalingam and Valambikai.

She slept on the porch. Kanthasamy slept on a coir cot in the front yard.

They talked for a long time before they fell asleep.

He mentioned that Maheswari's brother Veluppillai had fallen into a well and drowned and was dead a few days before anyone discovered him. "It was good that he died. A man can live with injury or disease. But when his mind turns, it's better for him to die."

"There are many people who seem to be suffering from mental health problems now, Kanthasamy appa."

"That's what I've heard too. In the old days they could take them to Moolaai. They could have them seen at Manthikai. Naya nmaarkaadu . . . Nallur . . . you know they could take them there and heal them then. Now . . . ?"

"Do you remember someone called Dr Nadarasa . . . ?"

"That was then. Who knows . . . who's still here now, or where they are?"

"There was someone like that in our area who became paranoid. They had him sent to Angoda through the Red Cross."

"Oh . . . they have things like that now? How does the sufferer know? The trouble is for the people around them. Velupillai suddenly went missing one day. Who was going to go look for him? They said one of his sons used to drop by occasionally, take care of him and go off. The boy came after he had been missing for a few days. There was no one at home when he came. He smelled something bad near the corner of the yard where the well was and when he went to see what it was, the body was rotting in the well. The boy is a tough fellow all right. He cut down two old portia trees in their garden . . . stacked up the wood near the corner where the toilet is . . . took the corpse to the pyre and cremated him before he left . . . House . . . garden . . . the whole town is a cremation ground now, child!"

"Hm." Arasi was submerged in her thoughts. Then, "What is Sellathambu doing, appa?" she asked.

"He went to Canada, didn't he."

"Oh . . ."

"Yes, it's been a year now since he left. The whole family went.

Sold off everything at half its worth and left in a hurry."

"Mhmm," Arasi responded in disgust. "So, you say there are still people left who can buy these things."

Kanthasamy said nothing in reply. They were both silent for a long time, deep in their thoughts. When she emerged from her thoughts and called out to ask him something, he was fast asleep.

From where she lay on the porch, she could see the sky. The same sky, the same stars, the same clouds, the same cool salt-spraying breeze; the night birds sang the same songs, there was the same distant roar of the ocean. It's only people who change. Nature doesn't. Life within nature doesn't change.,

"There are people left who can buy these things," she had said and thought about Kanthasamy not replying to that. He must have wondered if that was true. He must have fallen asleep wondering. Arasi asked herself, "There are people who can buy anything. What does that mean?"

It seemed to stretch out before her as a confirmation that life would continue on that soil.

Then she thought of Raji.

The girl had been adamant that she wouldn't leave. They had compelled her to go, almost as if they had grabbed her by the neck and thrown her out.

Thoughts kept drifting through Arasi's mind.

4

WHEN THE SUN RAISED its head in Chennai the clouds of dust rose as well. As the heat rose during the day, the dust grew thicker in the breeze, and ultimately would begin to settle over everything. The rays of sun that penetrated through the layer of dust would singe your back like an electric wire. Your skin would burn. As the exhaust from the vehicles mingled with the dust, the air became suffocating. The suffocation was doubled for those who had to walk along the streets in the afternoon. This must be experienced to be understood.

There were two chairs on the balcony with the weave unraveled on their backs. Sivabalan was seated on one of them. He kept his gaze directed on the setting sun. It was as fixed as though he were searching for a star to give him direction. Soon a star began to glitter in the distance. How far beliefs had travelled. The space between life and humans had stretched out too.

Even after all the loss and argument, why was there still turmoil in the family? As he thought about it, his mind felt like it was exploding. The future was a looming question mark.

Mala had come halfway up the steps and had sat where he

could see her, with her back turned to him. She was sunk as deep in thought as he was. She too was caught up in loss and confusion. She was thinking about the causes of turmoil in the family, while reeling from the distress it was causing her.

It was four years since they had got married. They had experienced so much in that time. Encountered so many obstacles. But there was more to come. It often felt to him that their love was tinged with bitterness. He was now living permanently in Mala's house. He was sensing a growing indifference to him now, as if it didn't matter if the broom brushed against him, since he had married into the house. But there was a feeling of resentment towards the father of the house. There was no need to hustle for rent or food. Sheila was sending them money. But the family had grown dysfunctional . . . its calm had deteriorated . . . grown turbulent. Each person an island unto themself. Each interacted with the other islands only when necessary. They hid their tears; their smiles were feigned . . . was this a life? He felt desperate sometimes to run away from it all. But where could he go? What could he do? In this state of confusion, he felt he might as well give up. The evening came with a threat. He didn't know if he should sleep or stay awake, and nighttime made him fearful. But he needed to think through things. Everyone does. Time threatens you with this fate, in different forms, in different shapes. Siva too had thought back over the past four years.

During the marriage talks, the two families had easily come to an agreement on the dowry. It was becoming the norm at that time. The details of the agreement were that within a year of marriage Siva must be sent to France, the bride's family taking care of all the expenses related to the wedding. The wedding took place as soon as they received Sheila's consent. Siva would never forget the days they had waited for that consent. He was amazed to think that even after they had got her parents' consent, they still had to wait for Mala's younger sister, who had the power to decide whether the wedding would move forward. He could understand it from an economic standpoint. But those days became unbearable as his dream and his longing grew. It was only as time passed that he realized that the marriage wasn't for love, but for a means to escape abroad.

A few months after his marriage, Siva visited a friend in Thanjavur and stayed over. He was arrested by the police, who had unexpectedly come to search the house. It took more than a week for the news to reach Chennai. Everyone was sympathetic. But they hesitated to do anything. Saraswathi had grown a little afraid too. Would they get Siva's address in Chennai and come to question her young son Senan, or even arrest and harass him? Finally, it was Viswalingam who went to Thanjavur, made enquiries and arranged for the money they needed and had him released. Siva's parents did not lift a finger.

Two months after his release, Kulasekaram and his wife raised the issue "You people said you would send Siva to France within a year of the wedding, now it's been eight months. There don't seem to be any arrangements being made."

"When he got arrested in Thanjavur, you kept quiet as if to tell us we could do what we liked. So why don't you stay quiet now?" Mala had retorted. This caused a rift between the families, and they visited each other less and less. The relationships between the children grew strained as well. Siva had a younger brother Param. His family had planned that Siva go overseas and then call Param over. Param, who had boasted that anna would go abroad and call him within six months, became more and more frustrated. Seeing Viswalingam on the street one day, he held nothing back shouting at him. Viswalingam was deeply hurt and went straight to Kulasekaram to complain about his son. Though Kulasekaram was secretly pleased at the incident, he summoned Param and

disciplined him; Viswalingam went away appeased. Before the
quarrel bubbling between the two families could overflow, Sheila
planned for Siva's trip through an agent. Siva's journey began
in the hectic travel period between Christmas and New Year in
December '93. Param accompanied him to Bombay to send him
off. The journey ended abruptly in Delhi. Siva's fake passport and
forged visas had come under scrutiny and been discovered, and
he was arrested. That was around the time the Jain Commission
investigating Rajiv Gandhi's assassination had picked up steam.
The country was in a state of agitation. As soon as Siva was appre-
hended, the agent disappeared, and it seemed that there was no
way to have him released. It was like a bull stomping on a man
who'd fallen off a palmyra tree. Mala had to trouble Sheila again for
help. They had spent more than three hundred thousand already.
But it wasn't going to be enough. Once again it was Viswalingam
who used the money Sheila sent, traveling back and forth to Delhi
for two and a half months to procure Siva's release on bail.

How those months refused to go away from his memory! The
shame and suffering affected him physically, and he wasted away
to skin and bone. It seemed even his bones could grow frail. A
kind of heat took hold in his chest, with oozing and dripping.
Even Thavamani, his mother, burst out at him once "I could have
given birth to a stone pestle instead of you, and it would have
been more useful. You were born sickly, and now . . . plagued with
bad luck."

He felt beaten even at home. His heart shrank under Saraswathi's
gaze. He had been caught by the police twice now. She didn't want
this taint to fall on her own son's future. He understood her anxiety, but it didn't lessen his resentment. His helplessness drove a
wedge between him and Mala too. Though he couldn't say what
exactly the cause was. Even when he felt less estranged from her,
the bitterness seemed to linger, tainting everything in the end.

The house was now known as Mala's house even though Viswalingam still lived. Saraswathi was alive . . . even Siva. It was Saraswathi who had managed the household thus far, but she had lost control over it recently. She had changed, as though deliberately. She went along with the tide. She buttressed Mala's control by submitting to it. There was no other way. Her worries about the country, land, house, all of that was stuck in the past. She reasoned that they could buy a house for what they were spending on rent now; the idea of profit had entered her mind. As soon as Mala's problems were sorted, they could send Senan to France, or another European country; and if the desire to continue sending people overseas took hold of her, who could blame her? Many were doing the same. She had to think about her children. It had been a few years since Poobathy had come of age. Thulasi, the next one, was rapidly growing to that age too. Sheila was more beautiful than Mala. Poobathy was even more beautiful than Sheila. Didn't Poobathy have dreams of her own? Saraswathi had the duty to consider this and act responsibly. And so she raged; she shouted.

Back in the village, if she had called out from the house you would not hear her at the gate. She had been so softspoken. Now when she raised her voice the neighbours could hear her. Time had wrought this change in her. As the years added up, so much was eroded away. Each was fated to change in different ways. It was only time's capacity to change that remained unchanged.

It had grown late. They could eat and go to bed now.

Mala turned and looked at him. Siva still sat with his back to her, staring into the distance.

"Siva!"

He turned.

"Come, let's eat."

He stood up in silence.

5

Chennai, India

VISWALINGAM HAD RETURNED HOME that day. He had left four days ago early in the morning, and returned just as the household was preparing to sleep. No one knew where he went, or what he did for his food and other expenses. No one cared. Care could only arise in hearts that felt love. That house . . . it was like a refugee camp. Everyone was alone there. Each had their own purposes. Each orbited within their own boundary. As long as the orbits continued in their paths, there would be no collisions. They all understood that.

They were all eating in silence, watching TV when he arrived. There was a small clothesline on the verandah, it stayed there rain or shine. There was an old trunk below it. This was all he had. When he got to the verandah, he called Poobathy, told her he had eaten already and went down to the well. There was a bathroom, but he had never found it as convenient as the well. He washed his upper body and came back. He pulled out a mat and pillow that had been rolled up in a corner of the room and went up to the balcony. He didn't attempt to see or speak to anybody. It was only when he bumped into Siva that he smiled faintly, like an outsider.

It was pleasant on the balcony. Stars glittering in the black sky. The coconut tree across the street rustled in the wind. The asoka and vembu trees whispered. Viswalingam spread out his mat and lay down. He ached all over. His knees, his ankles, his shoulder blades, his elbows, all hurt. His joints felt like they would snap. He had been travelling a lot. He felt that if he stopped, he would stop moving altogether. He could not bear to be here if he couldn't move. It was not the home he had thought it would be. They were not the people he had thought they were. You couldn't say that they didn't know that he travelled and was working. Yet . . . not a word of comfort, no loving conversation. They didn't even approach him for their needs. He would come forward himself and take care of a few things. From the way he mumbled to himself, "This is all for my past sins, I must finish paying for them in this lifetime," it was obvious how his spirit had shrunk.

Back when he had worked in the restaurant in Colombo, he would only go back home once or twice a year. Because he worked standing up all day until the veins in his legs stood out swollen, Saraswathi would take his feet on her lap and massage them. He would pull his feet away, saying, "That's enough, that's enough." She would tuck a betel leaf with tobacco into a side of her mouth, smile lovingly at him, and hold tight onto his legs. Now his feet were dry, the skin cracked. His toenails had become thick and dark and refused to grow. It was those feet she had held onto so lovingly . . . So deep was her love for him. The slightest brush of her tender breasts and he was aroused in an instant. She was as passionate as he was. She had never been betrayed. Nor had she betrayed him.

There had been around a dozen men rooming in the house where he stayed when he went to Colombo. They would stay up until ten or twelve in ribald talk, laughing. There were some who would run off on Saturdays and Sundays to Maradana and Fort

where the Sinhalese sex workers plied their trade. He felt his flesh
stir when he overheard their raw and ribald talk. But he stayed
firm. He was a disciplined man. She knew it too. He was skilled
in the art of love. But he only practiced his art with her. And
now . . . ? He had grown old beyond his years, and asthmatic. She
had lost herself in her family. But the needs of a wife, or a husband
extend beyond the physical to the realm of compassion. If that is
not understood . . . even a stray word can burn you with its fire.
He had been burned. Many times. But it was being shunned that
hurt him the most. When and why was he shunned?

It happened when his ability to support his family was taken
out of his hands. Sheila's fury . . . Mala's rage . . . all bore witness
to it. When the source of income shifted . . . Saraswathi rejected
him too. What value did he hold in the household anymore? He
was treated with disgust, as if he were no more than a blade of
grass . . . a worm.

He didn't try to sever his relationship with them even then. He
simply became another family within the same house.

He shrank and shrank away . . .

They pushed and pushed . . .

He was too tired to even think that day. But there was something else that had weighed on him over the past few days, heavier
than the stress he felt when he got home. Those thoughts defeated
his fatigue and preyed on his mind.

His back began to sweat from the warmth of the cement floor
beneath his mat. He leaned to a side so the breeze could cool him.

He had returned from Rameswaram that morning. He had
gone there on someone else's matter. But he had returned with
worries and concerns of his own.

He had gone to Rameswaram four days before, rented a room in
a lodge there and left the next morning for the Mandapam refugee
camp. The anxiety brought about by Rajiv Gandhi's assassination

had diminished by then. But since there was a court inquiry going on, new arrivals to the refugee camps and all activities along the coast had come under intense scrutiny. There was fear in the country that the Tigers would break the accused out of prison. Some such events had occurred in the past. But Viswalingam didn't have to worry about such problems as he wasn't easily identifiable as a Lankan. Many mistook him for a local, based on his appearance. His verty, short-sleeved shirt, his hair slicked back with oil, a yellow cloth bag from the temple in his hands, his mouth full of betel . . . He had the knack of quickly capturing the essence of pronunciation in a language. When he lived in Colombo, he learned to speak Sinhala as fluently as any Sinhalese, though he could not read a word in the language. It was what had saved him during the pogroms.

He had reached the threshold of death and been saved by a trick.

It was July of '83. Colombo was burning. Howls from atrocities rang around him. Fires raged, bodies and objects blackened to ash. He had crouched along the edges, watching, and hiding in darkness as he tried to make his way home. He suddenly found himself face to face with a mob, with no means to escape. Armed with knives, crowbars, and all manner of axes, they loomed terrifyingly over him. He thought his time was up. He even said a prayer to Nagapooshani. That was when the thought sprung in his mind . . . he could swear as well as any of them. He raged. "Kill those Tamils . . . rape their women . . . smash their children . . . Tamil dogs . . . ! Over there . . . they ran that way . . . !" The mob ran in the direction he pointed.

It took a while for him to come back to himself. But he returned home with a heaviness that he carried with him to the refugee camp. He had boarded a ship for India as soon as he could.

He was quick to adapt to the local idioms when he arrived.

He could just as easily sound as if he were from Madurai as from Tirunelveli or Coimbatore. You could say that he hid himself behind those mannerisms and dialects as he travelled.

His reason for going on to Rameswaram was so he could transport a young man called Manoharan from the Mandapam refugee camp to Chennai. He had been to many of the camps many times, with the purpose of reuniting refugees in the camp with their relatives living outside, or to assist them in going abroad. He had been to Mandapam too. He even had a few friends there. That was how he had become friendly with Nada.

He had gone to the camp that morning and was chatting with Nada when he suddenly heard about Suntharalingam's wife.

"Suntharalingam's wife? Which Suntharalingam?" he had queried.

"From Nainativu, apparently. They said if you mention Suntharalingam from the Party, people will know right away."

"He was known throughout the north at one time. Now . . . I heard he's living somewhere in Tamil Nadu."

"He passed away; didn't you know?"

"Oh God!" Viswalingam was taken aback.

"Yes, anna. Even his wife didn't know he had died. She had come here because she hadn't heard from the man for two or three years after he came to India. She had brought the addresses of a couple of people she knew here. But she had misplaced them during the journey . . . and she ended up here . . . "

"Then?"

"You know Ganesalingam in Madurai, he's a distant relative of my wife's. Occasionally they exchange letters. My wife had mentioned something in her letters, and the next week Ganesalingam and Suntharalingam's daughter-in-law, the one they say has been here a long time, came running."

"So, Suntharalingam's wife is in Madurai now?"

"I think so."

More than Suntharalingam's death, Viswalingam felt that his wife finding out about it only after she arrived was the bigger tragedy.

Death is cruel. Those left behind were to be pitied. But these tragedies kept following one upon another, each engulfing the other. Today's loss, death, and pity overwhelms yesterdays. All that was left was to visit her and offer his condolences as someone from her hometown.

He had done what he set out to do that day. He had taken Manoharan to his relatives in Chennai and received the payment for his troubles. He thought he would rest the next day and go to Madurai the day after.

It was a while before his tired and aching body allowed him to asleep.

6

Madurai, India

IN MADURAI, THE MAN who knew where Ganesalingam lived could not tell him the exact address. When Viswalingam asked, the man could only give him directions. When he got on the bus that morning Viswalingam had cursed himself for not getting Ganesalingam's address from Nada in his rush to leave Mandapam camp with Manoharan.

The city was just beginning to stir from its slumber when Viswalingam alighted from the bus in Madurai. They say that great cities never sleep. That was true, in a way. A few travelers, a man running a teashop, a couple of bicycles, autorickshaws, and Jutcars stayed away in the city. It was also the time when a sex worker in some corner stirred the last sighs of pleasure from her client of the previous night with her tricks.

Viswalingam drank a cup of tea to wake up his body and began to walk. He had been to Madurai many times. The streets had grown familiar to him. He walked along a deserted street.

He reached the Vaikai River bridge. He had to pass it and take the first street on the left. "If there's a water tank on the street, don't think twice, just keep walking until you get to the street that intersects with it. Then . . . straight across you should easily spot the house with the green gate. If you ask for Ganesalingam . . . the guy from Ceylon . . . anyone should be able to tell you which house it is," the man had said.

As the dogs were unusually quiet, he walked along the street with the water tank and drifted onto the street that intersected with it, and just like a miracle the house with the green gate appeared before him.

Only Valambikai was awake at the time. She was seated on the steps outside, looking out at the street.

He approached the gate. As she looked up, her face seemed to ask, "Who is this?" She didn't need to speak the words. She stayed silent because she had felt a flicker of recognition.

"Ganesalingam's house . . . ?" he ventured.

"This is it."

Once it was confirmed he stopped and asked, "Do you recognize me?" "From Nainativu. Viswalingam . . . "

It took her a few seconds to recall, "Oh . . . oh . . . I know," she said. "You're Mala's father, aren't you?"

"Yes, yes."

"Come in."

He walked in and sat on a corner of the wide steps to the house.

"I had brought your address as well when I came here. Lost it all on the way . . . "

He had been a little hesitant to see her. But as she began to speak easily, he forgot all about it. "I had gone to Mandapam camp a few days ago. I only learned about you by coincidence."

"I stayed in the Mandapam camp a few days . . . "

"They told me."

"You have been here a long time, haven't you?" She stuck to small talk.

"I came here during the riots of eighty-three. My woman and

kids came here in eighty-five."

He had never been an expansive talker. Now with grief working in his heart, it took some effort to get the words out. He managed to come straight to the point: "I only heard about Suntharam at the Mandapam. I couldn't believe things like this could happen. It has been so long, nothing about it was mentioned in the newspapers."

It was only then that Valambikai understood what he had come to say. That he had come not to see Ganesalingam, but her.

Her grief had diminished so much by then. Though it still was grief. The dormant thing began to rumble and rise.

He continued: "I hadn't been close friends with him and come to his house. We used to greet each other and make small talk only. Yet I was very sorry to hear that he was gone. A man you couldn't easily forget if you got to know him. Whenever he went to Colombo and passed by Kotahena, he was the only person who came inquire how I was doing. What an ending for a man like that . . . ?"

Back home even the young and infants were dying. Suntharam had lived his life and was an elderly man. So, it was possible to bear his death without being shaken by it. But to be away from his hometown, his country and die in this place; that would sadden anyone. Viswalingam went on: "How . . . suddenly?"

"Some heart problem."

"Tcha!" Viswalingam sighed. "There are so many medical advances now. They've discovered all kinds of new medicines. If it's not working . . . they do heart transplants now. In spite of all that, they couldn't save him!"

"I have been plagued by that question all these days. Still, would you believe it, anna. When he was in hospital, Raji had come there on some other work and seen him. She stayed with him and took care of all his matters. What do I say about that, anna?"

"Raji stayed and took care of him?"

"That child has lost so much and is now living in a camp. Still, she raised forty thousand rupees and had a pacemaker put in for him . . . and is still broken up because she couldn't understand what happened to her maama. It's all so sad to think about. But there is some consolation in all of this," Valambikai said.

"True. God doesn't leave anyone to die entirely alone and abandoned," Viswasalingam said.

"As if all she has done weren't enough, Raji comes to see me often. I am indebted to so many people. How am I going to ever repay all this?"

Just then Ganesalingam opened the door to the hallway and stepped outside. Valambikai introduced Viswalingam to him.

The three of them sat in the verandah talking. Ganesalingam's wife brought them some tea shortly. Viswalingam drank it and prepared to leave. Ganesalingam would not let him leave. Neither would Valambikai.

He rested a while after lunch and left saying he needed to see someone. He came back around eight, saying he had booked a seat on the ten o' clock bus to Chennai. He hurriedly unhooked the cloth bag he had left behind, hanging on a nail.

"Thiyagu is in the Trichy camp now. Did you know?" Valambikai said.

"Who—our Thiyagu? When did he come? How did he come . . . ?"

"You won't believe me when I tell you," Ganesalingam said, laughing. "Everyone else comes by boat . . . comes by plane . . . this fellow swam here."

"What? The rascal!" Viswalingam was astounded. "How is he?"

"He's well," Valambikai told him.

"Hm . . . " he began and was silent. Then he said to them, "If all goes well . . . in a while we'll all be able to go back home . . . "

Ganesalingam replied immediately, not bothering to hide his

discontent and disagreement. "Peace will not come to Sri Lanka just because two people agree and sign something. The war is happening in people's hearts—in every single one. The conditions for it have become rigid. There must be some fundamental change. Or else peace is just talk."

"That's true. It's not that I haven't considered that. We have lost so many lives, possessions, livelihoods . . . so much. Enough . . . this is enough. At least let us live a little now. There's some talk that the UNP won't return to power in the upcoming elections. Chandrika's platform claims that she wants to make the ethnic problem her priority. The TULF says that there's a definite chance of peace if Chandrika comes to power. These are all hopes. Who doesn't hope to live in our own town in our own homes?" Viswalingam sounded tired.

He took his leave from them shortly after.

Valambikai walked him to the gate and stood outside for a while. She felt some pride when she thought back on the past little while. At least a few people who had known her husband had come by to offer their condolences. She felt gratified that the man's life and death had some meaning. She didn't burst into tears at the thought of him anymore. But the more painful memories still brought tears to her eyes, trickling down her face. Her grief had become a monument to his memory now. It's the form that grief takes. That it must take. But he must be the only man who had left his country and died in grief at the memory of his people and his homeland. What kind of obstinate death had he chosen, refusing to return to his land when he had the chance?

His friend, the crippled lawyer who had moved to Australia, had come to India on a visit and rushed to Ganesalingam's house the very next day after his arrival. He had got to know Ganesalingam years ago when he stayed in India for a year, before immigrating to Australia. He had come to see him and share his grief at the loss of their mutual friend. He had not been expecting to find Suntharalingam's wife there. Seeing her, the man had broken down in tears. An eloquent man rendered speechless . . . stumbling. Collapsed in the face of unbearable sorrow.

Valambikai had observed her husband's every effort in silence, not tried to stop him. She had borne the burden of caring for the family and protected him from all such pressures. This because she shared his views. Her father, Chellappa, had been so devoted to Chelvanayagam he would have whistled his life into the wind for him. She had absorbed some of that devotion. But she had realized, after giving birth to two children, that a livelihood was important as well. Suntharam hadn't. It was the only resentment, albeit mild, that she had against him. Yet here were all these people visiting her to offer their condolences and giving voice to the meaning of his life. That little resentment too had dissolved now.

She turned to go back inside.

7

Chennai, India

KULASEKARAM APPEARED TO BE immersed in his newspaper. Even though anger flowed like a fiery river in his chest, he was able to maintain his calm with some effort. Siva was speaking to his mother. She was angry with him too. But her love for him would quench that fire. She needed to see her son at least once a week. She would tell Vasantha or Param to ask him to come over if they saw him in the street somewhere. He was there that morning because she had sent for him the previous day.

He never came in and asked her why she'd sent for him. He would sit on the ledge on the verandah, within arms reach of his father's chair. It was she who came out to see him, when told that he had arrived.

Vasantha had told her of his coming that morning. His mother had dropped everything she was doing in the kitchen right away. "Oh Rasa, you've just gone and fallen into a pit," she began in an annoying complaining voice. He would bend his head and sit in silence, his gaze shifting from her to his father, to his sister standing in the doorway.

His mother went on and on. She spoke tearfully of how lovingly she had birthed and raised him and how much money they had spent to extract him from the Movement. He gave her no word of comfort. He knew that she would burst into tears the moment he said anything. It was the only language she knew. Everything she had said so far had been instigated by his father. He knew how to peck at, needle, and sift through the mind, as if through sand. After she had said all that needed to be said, the only question she asked him of her own volition, was: "Have you eaten?"

He told her that he had eaten already.

"Don't lie to me."

"I'm telling the truth, amma."

"What did you eat?"

"Idli."

"Bought at the shop?"

"Hmm . . . "

"Who knows what idli . . . or what sambar . . . I don't like the food these people cook here one bit," she mumbled to herself as she went inside and brought out a plate of hoppers that looked like it had been set aside for him.

One egg hopper; one milk hopper. He ate them without demurring. He realized she had sent for him through Vasanthi just to share this special meal with him. Would a mother ever change?

He felt his eyes grow misty.

He washed his hands after eating and came back to sit on the porch.

"What does your sister-in-law in France say these days?" she queried.

"She called a few days ago. Mala spoke to her."

"What did she say?"

"She said we have to get hold of the agent we paid and get back at least half the money before we can do anything."

"Hm."

"She says she's planning on coming here next year. She'll talk to the agent herself and arrange to send me over before she leaves."

"Then?" Thavamani said in disbelief. "If we can't find the Bombay agent? That's it?"

He tried to pacify her. "How would we not find him, amma? I have told everyone I know about him. Senan has told his friends to keep an eye out as well. We'll find him."

"Don't just believe that and wait without doing anything yourself."

"No, amma."

"Tell him to remember that he has an older sister, Thavam. The years are creeping up on her. It's only after he goes overseas that we can think about getting her settled." Kulasekaram spoke without even turning to look at his son.

They didn't have any quarrel with each other. Then how had it come to this, that they couldn't look each other in the face when they spoke? Was it a resentment born of frustrated hopes?

"Do I need to be told this, amma?" Siva turned to his mother.

"Needs to be told," his father interrupted. "How many fellows have said they'll take care of their brothers and sisters and gone abroad and done nothing? Do you know how many have forgotten about all the money their families borrowed for them? I know . . . "

"How many don't forget and take care of everybody's needs, do you know? Everyone knows how Ranjan takes care of not only his brothers and sisters but even people in his extended family."

"If this boy felt that kind of responsibility, I'd be happy."

Siva stood up.

His mother walked with him to the gate. "What's the name of the girl younger to Poobathy? Thavam, is it? I saw her at the bus stand the other day. She has really blossomed so fast!"

Siva said nothing.

"Oh . . . and Poobathy goes out somewhere on Saturdays and Sundays. Where does she go, son?"

"Dance classes."

"That's useful," Thavamani said pointedly.

She remembered what her friend Rathi had said to her a few days before. "This craze for rushing overseas is dying down now with these boys and girls, Thavamani akka. In the old days they used to think of a girl as a burden. Now it's not a problem. They educate them up to the tenth grade . . . teach them dance, a little singing or veena and that's enough . . . the marriage can be arranged in no time. Mangalam's daughter went to Denmark that way."

He was afraid that if he stayed any longer, she would say something that would annoy him. For some reason, they didn't seem to like Mala's family as much as they had when they had arranged his marriage.

He said goodbye and left.

Vasantha felt sorry to see her brother unhappy after getting trapped by his parents' marriage schemes.

"Thavam, make some tea," Kulasekaram called out.

Thavamani and Vasantha walked back into the house. As she passed her husband, Thavamani threw a glance at him. Kulasekaram was submerged in thought, gazing in the direction where his son had gone.

There was a faint yearning in his gaze.

He was not really angry with his son.

He was only bitter.

He had carried high expectations of the boy since he was little. He had decided that since Siva would never excel at athletics, cycling or football, he must excel in his studies and encouraged him in that direction. He paid for his tutoring and his books without sparing any expense. Siva had worked hard and began to show some promise. It was then that he joined the Movement and went to India for his training.

His life's purpose, no, his very life, had been his plot of land. He had mortgaged it to the hilt and come to India to retrieve the boy. Siva had forgotten all about his condition when he grew up. His father hadn't. He lived in fear that one day his heart condition would return and claim his life. He had not been happy with his son settling down to a married life. His plan had been to get the marriage registered, let him go overseas, and come back for the ritual marriage; or take Mala overseas for the wedding. But circumstances had not allowed this. Once he got married, how could he ask him not to be intimate with his wife?

It was all these thoughts that preyed on him and stirred his anger against his son.

He was a farmer. A hardworking farmer. Some summers the well that irrigated his crops would dry down to its rocky floor in the heat. The crops would begin to droop. He was never discouraged. He would set explosives into the rocks, dig them up, and find a spring two to three feet underground. Not many knew that it was this kind of determination that had helped the people bear the deprivations of war now. This human determination to survive saw the cutting down of palmyra, wild berry, wild dates, and wild indigo, in favour of food crops.

Thavamani was reassured knowing that his anger, or sadness, was due to his hopes that Siva would make amends for the heart condition he was born with, and for their financial losses by going abroad.

All this went through her mind as she prepared tea at the hearth.

Vasantha watched them both, trying to understand what compelled her parents to act as they did.

8

Nantes, France

IT WAS A FRENCH town inland. Spring had begun. The trees decked in green glimmered in every direction. How beautiful it was with the gentle blue of the skies above and the lush pastures below. Not only green. There were reds. Yellows. Leaves and buds in hundreds of varied shades.

The dawn skies were spectacular that day.

The sun was a rad circle climbing up the sky in the east. It rose as quickly as though someone were pulling it. The French said that if the sun rose in a red tinged sky, it foretold a blazing hot day. Suthan thought about it as he turned away from the window.

Chandramohan had just returned from work and changed his clothes before entering the living room. "Did it bother you being here alone at night, Suthan?" he asked.

"I'm used to this town . . . and to being alone. I came here from Paris to be alone."

"Do you need to go out anywhere?"

"I don't need to go anywhere right now. But I'd like to take a walk along that street we used to walk on. Do you have time for it?"

Chandramohan hesitated. It had been years since he had forgotten that street and the person who had lived that way. He hadn't thought about the area since Suthan left for Paris. Sheila was an old scar. He had not thought of her departure as a tragedy or a betrayal, but as something inevitable, and he had forgotten her. Though it had been a civilized agreement, which they had come to for both their sakes, he could see that the memory still caused a pang in Suthan. So he hesitated before speaking.

He thought they might as well go there, at least to see how much time had healed the old wounds. He agreed: "You'll be here for a week, won't you? Let's see."

The two ate their meal and washed up.

"I'm going to sleep for a while," Chandramohan said. "When I wake up it will be time to cook. I leave at around three, after I've eaten. I have a heavy workload this week. I can't take time off. It's going to be hard for you to occupy yourself."

"Don't worry about me," Suthan said. "My head is heavy; crammed with so many things to think about. I came here to take some time to think through them calmly and come to a decision. I need a break in between, so I can think productively later. I'll read. Watch TV. I have two new videotapes, I can watch them. Time is not an issue for me."

Chandramohan went into his room to sleep. Suthan chose one of the new cassette tapes and played it while he stared out of the window. It was a full-length window that they called a French window. One side of the room had no wall and was entirely a window. It was remarkable. The window was all glass and gave a panoramic view of the outdoors.

Grass and bushes grew abundantly here. There was a row of canna lilies along the balcony, beautiful to look at: red, yellow, and even a few pinks.

He remembered the periwinkle plants that used to grow

rampant by the well and along the fence of their house back on the island. White and pink by the hundreds. There were even more in Kanthasamy appa's farm garden. Once he had been introduced to an Indian plant dealer. The man had asked him to find some periwinkle roots for him. Suthan had got together with Paramasamy and a few other boys from his school and scoured the town for periwinkles, uprooted them, heaped them at the back of Kanthasamy appa's plot, cut the roots, dried them, and bundled them up for the man. They had made a good deal of money. Seeing the quantity of plants they had uprooted, some of the townsfolk had grumbled that the species would be wiped out forever on the island. But the next monsoon they erupted through the ground in the thousands at the first rainfall.

Occasionally, when he was home for more than two days in a row, his father would pull up the periwinkles, heap them in a pile and burn them along with the garbage. He believed the plants attracted snakes. He must have seen a snake somewhere, some time in a clump of periwinkles. The jasmine creeper in the front yard had met the same fate once. Suthan had clashed with his father over it that day.

"People need to know how to appreciate plants and bushes. If they don't appreciate them, they should leave them alone for the people who do. They can't chop them down and burn them. A man could give his life for a jasmine creeper." Suthan had shouted at his mother within earshot of his father.

"That's all well and good. But what if it's someone else's life? Does the snake know who has a death wish and has built a frame for the jasmine?"

That father was no more. It had been four years since his passing. He had received a letter about it two months later.

When he thought about it, he felt that he understood the reasons for all his decisions and events in his life.

It wasn't confusion as much as humiliation that plagued him.

His quarrels with Sheila had grown from the condition of their finances. She had repeatedly told him, calmly and angrily, that he couldn't fritter away her earnings. She reached a turning point and her behaviour changed. She began to separate their finances into his and her income and purchases.

Once she had spoken lightly about their relationship in front of their friends. She had made their relationship sound like a joke, something to be mocked. "I'm not a married woman with a thaali; or even married in a civil ceremony; we're just in a relationship of convenience, living together," she said, and he felt himself shrink into a worm.

That was the day he had broken down.

Chandramohan and his other friends had pacified him, telling him that this lifestyle was the norm in France; people lived together only to fulfill their own needs. She had adapted to these foreign customs very quickly, he thought, and had lost her values, but he began to be more careful. He cut back on his drinking. He worked harder and increased his income. Although he couldn't make as much money as she did, he earned more than before. Things continued in this manner until that summer's night in ninety-three.

He had gone to a restaurant with his friends after work. He had been drinking and was slightly dazed when he returned. She stood aloof, staring at him.

He needed to write a letter in a hurry. He sat at the table with pen and paper, and she went into their room. When he went in to get something, she had popped a pill into her mouth and was drinking some water. "Are you feeling all right?" he asked. "It's nothing, just a headache," she cut him off. As he was leaving the room, he happened to spy a blister pack of pills on her dressing table. She quickly brushed it into the drawer, out of sight. He backtracked into the room and looked again at the table. Sheila stood up, blocking the drawer. "Step aside," he said. She didn't move. He pushed her out of the way and opened the drawer. The blister pack of pills was in there. He picked it up. It was just as he thought. They were birth control pills.

Why? Why without his knowledge? She was still holding back something. She had said once that they only lived together for convenience, out of necessity, and she still seemed to feel the same.

And he?

When he turned to ask her about it, she stood there, glaring at him, her eyes reddening.

He left the room in silence.

He turned on the TV. He flipped channels. Nothing seemed to catch his attention. He took the bottle of whisky and a glass from the small cabinet and set them on the side table next to him. He drank late into the night and fell into a drunken stupor on the sofa.

She had bought the sofa too. He had bought the house. It was close to Chandramohan's house, and they had bought it when it came up for sale. They had been living there for four years. It seemed to him that her resentment had taken shape after they moved.

Until then he had not worried that they had no children, though he had thought about it occasionally. He had wondered why she seemed unconcerned. What a lie those eight years of life together had turned out to be! When they first reached France, he had tried sending her to live in a friend's house, to see how things would go. Though she had only been a substitute for something he had lost, he found himself needing her near him all the time. And he stopped thinking about it.

It was only now that he saw the boundary she had drawn within herself.

He fell asleep with these thoughts. When he awoke, it was well into the morning. His head was heavy, his eyes burning . . . still a little hazy. He looked up to find Sheila dressed to go out.

She seemed unconscious of his gaze.

"Where are you going?"

"To see someone I work with."

"A copain? Or copine?"

She was bending down to put on her shoes, and she looked up at him in midmovement. Who are you to interrogate me? her look seemed to say. She turned back to put on her shoes and stood up. She picked up her handbag and slung it over her shoulder. She opened the door.

Rage roared through him. "Wait!" he shouted. "I don't care if it's a copain or copine . . . you can live there from now on."

"Are you telling me not to come back?"

"That's how it is."

"You can't say things like that to me."

"You're not my wife. I didn't tie a thaali on you; didn't register any marriage."

"So, I've just been some woman to you all these days?"

"You've never thought about yourself as a wife. So, I won't hold onto that anymore either. The minute you started taking birth control pills without my knowledge, you became a stranger to me. From that moment you mean nothing to me. I can kick you out, no problem."

"This is my house too."

"I hunted for the house. I put down the deposit. I took on the mortgage and paid it off."

He stopped there, waiting for her to say something.

Silence wove its way in and out of the room.

He knew she must be furious. He had decided to end things

that very day. But he didn't want to take advantage of her inability to react.

He went on, "Still . . . I won't forget that you've put your half into this place. I don't need a single franc of yours. You can come back in three months and get it. If I can't get the funds together, I'll sell the house and give you the money."

"Don't put yourself out. You brought me to France. I didn't pay a cent of my own money towards it. You even paid for the clothes I wore to come here. You can keep the house money in exchange . . . "

"No need. I didn't do any of that to have you indebted to me. It was charity. I'm not in the habit of taking account of the charity I give out and asking it back."

She left. Two people he had never met came one Sunday to pick up all her things and take them away. He sold the house four months later and gave half the money he received to a friend of hers to give to her and moved to Paris.

It was two years now, his first visit back. Memories overwhelmed him. Sometimes he felt that none of this was his fault. Sometimes he felt that it all was. He had a lot to work through.

9

Nantes, France

TWO DAYS LATER, SUTHAN and Chandramohan took a bus after four in the evening and got out at a spot overlooking the Loire River. They had coffee at a café near the bus station and began walking back in the direction of Chandramohan's house.

The newly washed street gleamed. There was very little traffic. A car, a motorcycle going in the opposite direction, the occasional bus or truck.

They walked slowly.

"Have you not seen Sheila at all since you left for Paris?" Chandramohan asked, turning to scrutinize Suthan's changing expression.

"Hm. I've seen her. Not face to face. From a distance."

He had lost the feeling of shock he'd had in the early days. But Chandramohan could see that he wasn't completely unaffected either.

"Even if you were in Paris, and Sheila was just outside Paris, the distance isn't too great. Don't you feel a wave of emotions sometimes . . . ?"

"How not to?" Suthan replied calmly. "It's a good thing. You gain some wisdom only through experiencing some kind of loss. A loss . . . a complete loss . . . a loss that you can stop ruminating over, that's the beginning of wisdom. I don't think of her often, but I do occasionally."

"True!" Chandramohan said. "As long as you worry about, it you learn nothing. Wisdom comes after forgetting."

The hum of vehicles and their differing opinions sowed more silence between them.

A twenty-two-wheel container truck rumbled past them. When the noise died down Chandramohan ventured, "So, you haven't got any letters from Raji, have you?"

"Why should she write to me?"

"If Raji had thought that way you would have never got to know that your father passed away. There would have been no one to stay beside him and take care of him in his final days. Even if it's not for the sake of a relationship, you owe her some thought . . . some respect . . . as someone who helped you."

"It's good that she doesn't write. In fact, it would be best if I never saw her again."

"Hm. It will be the Assembly's tenth anniversary in a couple of years, and the other day my uncle suggested that we celebrate it with a grand event in India."

"Yes, that seems to be the idea."

"You planning to go?"

"Let's see."

"You may run into Raji then."

"No, I won't."

"You may need to speak—"

"I won't. As far as I'm concerned, she died a long time ago. I'm not in the habit of talking to ghosts."

"Why are you losing your temper?"

Suthan was quiet.

"Because . . . they're not the same kind of relationships. You're not sad that Sheila left. But you're still sad about losing Raji."

"Let it be whatever it is. I don't want either of the two. Not now, not ever."

"You shouldn't hide from yourself, Suthan. You never forgot Raji, even when Sheila was around. After Sheila left, you've been thinking about Raji even more."

"Yes, that's true. I haven't forgotten her. How could I? After I made all the arrangements to bring her to Germany . . . and told her 'Just wait while I make a quick trip to Trivandrum' and left . . . the woman says she's going back home with her cousin and runs off. How could I forget her?"

Chandramohan understood his fury. He didn't want to ruin the evening anymore by dwelling on the subject. He had asked Suthan the question only because he wanted to know how he felt about the situation, not because he needed answers in a hurry.

Suthan walked with his arms crossed. He was trembling slightly, as though the outburst had drained all his energy. Chandramohan could see that even though he wasn't in the throes of turmoil anymore, he hadn't yet recovered from the incident. When a woman, be it wife or girlfriend, rejects a man, it's an emotional blow. Suthan had gone through it twice. He seemed to be eaten away by a festering wound.

It was a quarter past five. The sun descended golden into the English Channel. A few seconds later it was gone. There was just a tinge of red left on the horizon.

The wind blew fierce and relentless. As soon as the sun set the chill descended on them.

There were signs of a storm gathering strength in the Atlantic, and the BBC evening news had reported that the storm had wreaked havoc on the eastern coast of England the previous night.

It was a piercing cold. If you weren't used to it, it made

sightseeing and holiday excursions quite miserable. He could bear the cold and walk a little longer. But Suthan was shivering. As they approached a restaurant, Chandramohan asked: "Suthan . . . are you cold? Shall we get a whiskey? It helps with the cold."

"I don't need one."

"Just a small shot, and you'll be fine to walk longer. That's why I asked. If not . . . ,shall we just get the bus back?"

"No . . . let's grab a quick drink and keep walking."

He wanted to keep talking.

They might have been in the restaurant for about fifteen minutes. They each had a glass of whiskey and set off on their walk again. Some of their enthusiasm from the beginning of the trip returned.

"You tell me. When I start talking about something, you get upset. But you asked me to walk with you so we could talk," Chandramohan began.

Suthan smiled faintly. "You mentioned on the phone that one of akka's poems had appeared in a small magazine, and that it was great," he said.

"Yeah, it was a good poem. It was titled 'Told to a Friend.' I can't say much about the meaning. But it's the ghost of a woman speaking to her living friend, telling her who she should trust and who she should be careful of. Though it looks like a general warning on the surface, it captures the situation in Sri Lanka like a snapshot. It's the form that makes it so special. The feelings it expresses are remarkable. Where it says things like 'don't dismiss it because it's a thread, it can turn into shackles,' it's just excellent. I've discussed it with quite a few people. It's one of the most important poems of our time."

The darkened sky seemed to grow a little brighter.

They felt as if a cold net had been removed.

As they walked, they began to sweat.

Even though they were out in the open, it felt as if the wind had settled.

"What's akka doing now?" Suthan wondered.

His sister had stubbornly refused to go to Germany when he had called her, saying that she chose to live as a symbol of her land and her tragedies. He could still recall some of the lines of her letter. "*As it was his land, it is my land too. He has died trying to stop the torment of a daughter of this land, as a witness to the atrocities committed on the Tamil people. People like me must safeguard the memory of that witnessing and live on here.*"

She had inherited this sensibility from aiyya. She had shifted from her original position. You could say she had progressed beyond aiyya. That was what her poems revealed.

He was saddened to think that there was no way of knowing anything about her now. If amma wrote to him, he might learn something about her. Would amma write? When would she write?

She could have come to India with their mother. Had she stayed back in Colombo and sent amma off because she refused to travel on his money? When he called them in Colombo once, his mother told him akka had refused the money he had sent for her, asking amma to keep it for her own use. She had a temper. She was hypersensitive. She was just like their father; he would fly into a temper too. It would always take a while for him to calm her down. Did akka know that aiyya had died?

She would have been a comfort to their mother if she had gone to India. What was akka's life like now . . . ? With the ceasefire, the preliminary arrangements for peace talks, and the devolution package, this seemed to be a period of less trouble in Jaffna. They seemed to be getting the basics without any restrictions now, from what he heard. There was air travel between Colombo and Palali, and ships travelling between Trincomalee and Kankesanthurai. There was an opening for letters to travel back and forth. She could have written just a line. Even just to scold him. If there was any contact at all, he could get her to come to India when he visited there in two years' time, just to see her once more. All alone. She writes poems. She must be in her own head as much. Try as she might, she wouldn't be able to avoid thinking about him either. He felt overwhelmed as his thoughts piled one on top of the other, as he guessed at her reasons, and debated them in his mind.

"Suthan . . . !" Chandramohan's voice brought him out of his reverie.

"Hm . . . "

"What is it, so much thought?"

"About akka," he said, without turning around.

Chandramohan was sure there were tears in his eyes. But he couldn't see them in the dark.

10

Nainativu, Sri Lanka

YOGESWARAN HAD COMPLETED HIS father's last rites. He had lost all relations now, friends, loved ones, anyone he cared for. How could he make sense of the loss that seemed to pervade his life in some form or the other? All he had left to lose now was himself. But he didn't want that loss. She had followed him down the steps after he left her at Kamala akka's, after their time together in Mahabalipuram. "You're going back to the country now. You know the situation there better than I do. Be careful," she had said. She should have said that he could never come back to see her again. What she said instead, was "You'll stay there now. If I think about it, you will be the only kin I have left still living there. Even though I remain here, my heart will circle around that place where you are. There, you will have to do my part too. That's why . . . " She had faltered.

He didn't stay in Tamil Nadu for much longer. He got on a boat and reached Maniyam Thottam. He didn't go back to Tamil Nadu except for his duties. The urge to see or speak to her was quelled as quickly as it arose in him. Her words kept resonating in him that he should stay back and take on her share of duties as well as his, and he felt he must do something.

He taught his skill at navigation to many youths. He had experience that marked him as a master boatman and brought respect and attention. His life and the war were no longer separate. The rebel navy commander saw his dedication and eased up on his inflexibility. That was a great relief to Yogesh. But they had not asked for his help in the hijacking of *Irish Mona*, the ferry transporting people from Trincomalee harbour to Kankesanthurai. Did they think that his skills were limited to the Palk Strait and didn't extend to the Indian Ocean south of Sri Lanka? Or did the modern navigation tools make his hereditary knowledge of the waters obsolete? He tried to show them that he was willing to join the Black Tigers' suicide squad. But he was kept at a distance. He might be considered for advancement after some more close observation. Others familiar with the seas in that area were chosen to carry out several other attacks. He was not even considered for many operations. But something had happened recently that gave him comfort. He was chosen to lead an operation to observe and attack the Sri Lankan navy's artillery boats in the Valvettithurai area.

One artillery boat was destroyed, and the other heavily damaged in a sea battle. After that, he asked the head of the rebel navy for permission to visit his town.

"Home? Where?" the head asked.

"To Nainativu."

"Isn't your house in Thondamanaru?"

"I had a house in Thondamanaru. Not anymore. Now I live in Nainativu. It's not my own house either. It belongs to my aunt. My mother was cremated in that town. My father was cremated in the backyard of that house. Now that island is my hometown."

"You know that the groups opposed to us are very active on that island, don't you."

"I know. I'll go and come back without them sighting me."

Knowing his singlemindedness, the commander concealed his curiosity and irritation. "All right, go and come back. You get two days, that's all. You'd better be back here on the morning of the third day. You won't get away with any excuses like you did in the old days, Yogesh. You delay this time; you pay for it." He sent him off with this warning.

He left one afternoon and reached Nainativu at night. He spent the night in the house.

Beginning early the next morning, he roamed all over the island. He walked past Nagamma's temple, the temple jetty, Manimekalai Hall, and the Bungalow bridge and then turned west and headed past the Pillaiyaar temple, the paddy fields, the vihara, Manipallavam Library and reached the shore of the large lake. When the sun reached its zenith, he returned home.

He had worn trousers on purpose. He had hoped that anyone seeing him at a distance might assume he was Thiyagu, based on his height, and he had probably succeeded. There was no one he recognized.

Though Yogesh didn't know him very well, at least that half-addled Thiyagu would come talk to him in the old days. What had happened to him? Even his cattle pen had gone. Yogesh had got to know the teacher Sankarapillai during his trips back and forth. On inquiring, he heard that the man had roamed around Colombo trying to get his pension, and then gone to Ariyaalai to join his wife and children. He also learned that the priest at the temple had had a heart attack and died. Now his son had taken on the responsibilities of offering poosai. The young priest smiled as he spoke to him. But the keen intelligence he detected in the priest's eyes prevented Yogesh from getting too close to him. He occasionally glimpsed a Buddhist monk, who seemed to scrutinize him but kept his distance. It looked as though he was puzzled to see him. Who else? He didn't know many people or have many relatives left here. How could there be anyone in this village to ease the loneliness he felt?

There seemed to be some organization that had been set up recently in the town. Law and order were being maintained. The people looked on in dismay as all attempts at talks between the Movement and the government failed. He listened carefully as his contemporaries talked about the mulish stubbornness of the Sinhala government. He believed it when people said it would all end in war. They seemed to invite it with open arms.

Recent events indicated that it had taken hold in the eastern province. The fact that the arrests, interrogations, surveillance, tortures and other governmental atrocities that had prevailed in the north for so long were spreading to the east certainly seem to confirm that conclusion. At the same time, it seemed that there was another community in the east that remained indifferent. He saw it as a sign that the Tigers had lost the support of Muslims. He reasoned for himself that this was a result of the Muslims being expelled by the Tigers from the north. But he still figured that the war would gain ferocity in the east, spread to the hill country, and finally end in a definite victory.

He would see Raji again then. And only then. The embers that sparked inside you have leaped into me and are blazing like fire, quelling all resistance. Now you can be calm, he would tell her then, and she would understand. Her anger would subside, and she would be content. That night the moon that slanted outside his window, the clouds that roamed in the sky, the glittering stars, the dancing breeze were all witness to a union. He had heard that the gandharvas experienced this. "If you ask me to show you, would I / if you gave me money, would I / when my prince comes, I will light the lamp and show him . . . " Many times, he had heard the woman in the Sannathi temple wail to the sky in the torment of the night's desire. This is how the disciple Kanagavalli must have enjoyed her life of pleasure in the capital of Nallur and proclaimed her compromised virginity, he had heard some of the elders say. He would prove to her that he was the right man for her.

Yogesh stayed another night and had a dream. There was black smoke swirling in one corner of the sky. Waves of sound arose through it occasionally. Yet the island looked as beautiful as if it had been freshly washed in the first rain of the monsoon.

Though the sun blazed, the breeze cooled him.

He closed the gate over the frangipani flowers that had fallen in the front yard and locked it. He stepped out on the street and looked around.

Then he began to walk to the northern shore of the island, towards the dugout that had been dragged ashore.

The east grew bright.

11

Kachai, Sri Lanka

ONE MORNING, SOMEONE CALLED Bavanantham came to the house. He gave Arasi two letters saying that the teacher Atputharani had sent them. He said somewhat guiltily that he had arrived from Colombo two days before. Arasi wasn't in the least irritated. Sometimes time seemed to rush, sometimes it crawled, she understood that. She insisted that he stay and made him a cup of tea before she sent him off.

Only one of the letters was for her. The other was for grandmother Chella. She would have to walk to Mirusuvil to deliver it. Never mind. What else did they have to give each other? These days, this was all the help they could offer. She decided she would deliver it the next day or the day after and put it away safely. Her own letter was from Maheswari, who was in Canada. She opened it eagerly.

It wasn't maami's handwriting. Viji must have written it, she thought. It felt like maami was in the same room, speaking softly to her . . . as if comforting her in her distress . . . as if she were giving her advice . . . condoling with her.

Dearest Arasi,

Viji, her child, my son-in-law and I are all well here. I pray to Nagapooshani amma that you are keeping well too. I don't need to tell you how impermanent human life is. You would know far more than I how much life has deteriorated in our country.

Separations and deaths seem to keep occurring. Is human death a new thing to this earth? We weep at death. We must weep to become calm again. Then sometimes we wallow in thoughts about our losses. Step by step it eventually becomes something we only occasionally remember. You musty keep this firmly in your heart.

I can't find any reason why you should keep suffering these losses. First your husband. Now your father. Your sorrow must be terrible. Though you have lost many people it is better for you to think of the ones still living and find comfort in that.

For a moment she couldn't understand what Maheswari had written. What had happened to aiyya? When? It had been so long since amma had gone to India, and she hadn't written anything yet. Surely, by loss she meant that he was so far away! Oh God, I hope nothing has happened to aiyya.

Her eyes turned into pools, and with some effort she managed to dry them. Tears were, for the most part, easy to contain these days. But she needed to know exactly what had happened. She kept reading.

It was Mala who wrote to me. That virago daughter of mine is there. Having lost everything. Still, she goes on, without any decency, losing more. That one didn't write to me. Who knows where she got the arrogance? But one comfort, she was there in his last moments and did what was necessary.

The moment I found out I was more shocked than sad. It was I who dragged him from Sri Lanka to India. When I found out the games she was up to, I didn't have the heart to go back home. I decided then that it was a sin to even think of her as my child. The one younger to her is stirring trouble in Bombay, apparently. I don't have any relief even thinking of that one. I came to Canada because I never want to set eyes on either of them again.

I now think that it was the heavy impact of Suthan's behaviour that made Suntharam anna lose the will to return home. That and he was heartbroken when he heard about some of Suthan's impulsive decisions (check). I think his heart disease must have come about because of it.

Raji was fortunate to have been able to stay and take care of that good man in his last days. He had been good to her. It wouldn't have been possible for someone to wipe away such a huge disgrace so easily, otherwise. The people who plan to go overseas and get stuck here and there seem to be up to all kinds of disgraceful behaviour. There was a teacher called Nesamalar on the island. You know her, don't you? She has gone from Bombay to Calcutta and ended up in Thailand, where she did. I hear she had a child. Noone knows what happened. A boy from Tellippalai who was there at the time, is now here and he told me all this. Now all these kinds of scandals have come down to the level of simple information. They don't impact us the same way anymore. But there was a time when even a small suspicion had the power to destroy a young woman's life on the island. Suntharalingam had saved her, and me, from destruction at a time like that. If she was able to do any service for such a man, she should count herself lucky.

It was all clear to Arasi now. She erupted into sobs. The tears poured down her face.

She hadn't even found out about it immediately after he died. The letter seemed to imply that the news was two or three years old! Did amma still not know about it? Why hadn't she written? Had she not written because she didn't know how to write these words? Or did she write, and it never reached here? Or was she in such a state that she couldn't do anything? The thought made her cry all over again. She went back to reading the letter, the tears still streaming.

Stay strong. Now your mother isn't with you either. It would have been so much better if you two had been together at this time. This is all the work of fate. From what Mala had written, it sounds as if amma didn't know about anna's death when she got to India. I hadn't been getting any letters from you, so I neglected to write to you as well. It's a terrible situation to discuss news of what's happening in India from all the way here in Canada. Amma, Mala, and even Raji must be writing to you regularly, aren't they? It's only my letter that has been delayed. It looks like amma is still in India. I heard Raji went to see her when amma was in the Mandapam refugee camp. Then she got her out of there with the help of some people she knew and took her to the house of Suntharam anna's friends in Trichy. I don't know how your mother ended up in the refugee camp. Why don't you go to India and see? It will be a comfort to you too. And you could take amma back home with you. Just get a passport somehow and keep it. I'll make the arrangements for you to go and come back.

Think about what I've said and write back to me. Think about all the other issues except for money. Viji keeps telling me that she is eager to see Arasi akka. They are planning to go to India. Maybe I will too. If we are fated to, we might be able to meet in India.

With love,
P Maheswari

It was clear from the letter that aiyya had died. But the sequence of events made it hard to believe.

What a remarkable man he had been! "The mother who gave birth to you and the land of your birth are more precious than the heavenly skies," he had always said, and he had lived by that saying. That such a man should not be fortunate enough to be buried in his own land . . . the heart could not bear it.

The wind rose.

The dry leaves tumbled and swirled.

The breeze carried their debris.

The dust thickened in the air.

It had rained, but the soil soon dried. The villagers had hoped that it would rain again at least by September. If the wind rose and created such havoc, how would the clouds gather? How would it rain? The rains had been scarce the previous year. She was a farmer. The rains were important to her. Her garden well had reached rock bottom. They needed rain for the well waters to rise again. They needed rain to till the soil. They could only choose and plant the seeds then. The town depended on it. The supply of provisions was irregular. What could they do but farm?

The wind had drawn her scrutiny.

It made her peer at the sky.

She thought she could see about going to India the next year and folded the letter.

Her thoughts of her father were also folded away.

12

Mirusuvil, Sri Lanka

WHEN ARASI REACHED CHELLA'S house the sun was beginning to fall behind a clump of trees.

Some of the old lady's relatives were present as well—a husband and wife, an older man who could have been the father of either, and two little children—making the house lively but not noisy. The old woman herself seemed livelier than usual. It was the time of day when they shared stories. The adults were seated on the verandah huddled in conversation. She knew that if she went in she wouldn't be able to turn back quickly. But she went in anyway.

"Is that Arasi? Come in . . . come in." The old woman welcomed her lovingly. Seeing the letter in her hands, she said, "What . . . has a letter come? For me?" and came forward to receive it. She didn't to appear as excited she would have expected from a mother who hadn't heard from her children in a long time.

The old woman opened the letter and peered closely at it, reading. Then she folded it carefully back into its original form, returned it to its envelope and put it away in a table drawer before returning to the verandah. It was only then that she asked Arasi to sit, sat down beside her and asked her whether she herself had received any letters or not. She even asked what she'd heard from those letters.

Arasi didn't feel like hiding anything. It wasn't news that she should hide either. She told them about her father's death.

"Aiyayyooo! When?"

"More than two years ago."

The old woman was devastated. The others didn't feel as affected by the news, as the time that had elapsed since the death seemed to have dimmed its impact. But the woman's grief moved them. They commiserated with her, saying that no one should die away from their own land. They blamed the times. too.

Chella introduced the visitors to Arasi, hoping to dispel the sad mood. "This is the younger sister of my daughter-in-law who lives in Germany, and her family. This is her father-in-law. From Valikamam."

"Anything wrong?" Arasi asked.

The old man replied, "No problems up to now . . . "

"Then?"

"The problem is coming . . . and that too . . . more terrifying than anything that's happened so far."

"How can you be so sure?"

"The Palali camp is quieter than usual. That quiet . . . it's horrifying, child. I know all about it. It means the army is ready."

His daughter-in-law explained. "The camp used to be very busy before. I've seen it myself, the army trucks rumbling back and forth when I used to travel to Pandatharippu."

"The recent events are more important than any of this," her husband Ramajeyam added. Everyone's attention turned to him. He continued, "The weapons can't come over land. The air route is not safe. The Boys have RPGs. And it worries them. These folks can't do anything by sea either. So . . . they can only bring in weapons and troops under the guise of bringing food supplies for the civilians in Jaffna. The Red Cross usually accompanies the ships bringing food as a safety precaution. The ships, *Nakomo* and *Sea Nartaki*, that the Red Cross had rented came here under that arrangement. There were no problems for a while . . . "

"Then?" Chella asked.

"The Boys began to suspect that they were bringing weapons and military personnel disguised as civilians. At this time the sea mines set by the Tigers exploded and sank the Sea Nartaki. The *Irish Mona* was the ship the Red Cross used to replace it. The ship also ferried passengers to and from the islands."

Chella interrupted. "This was the ship the Boys hijacked at sea?"

"That's the one. The *Edithara* came after this. The Boys only suspected that the *Edithara* was carrying weapons. We were sure of it."

Arasi was shaken by the news.

This was all going on behind the peace talks.

She couldn't read the old woman's expressions. They were hidden in the wrinkles of her face.

For a while no one spoke.

One overt action and a covert action behind it? It's not for nothing that they call war a time of darkness. Along with its terrors it held mysteries as well, Arasi thought to herself.

Though she knew some of this from the Tigers' Voice radio channel, it impacted her more upon hearing it directly from someone.

The old man Sambasivam spoke up, breaking the long silence that had fallen. "We dropped all our earthly possessions in eighty-three and fled to a refugee camp . . . and suffered all kinds of losses before we reached here. Shanthi hates living here. I've pacified her so far, saying that we should look at Jeyam's work situation and see what can be done. Now, after hearing that the *Edithara* arrived carrying weapons, Shanthi cannot sleep. She wakes up with a start in the middle of the night, screaming . . . it's like there's a war going on inside her mind. I can't let her suffer anymore. As soon as the Kilali Road is open, we'll go to Colombo . . . and make arrangements to go to India."

Challa's mumblings found their way through the fog of her thoughts. "What does it matter if the weapons come by ship? By plane? Our boys can beat the army, can't they! They have the weapons they used to beat the army in Mankulam last year, don't they?"

What confidence! Arasi thought. Is it this confidence and bravado that has made a minority population arise as a great force and endure so long on the battlefield?

"When will your mother come?" Chella asked.

Arasi replied, "I'll only know amma's plans for certain if I get a letter from her, aachi. From what I see, it doesn't look like she'll come now. My sister-in-law, you know Raji . . . whom I've spoken about . . . she's taking care of her. Maami and Raji's younger sister are planning to go to India from Canada late next year. I think amma will stay to see them before she comes back. Maami asked me to go to India as well when she comes, and then return."

"You should go and come back. When people come all the way from Canada, it's good to go and see them."

"Have to think about the cost too."

"True. But won't your maami or her daughter help?"

"That's what she's written. But . . . "

Chella laughed. "You're so particular about your dignity even among your relations. Some folks here will ask for help from people they only know by sight. You're a strange woman . . . but then, you won't even accept help from your own brother. Just go, child . . . " She tut-tutted.

Arasi stayed silent for a while, she felt as if she were floundering in the waves. Then, "Aachi . . . I can't seem to leave this place," she said. Her eyes welled up with tears.

Chella was startled. "Amma my dear, look here . . . don't cry my dear. I know what's in your heart, child. I know the trials and tribulations that young women who lose their husbands go through, when they should be living in their prime. I lost my husband before I turned thirty also. It wasn't like the deaths we see now. The man had gone to Vavunikulam and was bitten by a snake. The man haunted me for ten years, showing up in front of me, or following me. I couldn't stand his spirit's suffering anymore and went to a Muslim who had come here to harvest paddy . . . and got him to do a spell and send him off in peace. I haven't forgotten anything, child. Love isn't just for sexual pleasure. You need it to remember them when they die . . . to live for them . . . for everything. Am I asking you to go to India forever? Won't you go see your in-laws, and bring your mother with you when you come back?"

The grandmother was a truly good woman. She had a heart that knew pain. She had her secret ways. She didn't trust anyone easily. Grandmother Chella was not one to live off anyone else's suffering. If she felt like it, she would become very close to you. If she didn't, she'd keep her distance. That was her nature.

A demonic darkness covered the north.

"There are signs of rain. Are you going to leave, child? If it's difficult, why don't you stay over and go in the morning?"

"No. I'm going, Aachi. Apart from my feet, what do I have to be afraid of?"

Chella came to the gate with her and tried again to convince her: "You can decide if you want to go overseas or not. But if you have the chance to go to India, take it. You don't know what state your mother is in. You can only be sure of bringing her back safely if you go."

"I'll think about it, Aachi. I'll come this way next week if I can. We'll talk. See you later, then?" Arasi said and stepped out into the street.

13

Kachai, Sri Lanka

ARASI WROTE A LETTER to Maheswari, agreeing to go to India. She sent the letter through someone headed for Colombo, to be mailed from there. Who could tell how long it would take to reach Canada? How long would it take to get a reply? It could be months. By this reasoning, she could estimate that it would take at least a year for her to go to India.

It had begun to rain intermittently. They were often forced to stay indoors. Then her mind would be overwhelmed with thoughts whirring at a fever pitch. No matter what was in the forefront of her mind, it was eventually overtaken by thoughts of her father and the grief. It would be good to go away for a while. She thought about going to the island. It was hard. It used to take a whole day before. Now it took a week.

There were many people in the island who thought about him and spoke about him. She needed to let them know of his passing. It was her duty. She thought she might go the following Saturday. If she sold some vegetables in the market on Friday, she'd make some money. It would help with the costs of her trip.

She was in her garden on the Friday afternoon when her friend

Pavalam arrived. She told her that the Kathirgama Swamy was back. Arasi felt that she needed to go to see him. She went to the temple around dusk, taking Pavalam with her.

The burnt tree Amman no longer had a burnt banyan beside it. It had grown again and flourished very quickly. It was the same tree she had seen many times before. It was only that day that she understood its wonder. It had been struck by a bomb and was half destroyed. It had remained withered for so long everyone thought it would rot. Yet suddenly it had had grown and was now lush again; was it by Amman's grace? It was in this state of wonder that Arasi reached the temple.

Someone was just leaving after receiving their blessing. As Arasi and Pavalam stood waiting at the entrance, Bandaram saw them by the light of the glass bulb there and came to lead them inside.

There was a clay lamp glittering inside as always.

They could see the silhouette of a gaunt figure through the darkness. As they got closer, they saw his eyes rolling.

The swami had been complaining, "I don't ask for money. But when the faithful come, they could wrap up a lemon, a betel leaf, or at least a hibiscus flower in a knotted cloth to bring me, couldn't they?" Pavalam had reminded her, and Arasi had brought a lemon and some betel leaf. She bent humbly and left them in front of him and backed away.

The swami stood up and looked at her.

His eyes fixed on her, motionless.

Did his eyes say that he remembered that she had been there before? Would he remember what he had said then, too? Though they were not meant for her, they were connected to her. He had said they should go to Thiruvarur with puffed rice. If things didn't work out, that meant they needed to fulfill something else before coming back. That was the hidden meaning of what he'd said. It had come true, Arasi thought.

The moments passed as he remained unmoving, and then he spoke. His eyes remained closed. "Eh . . . Sinnathangam! She has had to bear a lot. Poor thing, I told her to go with puffed rice. The mother left. Now it's her turn. Give her some comfort, Amma. She's alone, Thangam. Don't let her suffer any more . . . yes . . . hm . . . oh . . . yes yes . . . " the swami said to himself. Then he opened his eyes. They burned red as embers.

Suddenly something dark flew by, flapping wildly, smashing into the walls and the roof. It took Arasi some effort to stop herself from crying out loud. Then it dawned on her. It was only a blind bat, nothing else.

The priest went on: "You will have to make a journey. Go alone. Even though you go alone, it will turn out that you return with a companion. Go alone. Good things will happen."

Pavalam had been standing behind her, a little apart. She was afraid that he might be naked, one of those hermits who wear the sky. It was dark. Would nakedness surpass the dark in her fears?

As Arasi turned away, thinking it was time to leave, the priest thundered: "Wait! I have not given you leave to go."

She clasped her hands in worship, words deserted her. The swami nodded in approval.

"This lineage of five generations of yogis will end with me. I will attain nirvana by the year two thousand. So, I will prophesy no more. I need to do some things for myself. I'm going to Nallur from here. Or I will go to Columbuthurai, where my guru attained nirvana. I plan to spend my time in silent contemplation there. I will not move after that. In the year two thousand, this island will experience a great tragedy. The light of wisdom will shine bright here then. But there will be no one to see it. If you can, try to see it. I won't be here to see it. All right, you can go. Om Sakthi."

The two women walked out.

"Pavalam akka!" Arasi said as they walked along.

"What?"

"You could have come to the front too . . . "

"I was afraid, Arasi."

"Did you hear what the swami said?"

"Hm. That he won't prophesize anymore? I heard."

"Then I am the last person to hear him. He will take on his silent contemplation and reach nirvana by the year two thousand. Why, akka, will all of this happen?"

"It will."

Arasi left for Nainativu the next day.

Many knew of the increase in armed personnel at Elephant Pass, Poonakary and Palali. A few NGO newsletters had confirmed the situation. Yet most of them felt no need to flee, unlike Sambavasivam and his family. Even if they wanted to flee, where would they go? What would they accomplish by fleeing their homes and their productive farm gardens? So, it became their war. The opposing groups who had conflicts among themselves and with the Tigers soon rid themselves of their "alternate" status and aligned themselves with the government as alien political groups. The voice of the TULF was the exception. But some noticed even that growing faint. The loss of voice among the groups was inevitable. It was understood as their attempt at political survival. Some said it was because many in the groups now received a monthly salary from the government.

Arasi felt a new sensation agitating inside her when she set foot in Nainativu again.

She was carrying the news of a death with her. No one is dead while they are believed alive. In the same way that no one is living while they are thought to be dead. Was this one way of understanding that a person's life is not in their own hands? Suntharalingam was dead. To those who knew this he had died that day. To her, he had died only recently.

She went to the goddess Amman first. The young priest welcomed her affectionately. She performed her worship of the ritual flame and said her goodbye.

Some of the houses on the island had fallen to ruin. Thiraviyam's was one of them. She had heard from an acquaintance that he had a good job in Colombo now. If she had to go there to get a passport she thought she'd inquire of his whereabouts and visit him.

She passed the street where Nesamalar's house stood. The teacher who had lived at a well-known address had died homeless. She had asked aloud why a woman who had been educated up to her A Levels and had a good teaching job would run away in the desire for a foreign country, and Kanthasamy appa had admonished her for it. She too was a symbol of this ruination.

She walked further along and arrived at Raji's house.

There were signs that someone was inside, and she stopped. Who could it be? As far as she knew the place had been shut down since Velupillai died. She wondered if his son Yogesh had arrived.

She called out from the entrance: "Anyone home? Anyone home . . . ?"

A young man. Average height. Muscular body. He came out of the hall and peered from the verandah. Seeing her, he walked closer: "What is it?"

"Oh . . . I was just calling. There's no one living here, and when I saw the door open, I wanted to see who it was . . . "

"Who are you?"

"Maheswari is an in-law of mine."

"How is that?"

"Her daughter is registered to Suthan. I'm his sister."

"Oh!" He seemed to recall hearing of her.

"Arasi?"

"Yes."

"I'm Maheswari's brother Velupillai's son. Yogesh."

"Oh! Aren't you from Thondamanaru?"

"Mm. Our house was crushed in a bomb blast during Operation Liberation. We came here then. After my father died, I don't really have any family. I don't know where the few remaining relatives are. I come by here occasionally and stay a day or two and go back. I lit my mother's pyre in the Nainativu cremation grounds. I stacked up firewood in a corner of this property to light my father's pyre. You're standing outside. Come in, please."

"That's alright . . . "

"No, please come in. You've come all the way from Kachai . . . come rest your feet for a while. You'll have to walk all the way back."

She went in.

Yogesh! She recalled the name very well. He was the one who had brought Raji from Chennai to Rameswaram in May or June of ninety-seven. Raji had stayed with him for a while after that. Maheshwari had written all about it in one of her letters a while back.

She needed to speak to him.

There were no chairs on the verandah. She sat on the ledge of the verandah, her feet on the steps, and launched the conversation. It sounded as though she had begun to speak in a hurry; she didn't waste time on small talk. "You're like a thambi to me, I need to know something. You won't take it the wrong way if I ask you?"

"You're an akka to me not only by age, but also through our relationships. It brings great joy to think of each other as kin. I won't get angry. Please ask whatever you wish."

"Raji and Suthan had their civil marriage, he joined some group after that, then went to India, then left the group and went somewhere in Europe . . . now he's in France . . . you must know all this, already."

"I know," he replied. He smiled, but his brow furrowed slightly, not knowing where she was going with this.

"Raji and I have a friendship outside our relationship through her civil marriage to Suthan. It's a friendship that grew because we played together as children and we share many of the same thoughts and ideals. She could have really come up in the world. But somehow or the other she has ended up in a refugee camp . . . not that I think it's a disgrace to be in a refugee camp, that's not what I'm saying. I know we can hate our fates, but not our circumstances."

"That's true, akka."

"So, it's not about her being in a refugee camp. I just want to know what compelled her. I only know that she refused to go overseas with Suthan. I don't know anyone who can tell me the truth of what happened. Her actions could be the result of her stubbornness or her touchiness, but she wouldn't have taken things this far without a valid reason. Something terrible must have happened to her to push her. But that couldn't have been the only reason. You were with her when all these disruptions happened. You must know something about it. I'll be going to India after next January. Her mother and sister are coming there from Canada. There's no way we can avoid this topic. If you tell me what you know, it will help us think about what we can do."

She leaned forward slightly, her gaze penetrating as she finished speaking. It seemed as though even his deepest thoughts could not escape her keen observation. Unable to meet her gaze, he would try to avoid it.

He could help Arasi. It was just hard to determine to what extent. He couldn't tell her everything. He understood that Raji had intended the last night she had spent with him as a severance of all her relationships. That could be the reason that Arasi needed. But could he reveal that?

Arasi's intent was important. There was no reason for him to reject these good intentions of sincere, loving people. His thoughts of Raji had gone beyond yearning. They had turned to adoration. He had turned his deepest attention elsewhere now. He had been resurrected as a warrior. He was a seafarer. Though it was not his ancestral trade, he learned the arts of the sea with a remarkable aptitude. Though modern techniques and instruments had come into practice now, no one could approach his kind of expertise. Mother Ocean allowed only him to draw close to her heart; she played with him and rocked him in her lap. Still, he often felt listless. He was still only treated as a helpful outsider by the Movement. He took on the most difficult tasks. He carried out amazing feats to prove himself. He quit his smoking habit without anyone asking. Yet he was never brought into their inner circle.

He had come to this conviction about the struggle because of her. He had no intention of renewing his relationship with Raji. They had become strangers to each other, it was better that they remained strangers.

As he made up his mind, her voice interjected. "Why are you silent, thambi?"

He smiled faintly. He said, "I'm not in the same circumstances as I was back in eighty-seven, when I took Raji from Chennai to Thanjavur, or when I saw her once again four years later. You may have some idea of what my activities are now. I'm a seafarer. The sea is where I exist now. I hope and pray that my end will be in the lap of Mother Ocean too. I may leave out a few things for the sake of other people, but I don't lie. You can trust me in that."

She was silent.

"I don't remember her saying anything specific to me about any one thing or one person. I figured things out based on a few half-spoken words here and there. It will hurt you if I say what they are . . . "

"Don't worry about me. I can withstand any shock. As long as I know the truth. Tell me."

He still hesitated. As she pressed him further, he spoke. "Whenever I saw her, I had the impression that she was burdened by the belief that she had made a mistake. She kept saying at the time that she should not have fallen in love with Suthan, that she shouldn't have agreed to the registration . . . "

He lowered his face to look into hers.

"Go on, I'm listening," she said.

"She was distraught. She had heard about Suthan taking Sheila away with him. But she wasn't broken up about that. She felt cheated by the secrets that Suthan had kept. At one point she was determined that the relationship should not continue under any circumstances."

"So are you saying there's no chance that she'll want to go back to her old life?"

"It's hard to say for sure."

"Mm," she replied softly.

He spoke almost as if to himself: "The path of a river is determined. The path of fate is somewhat predetermined too. It's only the heart that wanders without direction, like a breeze."

She looked at him in surprise.

It was clear he had given himself away.

"I only wanted to live an ordinary life until four years ago I. It was only then that I decided I would die a warrior's death. I made the decision because of Raji."

"Why because of Raji?"

"What can I say if you ask me why, akka? A love . . . a caring . . . an offering . . . that's all I can say . . . "

The reply puzzled her. Yet she felt she could guess. But she couldn't dwell on the thought very long. His expression in that moment made her fearful.

He seemed to return to normal and went on talking happily. Eventually, he said, "I had been confused for a while, thinking that TULF Suntharam and Suntharalingam were two different people, akka."

"And now you know it's one person?"

"I know."

"In truth, now he's no one at all."

"I don't understand!" he said.

"Aiyya is not alive anymore."

"Oh!"

"It hurts even now when I think of how he died. It's been almost three years since he died. He died in India, and I only heard about it a few months ago. Amma didn't know about it either, and she left for India to find him a year and a half ago. How she must have suffered when she heard the sad news. My whole body burns when I think about it. Aiyya never knew a moment of peace or contentment even when he was alive, thambi. He never even wore a watch on his wrist. I've never seen him ride a bicycle. The political parties have held their marches every now and then. Everyday was a march for him. Aiyya only went to India to accompany Maheswari maami. I don't know why he didn't turn back after. He lay in a hospital . . . had a pacemaker put in because of his heart trouble. He died from this illness. But I am certain he wanted and prayed for that death and accepted it. That's a mystery to me. I need to find out more about it when I go."

It seemed even the breeze stood directionless.

After a while, Yogesh spoke up. "It is a time of loss for Tamils. So many kinds of losses. There will be a reckoning for all these losses, akka. Don't you worry."

She rose to leave.

It had grown late in the evening.

14

Kachai, Sri Lanka

IT HAD RAINED ALL the previous night. Occasionally they heard the clouds crashing into each other. Lightning flashed. A torpor had fallen upon the earth at dawn, a strange darkness covered it. This was not unusual in October. But the melancholy was unusual for Arasi.

She had been later than usual in getting to the farm. It was fenced in on all four sides like an estate. There were mango and jackfruit trees and moringa trees scattered here and there. There were two long tracts in the middle. One row held creeping gourd vines: snake gourd and bitter gourd spread out. The other row held five hundred knee-high chilli plants. In this plateau they held firm even in the rainy season and bore fruit. When green chillies cost a fortune, it was a crop that was sure to bring in some income. Half the crop remained to be harvested, but she didn't feel able to do anything that day. She tried to figure out when she was supposed to get her menstrual period. By her account it might be that same day or the next.

She walked over to the ambalavi mango tree and sat on a rock beneath it. There was a sudden tremor, like thunder, in the distance. It must have been around Elephant Pass or Poonakary. She wondered later if it had really been thunder.

Pavalam arrived and sat down, exhausted. "People have started leaving the Valikamam area."

"Why is that, akka?"

"The Boys have announced that people have to evacuate the town."

"Ammaalee!"

There were at least five hundred thousand people in Valikamam. They were all packing up and leaving. Arasi shivered, unable to even imagine it. The destruction of property, theft, the emotional strain, the injuries to their dignity . . .

They stood up, silent as statues.

It began to rain.

The streets filled with puddles.

Far away somewhere in the north the great tragedy of children, the elderly, women, men, and goats, cats, hens, even dogs migrating south had begun. With their belongings packed on their heads, their cycles, cars and vans, knowing nothing but a direction, they migrated towards a wasteland. A mass migration.

For the people of Jaffna, a plot of land and a house were like icons in their lives. Their culture had been erected through these. This was how house and land had congealed into dream and devotion and their lives had gained shape and order. The culture of the coconut frond fence shaped the discipline of both women and men. Both eastern Sri Lanka and the hill region were Tamil areas that needed to grow through education. At the same time Jaffna seemed to manufacture pedagogues. Even though the Jaffna Tamil did not wish to leave the boundaries of his house and plot of land, he valued the Tamil communities that withered from a need for education. That house and plot of land were the reason the Tamil language did not spread widely.

Arasi could not help thinking of Raji then.

Raji had felt that passion. She spoke up even in those places where she was excruciatingly aware of being shunned as an islander. Those geographical boundaries had shrunken now. Would the cultural bonds of their people shatter with all this migration? All villages are my village. Which Tamil's mantra was this? Was this the conflicting desire of a race that was of average colour, average height, average build and lived a small circle of house and land?

Human destruction . . . human destruction . . . stretched out before them, Rakini had written back then. Wasn't this human destruction being sowed even now?

1997

15

THE RED CROSS HAD reported that there were around a hundred thousand refugees living in hardship in the Vanni forest without any amenities. The great tragedy of 1995 was continuing into 1997.

February had dawned. A gentle breeze blew in the soft wintery sun. But it didn't bring them any comfort. When they were hungry, they found something to eat, if not right away, then at some later time. When they felt sleepy, they somehow managed to sleep. But the anguish they felt now, the humiliation, the trauma of seeing death up so close, none of it diminished.

Chella finally agreed to leave Mirisuvil.

Her daughter and her family had fled to her when they were displaced from Pandatharippu.

Thanasekaran had once left Mirisuvil saying he wouldn't set foot in Chella's house again, not even for her funeral. But when they became desperate, they came running back. Chella hadn't even known that their oldest daughter had married, but by the time they came to her the girl was already widowed. She still wore a black pottu on her forehead and held a dream in her eyes. She may not be looking out for Thevakumaran, who used to come by on his motorcycle, but she needed some Thevakumar* to keep on living, didn't she? When the stirrings in her flesh beat their wings, wasn't it Motorcycle Kanna who came to comfort her? She had grown a child in her belly but was taken with stomach pains for some reason in the fourth month and miscarried. They say the thevas are beyond death. Could bullets kill them? That was how her Thevakumar had died. The shame of it was that they had tied him to a telegraph pole and shot him. Her younger sister was of an age to have her saamathiyam.* Rahulan, younger than her, was a frail shivering mouse of a boy.

Chella was moved to tears when she saw them. She said, "Please, come inside." Thanasekaran had prostrated himself at her feet in remorse. She hugged her grandchildren and cried.

The army had possession of all of Jaffna. Operation Riviresa had succeeded. The defence minister had raised the Sri Lankan flag, and the troops stood to attention at the Mayor Durayappah Stadium in front of Jaffna Fort, as if they had captured a foreign country. Below it, they flew the Nandi flag, the insignia of the Nallur dynasty, a symbol of the Tamils.

Though she fretted as she heard this news, Chella had remained where she was. But the growing migration of displaced people into the Vanni forest made her rethink. She heard of army attacks in Thenmaradchi as well. The landscape of Thenmaradchi had discouraged the attacks, because the land tended to break up into little islands whenever the water levels rose, so though the attacks had been intended to stop people from migrating to the Vanni, it spurred them to flee even faster. They all trembled in the fear that at any moment ten thousand soldiers would advance from Elephant Pass to capture even more ground from the Tigers. If the troops left Elephant Pass, they would capture Palai, then Eluthumattuval, and finally Mirusuvil.

It was then that they heard the news that Colombo was engulfed in smoke after the rebels bombed the oil refinery in Kolonnawa. Chella didn't hesitate anymore. She decided that they wouldn't be able to avoid the troop movement from Elephant Pass. "We should go to Vanni too. Thavarasan is in Murasumottai, we'll head there," she announced.

Now, in the gentle morning sun, Chella seemed withered and lost in her own thoughts. She had been that way since the day they arrived in Vanni. It had been worse after Thavarasan returned from Thenmaradchi the previous week. Perhaps she wouldn't have been so distressed if he hadn't told her about the condition of her house. "They have removed everything and taken it away; not just the doors, windows and gate, but even the well sweep from the well."

She had built that house the way a bird gathered twigs for a nest. It had its own history. It was built on relentless labour . . . and unflagging hope.

Her daughter arrived. "What is this, amma? You seem lost in thought wherever you are?" When she was met with silence, she said, "If you were going to be like this, you shouldn't have come. We would have gone somehow . . . reached some place."

"What could I do, Thilakam? I couldn't bear to see your Nesam and Rahulan suffer anymore, so I came."

"Then stop worrying. We had to leave home to save them. Are we the only ones? Hundreds of thousands have come."

"That may be. But to build that precious house . . . well, you know, don't you?"

"I know, amma. He and I, and the children were all there then. You dug the foundation, you carried rocks, you carried sand . . . you worked like a coolie from building the walls to thatching the roof . . . "

Tears flooded Chella's eyes. "How will I burn on my funeral

pyre . . . after leaving a house I suffered so much to build? Think about it."

"There will be an end to all our suffering, amma. The day will come when we can return to our own homes and live our lives, just wait, and see."

"I don't believe that, Thilakam. I don't think the Boys will be able to recapture Jaffna after being beaten so badly."

"They can, amma. They always manage. Even when the Indian army came, that's what they did. It's because I have faith in them that I have stayed on here and haven't gone back to Pandatharippu even when the army told us to return to live there. How can I forget the humiliation of fleeing with just the clothes on our back when the army attacked us like that?"

"Isn't one of Thanasekaran's younger brothers in the Movement?"

"Two of them are."

"That's why you're so convinced in your belief. Victory and defeat come in turns over and over. The Boys beat the army and they run . . . the army beats the Boys and they run . . . "

"That's how it goes in war, amma . . . "

Chella was silent.

16

Colombo, Sri Lanka

HE HAD NO IDEA why he kept on sweating so much. It was early in the summer and the first flashes of heat were beginning to spread.

He was lying down and looking out of the small window and could see a trail of clouds through which the moon travelled. It looked like a round pot that had been crushed slightly, just shy of being a full moon. For the past few days, or perhaps even weeks, the nights had not passed easily for him. Even if he stayed awake for hours before turning out the light, sleep refused to come. He had not felt this restlessness in his early days in Colombo. His new circumstances and his new worries had banished Swarna to a corner of his mind. No longer. He frequently felt the loss of her in his body. Abayan was up to his shoulder in height now. Mekalai resembled her mother in complexion and form as she grew. He felt a delight whenever he visited them in Thunukkai. Yet the growing stirrings of his body made him forget all of that. Siva was a couple of years younger than him. He was still unmarried. He occasionally went out on the town, and sometimes stayed out all night. He was sometimes seen on his motorcycle with a girl called

Helen from the prawn-packing factory. Where could Thiravi go?

At times even the moon tormented him. He remembered how they had lain side by side on the verandah of the house in Vavuniya, looking at the moon peeking between the leaves of the coconut and mango trees; how they had talked, marveling in the flecks of light it cast on the other's face. So many delights to the senses! How many embraces, unions.

Just as his nights were troubled, his days were sometimes languorous. Recently, his afternoons had been more exciting. Anil had reduced his workload somewhat. He was working on a book, titled "Approaches to Solutions for the Ethnic Conflict: Rights and Wrongs." It had been implicitly critical of the devolution package. The book analysed the gaps in previous accords and their failures. Anil was determined to have it released in English, Tamil, and Sinhala. He had asked Thiravi to translate the book into Tamil, and he'd given the task of translating the book into Sinhala to his friend Anura Wickremesinghe. The original was in English. He would occasionally ask Thiravi to read through sections he thought might be contradictory and asked his opinion. During this process, Thiravi's torpor vanished.

One Tuesday, Siva had taken his truck to Vavuniya.

Thiravi sent off a fax containing the day's news and left the office at around three in the afternoon. Anil had told him not to take out the motorcycle without a license. He used it in emergencies, but he didn't like using it to travel to and from home. He took a minibus instead to Kochikade and got out at St Anthony's Church. He waited to cross the street to visit his friend Thomas. A woman who had been talking to Thomas took the paper on which he'd written something and was about to leave with her companion. It was only as he crossed the street and approached the video rental store that he realized that the woman was Arasi.

On seeing him Thomas pointed, saying, "He's saved you the

trouble. Thiravi is right here."

They exchanged smiles and asked after each other's welfare. Thiravi asked her when and why she had come to Colombo. She told him she planned to go to India.

"When?"

"I've applied for an emergency passport to get the visa . . . but it will take another two weeks before I can leave," Arasi replied.

He got the address of the lodge at which she was staying. "If I can . . . I will come and visit you by Sunday," he said.

It was five o'clock. Arasi and her friend Subathra took their leave and went into the church. Thiravi went home.

It was only when he lay in bed that night that he realized that though they had talked lightly about their hometown, and the condition of the country, they hadn't spoken at all about a couple of people. It struck him then that they had both been reluctant to speak about them.

That shared reluctance made him wonder even more about Arasi.

He had read some of Arasi's poems in the papers. He wasn't a fan of poetry, but he could tell good poetry. Her poems always ended in a query or seemed to be the answer to a query. This much he had noticed. He hadn't known at the time that she was the author of those poems. It was Siva who told him once when they had been thinking about her. "Arasi writes beautiful poetry; did you know?"

"Is she the poet Arasi?"

"Mm."

"You never told me all this time."

"I only found out recently. A relative of mine told me." He had been surprised. Her brother had done his BA, but Arasi had only received a tenth-grade education. He wondered what had prompted her to this pursuit. Poetry was a distillation. He felt that all the meanings we hesitate to speak in prose came pouring out at a glimpse of poetic language.

It was ten o'clock when he reached her lodge the following Sunday.

The lodge was in a state of excitement. centred around the telephone in the middle of the reception. It brought news from Canada, England, Switzerland . . . from all over the world. Thiravi felt as if the whole lodge hung on every word as each person asked in turn . . . would the sponsor work out, how was everyone over there, we need money urgently, can you send it soon? All their needs were addressed in that circle.

He walked past them and up the stairs.

Arasi and her friend Subathra were in their room.

Thiravi and Arasi brought two chairs out to the lodge's balcony and sat down facing the street and began talking. Subathra sat off to a side, saying she had to wash her clothes.

Slowly, hesitantly, they began to broach the topics they had avoided before. Suddenly Thiravi asked, "Do you still get letters from Raji?"

She shook her head, no. "She doesn't write anymore. Or maybe she has written, and I haven't got the letters."

"Why wouldn't you get them?"

"I hadn't got a letter maami had sent me after so long. I had given her a Colombo address and I got it sent on to me."

Thiravi was silent.

"Do you write to them?"

"I did. I stopped when I wasn't getting any replies."

"Did you write to Suthan as well?"

"I've only written to Suthan once in the past ten years. I wrote it as a reply to a letter he had sent me when my husband died. He was in Germany then . . . "

"And now?"

"Now he's in France."

"Oh."

"He's taken Mala's sister with him and is living with her."

"I don't understand . . . you're saying . . . "

"Raji told him she wouldn't go to Germany. So, in a rage he took Mala's younger sister with him when he left."

Thiravi felt the anger mount in him. "Then . . . where is Raji now?"

"Raji is in a refugee camp in India, apparently."

"In a refugee camp?"

"Yes," Arasi replied.

"How can you be so sure? Especially when you don't get any letters from there?"

"I ran into Yogesh unexpectedly in the island once."

"Who's this Yogesh?"

"Raji's uncle's younger son. You remember . . . there was a proposal for Raji . . . and it got disrupted . . . "

"Gunam . . . "

"Mm. That man's brother."

"Okay."

Arasi told him all she knew.

After all that, his own grief . . . the atrocity . . . seemed not as profound.

He was stunned. Then, "It's true that some are devoted to the land. Still, when a country is in the midst of war . . . when a generation that takes going abroad as its only goal . . . it's incredible to see such devotion to her homeland. And too, she has an extreme stubbornness, I think," he finished.

"She does have a lot of that," Arasi admitted.

The breeze blew in gently from the sea far in the north. The tugboat pulling a ship that had just left or just arrived at the harbour raised its siren and it echoed through the sky. The pinnacle of a

Buddhist vihara glowed white below them. The triangular leaves of the Bo tree in front of the vihara susurrated in the breeze.

Thiravi got up to leave.

"When will you come again? If Siva comes back, bring him with you. I'll know when I'm leaving, by next week. If you give me a letter, I can take it to Raji," Arasi said.

"I don't have any news for Raji."

He said goodbye.

At whom was he angry? At whom should he really have been angry? Arasi was puzzled.

17

Colombo, Sri Lanka

SOME HASTY MOVES IN Sri Lankan politics had become merely news items. The devolution package had been abandoned. This was clearly the work of some Sinhala movements that had grown strong in the wake of the capture of Jaffna. It was accepted that war was the only means to peace. Suthumnelu, the president's white-lotus movement was seductive but not one of its petals was dedicated to peace.

Anil had openly challenged the Minister of Foreign Affairs, pointing out the basest elements of their propaganda. Though it hadn't affected his acquaintanceship with the Minister, it had hardened the SLFP party members gathered there against him. The next morning one of the Sinhala extremist presses asked whose representative he was: whether he worked as a representative of the foreign press, or a representative of the Tigers.

From that day on there was a strange crowd in front of his office. They were rough in manners and looked tough. Always, an eye watching. Especially watching Thiravi. "The news is grasped in an honest way. News is not just a simple event. The event is only a part of the news. The duty of a journalist is to investigate its context. The best kind of reporter is the one who can present the background information along with the event. Paint me in whatever colours you want, however you want. I will do my duty, no matter what. No one can intimidate me," Anil bellowed over the phone to someone two days later. A couple of neutral Sinhala newspapers had written in support of Anil's actions. Then the smoke died down. Anil calmed his tone as well. It was only then that Thiravi was able to go to and from work in peace.

That day he thought of Arasi. He called the lodge and asked to speak to her.

After a while he heard her voice.

"Hello . . . who is it?"

"Thiraviyam."

"Oh, it's you? I was going to call you in a while myself."

"What's happening?"

"Nothing much. I got my visa, that's all."

"Oh. When do you leave?"

"I need to book a ticket. I've made inquiries. I think I may be able to leave this week. I need to see you!"

"Now?"

"Maybe in the evening?"

"Can you come here?"

"It's Wellawatte, isn't it? I'll come."

When Arasi got there that afternoon, Thiravi was waiting. They walked along Marine Drive and crossed the railway tracks and reached the beach.

It wasn't the kind of beach to relax and take in fresh air. Though it had been that at one time. It was an area densely populated with Tamils. In the evening it had been full of elderly folks strolling, sitting to rest their limbs, and children running around playing games. It was better to hide their identities and not draw unnecessary attention to themselves. Even if they didn't sit down, many of them walked along the beach towards Bambalapitiya, or in the other direction, towards Dehiwala. The walks were leisurely. Dehiwala had a huge beach. They could sit and talk there. As long as no one realized they were Tamil.

The sun set slowly into the ocean. The sky was tinged red. Soon the darkness descended on the earth. It was still possible to walk in the dark. Now, when her identity wasn't obvious, Arasi felt her fear dissipate a little.

They approached the Dehiwala beach.

"Shall we stay here awhile, Arasi?"

"Let's stay. I'm in no hurry."

They sat down, giving the appearance of a married couple, close but not too close. They both sensed this and something sparked in their hearts. It would be a lie to say otherwise.

Even now, in those times when Venus emerges in the sky, she occasionally wakes, her hand reaching out in search of another's. She had bloomed as a woman and known the frustrations of lone-liness and wept in anguish. It isn't possible to be human and not know and feel such things.

They spoke about the island; they spoke of the days when they had been able to fall asleep as silence brushed them with its wings. They spoke for a long time. At one point Arasi asked, "You've been here all this time. You've been connected to the newspaper world as well. In your opinion, what on earth is going on now? What is the solution to all these problems? Is there no solution? What do you think?"

The splash of the waves didn't let her words carry further than his ears.

"It's clear that the government is dragging its feet on a politi-cal solution after Riviresa. It's not possible for India not to impact its politics, whether as a neighbouring country or as an Asian power. India must do its part for Sri Lanka's peace. The Sri Lankan government refuses third-party arbitration. And the Tigers say that the third-party arbiter must be a European country. There are many ways towards a solution. There's just no will."

After a while, she said, "Get up, let's go. It's past seven now," and rose.

He stood up. They didn't speak in the minibus. They got out at the fish market, and Thiravi took her back to the lodge and walked back home.

His heart was in a state of tender ecstasy.

When he had the conch store, someone had found an unusual valampuri conch in the seaweeds and brought it to him for sale. He had never seen a valampuri of that kind before. The conches were usually white. But this one was flawless and gleamed with a milky hue. He could have bought it if he had the money. But he didn't have the asking price on him then. There was no way for him to raise the funds either. Even if there was, it would have taken time. He had no option but to return it. Dejected, just before he returned the conch to its owner, he held its mouth to his ear. He was entranced. It tinkled with the laughter of pearls. The sound rose. It touched his soul and resounded. He couldn't think of giving away that valampuri conch after that. He removed the ring off his hand, sent it to be pawned at Thangamma's house, and bought the conch.

The memory of that wondrous valampuri came back to him then.

18

Walawwa, Sri Lanka

THE RIVER RUSHED BY. The water sparkled in a silver stream. Such beauty. As the water rushed around the rocks it splashed and sent up little fountains. The wind carried the spray farther out. On either side of the river, the land was lush, like a green saree spread out. From somewhere there came the beating of a rabana.* The sound of women singing wove through the breeze. It told of the coming of a festival. As the wind swirled, the scent of mud arose from somewhere.

Sankarananda was used to all of this, having lived in that village by the jungle.

He awoke, not wishing to sleep anymore. He picked up his cloth bag. He took out an envelope that had been carefully placed inside and looked through the scraps of notes and notebooks in it. There were several capped blue ballpoint pens in the envelope as well.

The bhikkhu closed the envelope and put it away, satisfied that it was safe. The contents of the envelope were the symbols of the continuation of his life's greatest mission. They were offerings to his teacher—a dedication.

In the spray of the Walawwa River, he wrote the great history of Lanka. It was all the monk could do to redress the present disturbances, injustices, and the apocalypse. It was the revelation of almost half a century. The elderly monk had prepared Sankarananda to finish the work he had left undone. And Sankarananda had taken on the fulfilment of his late teacher's wish as his mission in life.

He lived on rice that he received as charity, traveling from town to town. A few dreamers hosted him for a few weeks. There he stayed and wrote his great history. At the end of each period, he returned to his samsara life. As he had declared to Gunananda Thero, he preached goodness wherever he went. Sometimes he spoke through Jataka tales. Sometimes he spoke of history through stories. They amazed the people. Filled them with wonder. They were stories the people had never heard before. Then he would reach a small town. He would spend his time in reading, taking notes and meeting people. It was as he was wandering that a woman who had lost her son came running to him, weeping as she fell at his feet.

"If you had only come here two years ago, I wouldn't have lost my son!" she wailed.

He looked at the people around him, puzzled. They told him that she had received news from the frontlines that her son, who had joined the army the previous year and gone to war in the north had died.

He left the place in sorrow. But he didn't lose his fervour for work.

The writing was effortless.

There were many gaps in their history. But recently they had been filled with many biased accounts. He knew them all and removed them to write what he had learned. It could be described as a historical account that looked upon the truth and wasn't cowed into silence.

Much later, as he was visiting a town, he caught a glimpse of a newspaper headline: "The army is victorious in the north! Five hundred thousand Tamils flee the north!" The bhikkhu was shocked. He lost heart . . . to write, read, preach, or meet anyone. He left for Vanni.

The Vanni forest was new to him. But forests were not. He had even trekked through the Hanthana forest once and gone from the Chandramouleeswara ruins to Koneswaram.

Hanthana was dangerous. It was known for its ferocious wildlife. He had to fear for his life from the arrows of the mountain people who didn't speak his language. There were stories that some tribes of Veddas who ate human flesh had lived there since prehistoric times. The bhikkhu had travelled across easily.

He had never before known the kind of grief that had settled the Vanni forest now. People wandered around under trees and ramshackle huts. The only thing distinguishing them from the ancient tribes was that they covered their bodies with clothing. It was a picture of human ruin.

The people looked at him with unsympathetic and hateful eyes because of his saffron robes. Realizing that none of them were about to act on their hatred and that he couldn't avoid stepping further into the forest if he was to understand the atrocities, he forged on. It was growing dark. The darkness was of the rainy season. There could have been a raincloud above. The tree cover hid the sky, the stars, and the moon. It was the guardian of the great darkness. A young palai tree stood a little further in. The bhikkhu approached it.

Palai trees were favoured by fire ants. Whether it was fruit season or not, it didn't matter. The monk knew this from experience. But perhaps because it was the rainy season, he could not see a sign of any fire ants. The bhikkhu put down his bag, leaned and sat against the tree trunk and looked across.

There was a hut a little further away, alongside a yaavara-nai tree, with some women inside. A few children. A little further away from the entrance of the hut, a man sat with his chest wrapped in a towel. He appeared to be in some discomfort. An overgrown beard. Unkempt hair. Bony hands, elbows. Was he an invalid? But the fierce expression in his eyes banished the thought from the monk's mind.

He had to spend the night there. There was no way to return now. Even if he were able to return, he couldn't leave without knowing why he had come here. He had a piece of bread and two small kathali bananas to eat. If he had some water, he'd be all right. He could ask the people in the hut across from him.

The monk arose and approached the man with the towel around his shoulders. The man sat unmoved. As the monk approached the hut, the men and women from the surrounding huts approached slowly and surrounded him. They might have thought he was attached to a human rights group or the Red Cross; maybe he was there to assess their needs to distribute ration cards. Did the monk understand why they surrounded him eagerly?

The man with the towel watched the monk with a look of surprise. The monk squatted in front of him and asked, "Are you from Jaffna too?"

Too stunned to speak the man nodded.

"Where in Jaffna?"

Marvelling at the bhikkhu's Tamil, the old man replied, "Anaikottai."

"Have you heard about me at all?"

The man shook his head, no.

"The preaching bhikkhu, they call me."

"Oh . . . is that you? I have heard about you, swami."

A note of respect had crept into his voice. The bhikkhu realized that the man had indeed heard about him. It gave him some happiness.

Inside, in the hearth, embers crackled, and sparks flew out. He supposed this was the time they cooked their food. He now understood the reason for the children's complaints and cries.

When the people realized he was not who they had hoped he would be, they began to disperse.

"I'm hoping to sleep here tonight. I have food. I just need a little water to drink."

"There are a lot of Boys from the Movement here. If they come, they will make arrangements for you to sleep somewhere."

"I don't need any of that."

The old man turned and called to someone inside the hut. "Rajam! Rajam!"

"What is it, aiyya?"

"Bring the swami some water to drink."

"Let it cool, aiyya. I just took the pot off the fire," Rajam said.

"Wait a while, swami. She has left the water to cool. It will come," Rajam's father said, looking at the monk.

"I can drink fresh water, that's all right."

"You must boil the water before drinking it here. When we first got here, we drank the water without boiling. Ten of the adults got cholera. About twenty-five children got sick and five of them died. So now we don't drink the water without boiling it. There's no shortage of firewood here."

"That's true," the monk said as he crossed his legs and sat down to wait.

"You came here after Riviresa*, then?"

"Yes."

"What did you do for a living back home?"

"I was a teacher. I've been pensioned for four years now."

"Do you get your pension regularly?"

"What do you get regularly these days, for me to complain

about not getting my pension?"

"That's true," the bhikkhu said and was silent.

The monk wanted to keep probing and asking the man questions. A few people had told him that Operation Riviresa, or Sunrays, was a desperate ploy on the part of the government. He thought it might be useful to speak about it with the old teacher. So, he tried again.

"I used to be a Thero a while back, at the Nagavihara, in Nainativu."

"Oh . . . so that's why you speak Tamil so well, swami."

"I was there for seven years. I have a friend called Sankarapillai there . . . he's a teacher as well. But never mind, what is your name?"

"Sanmugam."

"You had your own house in your town?"

"There are few families in Jaffna who don't have their own house, swami. Even if they're living in poverty, they'll have a small farm garden and a hut. You lived in the island for seven years, and you still don't know this?"

"You're right," the bhikkhu replied. But he didn't stop there. "Have you gone back to your house, since you left?"

"Where would I go? What would I see?" Sanmugam said in resignation.

"Why?"

"What a house, swami! We scrimped and saved . . . joined a seettu* and built that house. What banana, mango, jackfruit, lemon, pomegranate trees we had! I turned that plot into an oasis. Just outside the window at the front of the house we had two young king coconut trees. One of them had just produced an abundance of fruit. We never had a chance to cut down a single fruit for the pleasure of drinking its water. We had to abandon all of it and come. Two years now . . . Do you think any of those houses still have their fences and entrances safely locked up? No, swami. I can't bear to go back and see it all in ruins . . . my heart will break, and I'll drop dead on the spot."

Sanmugam wiped his face with his towel and calmed down. The scenes of that exodus unfolded before the monk. He felt himself carried along on every word from the old man's mouth. He felt what they felt. The bhikkhu could clearly see that the man was reliving everything he had experienced. He listened without interrupting.

"With their belonging . . . without belongings . . . on cycles and tractors . . . walking and running behind vehicles . . . oh god, how many temples we visited, how many festivals we observed, how many fasts we undertook . . . none of it helped. It was all for nothing. We fled . . . how we fled . . . that's what the Boys told us to do. That's what the Sinhalese government told us to do."

Mosquitoes began stinging. The bhikkhu had covered himself with his robe. Sanmugam had wrapped his towel around himself. But the mosquitoes found every gap and stung them. Where could they go to get away from the mosquitoes? Yet neither the speaker nor the listener was aware of them.

The migration was like being pulled up by the roots. It could take on different dimensions. No dimension could be far from the truth of destruction. It wasn't only the loss of a house, farm garden, land, jewellery, clothing, and belongings, but also health, wellbeing, culture and so much more.

When would they be safe again? How?

"Could you have avoided fleeing, Sanmugam? You would have had bunkers . . . couldn't you have hidden?"

"No one wanted to leave, swami. It was only fear . . . fear . . . utter fear that made us run. An Avro comes roaring in the middle of the night and drops bombs. We wake up, startled, as if from a nightmare. We hear napalm bombs falling and houses crumbling.

Bullets from the helicopters' fifty-caliber guns squeal past. I drag the children out and come stand on the road. My neighbour was a man called Vadivelu. His house was built on the money his son had sent back from Saudi. He had just finished building it. Twice the size of our house. Built in the American fashion . . . amazing to look at. It was when I began running that I saw Vadivelu standing in the middle of his house with his wife and children. The wife and children were shouting. He stood there like a madman, wouldn't budge. Finally, he brought them outside and told them to go and went back inside. I called out to him, 'Vadivelu don't go . . . come back . . . come back!' His wife was wailing. The children crying, 'Aiyya, aiyya.' 'Take her with you, teacher . . . I can't leave my house,' he said, and he went back inside. The next second, I felt like my eardrums burst. When I looked . . . his house was razed to the ground. Here and there fires burning . . . and this in the rain. How could we not run, swami? We knew only one thing at that time. To run. With your children if you can; or alone."

Rajam brought the water to the bhikkhu.

He took it and walked away.

What he could see of the sky through the branches looked grey. No stars . . . no moon. Bare sky. A grey sky. He stood staring at it.

He was relieved that at least it hadn't rained.

Eventually he slept for a little while.

Somewhere there was a disturbance . . . he heard a soft lament.

He felt in his heart that Lankapura was in darkness, and wolves howled down its darkened streets.

The next day he asked Sanmugam about the lament.

"That's normal here, swami."

Human ruin . . . human ruin . . .

The words echoed in his heart until he left for Vavuniya.

19

Vavuniya, Sri Lanka

WHEN HE GOT TO Vavuniya, Sankarananda decided to spend the day there.

That pale, slender figure who had disappeared behind the curtain of death frequently haunted him when he visited the place. At those times he felt he must get as far away from the place as possible. He felt that there were more people about in Vavuniya now. He also noticed a difference in the atmosphere. Though there was a lot of activity, the people seemed to move always apart from each other, like nelli fruit, and always in a hurry. This was due to an underlying tension. The people rushed through their tasks at the same speed as when they arrived, got into their vehicles, or walked away hurriedly. Did they fear that anything could happen to them at any moment? That was it. There was always something happening somewhere, all the time. The Sinhalese felt this fear as the Tamils did. They too were running like rats escaping a net. Cycle bombs and landmines didn't discriminate between race, religion, or language when they exploded.

He thought about Thiravi a lot these days. He felt he must see and speak to him. When he last saw him, Thiravi had mentioned that he planned to go to Colombo. Had he left already? Even if he hadn't, Sankarananda could not bear to go to that house after the horror of what had happened to Thiravi's wife. He went to Siva's apartment. He was told at the tea shop downstairs that Thiravi and Siva had gone to Colombo. Siva visited his apartment only once or twice a month.

He went to the vihara.

The sad plight of the half a million refugees from the north poured more sorrow into his heart. It was the peak of tragedy that half a million people were displaced, and that during the rainy season, when the nights were pitch black. He knew that similar migrations had happened in the history of the world. That early great migration had happened in the years before Christ and was spoken of in the bible. It was divine will that the Jews went to Egypt. They suffered untold agonies there. To safeguard their beautiful women, they underwent great travails and sorrows. A husband disowned his wife in order not to be seen as giving her over to the king. Or he was forced to take her to the king. They went through these atrocities for four hundred and thirty years.

One day, another command bid them to return home. "Don't fear! Leave this place and go to your own land. The land is ready to welcome you. Famine and drought have vanished. Here, the pharaoh has decided to wipe you out entirely. Before he begins his evil plans, flee from here!" God sent his message through Moses, who was to lead them through a long stretch of their journey, and through Aaron.

The exodus, a journey unknown to the puranas and the epics until then, begins at midnight. People in rows, numbering like pebbles. Six hundred thousand women. With the men and children. They ran. Walked. Hobbled. They walked through deserts. Through wilderness. And valleys in between.

Hunger . . . sleep . . . fatigue . . . deaths . . . diseases . . .

Once.

The sea ahead of them. Waves leaping and crashing, demanding sacrifice. The floor of the sea opened its belly to swallow those who were trapped.

Fear . . . despair . . . wailing . . .

God tells Moses to hold out his staff over the ocean.

As Moses obeys and stretches out his staff, the ocean parts in two and a path opens out in the middle. The people rush through. On either side the sea rises like a wall. Filled with awe and fear, the people who have journeyed so long rush through.

As they are almost across, Moses sees the pharaoh's war chariots chasing after them. The people are inconsolable. If we were to die, we could have died in Egypt, they wail . . . why go through all these trials? If we had died in Egypt, we'd at least be buried in graves.

God commands Moses to hold his staff over the ocean again.

The pharaoh's chariots have come halfway across the parted sea.

Moses holds out his staff and the cloven ocean closes in again. As the walls of water crumble, the whole ocean resounds with it. It sees the two expanses of water crash together in full force and rise . . . to form a giant wave. The pharaoh's army is engulfed in the belly of the ocean, with not one spared.

The people journey forward and reach their promised land. In a way it is a return migration. But it held all the trials of a journey into exile.

What could he possibly do for these Vanni refugees? He was not the sort to get easily tired or discouraged. He did feel the small aches and pains of old age. That was all. He needed a crutch. He used one occasionally.

Perhaps . . . that was all he could do? He tried to calm himself.

Some electric light . . . then a darkened area . . . he could see all of it. That was the place where he and Gunananda had got into an argument. That day he had shaken that political science graduate from Vidyalankara to the core. He had not seen him since. He had no intention to see him.

Gunananda was an individual in a movement. Sankarananda was a movement of one. Yet thousands upon thousands of people came to hear his words, to see his face, and to receive words of comfort from him. They were the symbols of the strength of his prayers.

It would dawn again in the east.

He sat peering into the darkness, thinking.

20

Walawwa, Sri Lanka

THE BHIKKHU SANKARANANDA LAY sleeping, stretched out inside the vihara by the riverbank. His head faced the south, towards a silent stretch of land. He heard the sound of the rabanna from a distant village in the north. He remembered that the Sinhala and Tamil New Year would arrive in two days. There were few sounds of rejoicing for the upcoming festival.

It relaxed his body to sleep with his arms and legs stretched out. Sleep came easily.

For some reason he realized then that he was lying north to south. He though of the words attributed to the child Dutugemunu: "With the Tamils to the north and the ocean to the south, how can I stretch out to sleep, mother?" This would not figure in his history.

There were two chapters of the great history yet to be written. There would be a restlessness and unease within him as long as they remained unwritten.

Buddhathattha was walking towards him as he lay their unmoving. The bhikkhu awoke with a start. It was only then he realized it was a dream. Was this because he had thought he must give the first three chapters he had written of the great history to Buddhathattha for safe-keeping?

Buddhathattha was lame. He had been in the army in the north for a long time. Once, while they were in a truck, a landmine had exploded, killing eight soldiers, and leaving him with his right leg paralysed. He lived in Punchi Borella. Sankarananda had met him unexpectedly. "What happened to your leg?" he had asked sympathetically. "I lost it in a landmine," Buddhathattha replied. "War is cruel. Either you lose your life, or you lose a limb. You keep losing something or the other," he said, smiling unexpectedly at the pitying face of the monk. That was how they had become friends. The friendship grew slowly. The bhikkhu never forgot to visit him when he went to Colombo. That friendship had come at an opportune time. Buddhathattha supported the monk's work wholeheartedly.

The bhikkhu thought of his dream and laughed.

There were many people like Gunananda. Some of them had shaven heads, some not. They had support from the religious institutions, as well as all manner of other forces. They would cause a river of blood.

Thirumalai was a sacred place. As sacred as Keerimalai. It had a history beyond record. It was difficult to assess its history without a prodigious amount of learning.

His teacher had spoken to Sankarananda with confidence: "Trincomalee history is Tamil history. History tells us that ancient settlements appeared in the north, south and west. But there were Tamil civilizations there thousands of years before the time of those settlements. The east was their core. The puranas and epics must be thought of as imagination that emerged from truth. If there was no truth there would be no fabrication. The parallels are the proof of the dream."

"Ravanan's story is not merely a fantasy. Neither is Raavana's

Cleft. Some nights when I'm asleep I hear the crack, crack of rocks splitting in the northeast direction. A shoulder that could move mountains . . . breathe like a gale . . . eyes glittering like the sun . . . his magnificence lifting a long sword to split a mountain in two, that's the vision that comes to my mind. What do you think of that, Sankarananda?"

Sankarananda had sat in silence. He could never let his imagination roam in such directions, like those who sit at a keyboard. But he felt something.

"Listen, Sankarananda. There was a powerful dynasty in the east that held the sacred mountain as its capital. There was a tribe that they had been vanquished in the northeast. That was the Naga tribe. Then a mixed race of people emerged. That race governed the north and the east. Then somehow, that eastern dynasty declined, like Babylon, Turkey, Egypt, Greece, and Rome. If there had been a proper archaeological study conducted in Trincomalee, all these truths would have been revealed. I tried in my time. But I couldn't carry it out. You must fill this vacuum."

The sound of his teacher struggling with each breath as he spoke echoed in his ears even now. But as he contemplated those words, more puzzles emerged. He was filled with amazement. And awe.

Was this a land where history had leaped and played?

He had gone to Koneswaram once. It looked like an abandoned house. It had forgotten the rituals of worshipping the supreme god, Siva. He had felt deeply troubled. He spent some time looking around the temple. It was a beautiful structure. The waves beating below. The three mountain peaks that took turns lifting the sun. From the street just outside the temple Raavana's Cleft, its base too far below to be visible. It was always shrouded in darkness. The white foam contrasted in splashes against the dark rocks.

He went outside and walked around. Fields of sugar cane, pond dams . . . what lushness! The forest, river, and sea surrounding him compelled him to stay. And here he had written the core of his historical text: the Chola incursion, the reign of their representatives, the story of Rohanam, and the architecture.

Now he could begin his journey.

The sun's rays had spread everywhere like a river.

But below the trees, the shade was still dark and cool.

21

Chennai, India

CHANDRAMOHAN HAD BEEN READY to leave for India in
April. It was the Indian High Commission that dragged its feet
giving him a visa. He had grown discouraged . . . but then they
gave it to him just before Theepavali.

He didn't engage in any business for the first three days in
Chennai. Katpaham maami's son Thivyan had been in India
for five years and knew Chennai inside out. His older sister
Perunthevi was studying at St Mary's. Those three days the three
of them enjoyed themselves visiting the cinema, temples, Golden
Beach, and the MGM.

It was on the morning of the fourth day that he picked up the
addresses he had brought with him and thought about the places
he had come to visit. He had a few letters and parcels to deliver
directly. Raji's matter was the most important of all to him. You
could say he had come mainly for this reason. He had also wanted
to meet some literary figures he admired, and to speak to some
volunteer organizations about celebrating the tenth year of the
Assembly.

After breakfast, he took Thivyan with him to show him the way and took an auto to meet Kamala. It was only when he got to her place that he heard she had moved to Porur. The neighbours were unable to give him her new address. They said perhaps Mala's family might know. So he had to go there. He was in no rush. He thought he might have to deal with some problems or tensions when he visited them. It depended on how much Sheila had told them about her split with Suthan. That was why he had tried to meet Kamala first.

Saraswathi peered out when she heard the gate open. When she saw two people she didn't recognize in the doorway, she called out, "Mala, go see who it is."

When Mala came to inquire, Chandramohan told her why he was there. Though she was hesitant at first to give the address to a stranger, many people had already showed up asking for Kamala's address, and she had given it to them, and this man had come all the way from France, so she made up her mind and wrote it down for him. Once they realized from his conversation that he was a friend of Suthan's, Mala and Saraswathi would not let him leave so easily. They compelled him to come in and have at least a cup of tea.

Chandramohan and Thivyan went inside and sat down.

He made small talk with Mala. It was only after Saraswathi had brought the tea that the tone changed. "How is Sheila, thambi?" Saraswathi asked.

He was amazed by the excitement and the warm welcome he received when they learned he was Suthan's friend. He also realized that they had asked him how Sheila was, because they thought she was still with Suthan.

He could have said, "She's doing well and kept up the pretence." But he felt he needed to let them know that they had split and help them accept it somehow. This mainly because he knew that they were still in touch with Raji, Maheswari, Arasi, and perhaps even

Rajendran. Though Kamala could help him somewhat with Raji, he thought he might others to help him accomplish what he had come for.

He thought that he didn't need to go into the fact that Suthan and Sheila had separated right away and alarm them. He decided he could suggest that indirectly and explain later. "I think Sheila's fine. I haven't seen her in person for . . . maybe . . . a year," Chandramohan said.

"Then you didn't see Suthan before you came?"

He realized that she had caught on that something wasn't right.

"I saw Suthan when I went to Paris. But . . . Sheila is not in Paris with Suthan now."

"She's not with Suthan?"

It wasn't a question; it was an expression of shock.

"Why . . . didn't you know? Didn't Sheila write to you about it?"

Saraswathi was now in tears. All manner of thoughts raced through her mind. Could it be? Could Sheila do something like that? It would not have affected her as much if it had been Suthan who had done it, she could have borne it somehow. There were lots of reasons why she would not write. She never acknowledged her mistakes, or her defeats to anyone.

"Wretch . . . she never wrote anything to us, thambi. What is the problem between them?" Saraswathi asked when she had come to herself. Her voice still quavered.

"I don't know what happened. It was Sheila who suddenly got angry and left the house. Suthan never explained anything to me. I thought I would wait till they cooled down and ask, but Suthan sold the house and moved to Paris."

"Sold the house?" Saraswathi panicked.

"There's four hundred kilometers between Paris and where I live. We occasionally see each other. But . . . aren't you sending Sheila's letters to a new address?"

"Yes."

"Didn't you wonder why the address has changed?"

Mala replied, "What did we know? She said, 'I have a new job . . . write to this address from now on,' and sent us an address . . . so we write to her there."

Chandramohan stood up. "I have a lot of work to take care of. I have an auto waiting outside as well. I'll see you then."

"How long will you be here?" Saraswathi asked.

"For two weeks maybe."

"Tell us where you're staying, we'll come and visit you. We should talk more about all this before you leave . . . "

"No, don't worry. I'll come back and spend some time with you."

"Don't forget."

"I won't."

Chandramohan left with Thivyan.

22

Chennai, India

KAMALA HAD LEFT ANNA Nagar for Porur because she knew a few people there. She had lived on the second floor of a house in Anna Nagar. It had been ten years. She was tired of climbing up and down the stairs. On top of that she had developed arthritis in her knees. She asked the old Shathri lady about the place and checked the layout of the house to see if the entrance of the house suited her before she rented it. So even when the ground floor became available in her old house, she didn't want to move again. Though the new place didn't have any luxuries, she and Nagaraja didn't have to struggle to welcome people to their home when they arrived. Her two younger brothers lived overseas. Satkuru was in Canada, and Satkunam was in Switzerland, so they helped her occasionally. They lived quite comfortably on the money that was sent to them, and they had no children themselves. So, they didn't face many of the struggles that others did. Nagarajah had developed a chest infection that left him with breathing difficulties when they took the boat across from Sri Lanka. Even from childhood, he had suffered occasionally from asthma, like his mother. He had suddenly developed a serious asthma attack as they waited four days for a boat on the Mannar shore. Even after they arrived in Chennai, he took great care. He could not stand either the damp or the dust. He was eventually cured because he took care of himself, and because he was able to find the right doctors and medication. Later, Kamala wrote to her brother Satkuru, asking him to call Nagaraja to Canada. After a full year of waiting, they were able to save up for the cost of Nagaraja's trip to Canada. Then Nagaraja called asking her to get their own house in Porur. As they didn't have to worry about the money, Kamala agreed and moved to Porur.

When she got there, she became lazy. Two idlis in the morning, or some Ceylon bread. Sometimes she made thosai. She cooked her afternoon meal. She didn't bother too much with dinner. All she had to do was sleep and wake up. Her body swelled up like a pumpkin. Her bosom had grown disproportionately. She was not happy with these changes. She had developed the shiny pallor of an invalid. She could have put up with that. But what she could not bear was how her hair had suddenly turned grey. She didn't mind a few strands of grey. She was old enough to expect that. But more than half her head going grey . . . ?

Kamala was lying on the marble floor of the hallway. She had already had one nap of the day. It was starting to get cold earlier. She felt too lethargic to get up. It was around five in the evening. She might as well get up, she thought, put some water to boil, wash her face and make herself some tea. She sat up.

An auto arrived at the gate. Chandramohan got out, stood hesitating at the entrance before pushing the gate open noisily to announce his arrival.

The door to the house was open. He stood on the doorstep and rang the bell; Kamala came to the door. "Who are you, thambi?"

"Is there a Kamala akka . . . "

"That's me. What is it?"

"My name is Chandramohan. I've come from France. A friend of Suthan's. I need to speak to you about something."

Surprise and joy mingled on her face as she absorbed what he had said, then she replied, "Come in."

Once she had gathered that he knew about her, and that he was close to Suthan and knew about Raji and had gone to Mala's house and spoken to them, and that he had got her address from them, she left him, saying, "Sit down, thambi, I'll be back in a minute." She came back five minutes later with some tea.

As he drank the tea, he answered all her casual questions.

When he had finished the tea, there was a lull in the conversation, and Chandramohan asked calmly, "You know Sheila, don't you?"

"Of course! She has been in and out of my house. Why . . . what's the matter?"

You could say that his calm tone had unsettled her. She realized that he had come to speak to her about Sheila, and about her people.

He began, "When Sheila and Suthan first came to France they stayed in my house. For four years."

"And then?"

"Then they bought their own place and moved out. The house was close to ours. Now they've sold the house. Suthan lives in Paris. Sheila, just outside of Paris . . . "

"I don't understand any of this."

Chandramohan explained it all to her.

"Has it been a long time, thambi? Since all this happened?"

"Four years."

"Four years . . . ?"

"Maybe more."

"Tcha . . . " Kamala exclaimed in surprise: "No one here knew she had problems at all! It's been a year, or a year and a half since I moved here. But I go to Anna Nagar once every few months. Mala didn't breathe a word of this to me either."

"I had hoped to meet you before I went to visit. So, I had originally gone to your old place. When I realized you had left, I had to go to Mala's place to get your new address. Even as I was going there, I wondered if they knew about this matter or not. If they didn't . . . I wasn't sure how much I should share with them. As soon as she heard that there was a conflict between Sheila and Suthan, her mother was rattled. I got out of there saying that I'd come back and talk to them later in detail."

Kamala was silent for a while, then she asked, "What's really the problem between Suthan and Sheila?"

He hesitated, wondering if he should tell her everything. He realized that he had to. He had to surrender to the fact that there was no way of moving ahead on the issue without disclosing all the facts to someone.

"Sheila's behaviour became the problem. She goes about all over the place . . . spends money on whatever she fancies, Suthan wasn't happy with it. I think they fought about it now and then. One day it all came to a head . . . and it seemed that Sheila moved out. It was only after she moved out that it came out that she was in a relationship with the Algerian boss of a clothing company. She's not with him anymore either, I hear."

"She had it coming!" Kamala fumed. "Suthan deserves even worse. He grabbed the first girl he could because he heard that Raji had gone back home; he didn't give it a second thought and dragged her with him. That poor Raji is suffering in a refugee camp after she drove away her mother and siblings. How will their crime against her not come back on them?"

He waited until her fury had subsided and went on, "It looks like there'll never be any reconciliation between Suthan and Sheila. I don't really care about Sheila. She lived with us for four years, like a sister, it's true. But she can take care of herself. But . . . I feel sorry for Suthan . . . "

"Why, is he pining for her?"

"Yes, akka. He's only begun pining now. But not for Sheila. For Raji. He's been thinking about everything that has passed and feels very bad about it."

She got up to switch on the light.

She looked out the front door and turned to him. "Thambi, the auto you came in is still at the gate? Could have given the man some tea."

"It's okay, akka. It's time for me to leave."

"Lots of mosquitos. We usually close the doors and windows by six o clock," she said as she began closing the front windows.

"Suthan is . . . he doesn't take care of himself . . . he's started to look like a mad man."

Kamala looked thoughtfully into his face. She listened to him with the same care.

"Some of his other friends and I have been talking and have come to a decision. I thought I should talk to you about it and see what you think. That's why I came."

"Talk about what?"

"I need to know a little bit about Raji. Is she still in the camp?"

Her brows furrowed. "Yes."

"Apparently, she had said she was going back home in eighty-seven. Didn't she go then . . . ?"

"She went. But at the time the fighting had started between the Indian army and the Tigers. The boat turned away at Mannar and went back to Kodiakkarai. She ended up back at the camp."

"Hm . . . " he murmured and was quiet. Then he broke his silence, "Akka, don't get upset. I'm going to ask you something. We heard that a boy had gone with her . . . "

"He did. The seafarer. A boy who pilots a boat. He's her uncle's son on the mother's side. He swam across to the Tamil Nadu shore once when his boat was shot down by the navy, and he was injured. The boy was half dead when Raji found him somewhere and helped him by bringing him here. We took care of him for two weeks," Kamala said. She was about to say something else but ended with: "He's a decent boy."

He listened in silence.

The rain began to splatter outside.

Heavy trucks drove down the Porur highway, honking at the other vehicles to make way.

Kamala sat looking at Chandramohan.

She had always thought of Raji as a sister. She worried about her future. She knew that a tenderness had crept into her relationship with Yogesh. Though she had disliked this layer of complication, Kamala respected Raji. Her story was indeed a tragic one. She knew that the relationship with Yogesh had broken off at some point as well. She had thought it was for the best. Raji might still harbour feelings for him. Who could peer into other people's hearts anyway? Many stories had come about him through hearsay, over the sea. A few had been reported in the Tamil newspapers overseas as well. She and Raji had talked about them too.

"We know you have a good relationship with Raji. If Raji can think of Suthan's past as a bad dream, we can try and bring the two of them back together. I don't know how to explain this exactly. Can you talk to her . . . and maybe try something to help it work? But first tell me about your thoughts on this, akka," he asked.

"We must certainly try," Kamala said, and broke down, her body shaking with sobs.

It showed the depth of her feeling. Who were they to each other . . . and how had they formed relationships and entitlements to each other as human beings? Chandramohan's heart melted at the thought.

Kamala came to herself and said: "For how long I have waited and hoped for a light to enter her life! If we unite these two and give them a new life . . . you don't need to go to the temple . . . you don't need to give out alms . . . this alone will bring you great merit in life, thambi. I'll speak to Raji and see. When are you planning to return to France?"

"When I left, I was planning on returning in two weeks. I can extend my stay if needed."

"We can't rush into this. But I'll talk to her and let you know. I'll have to send her a letter and ask her to visit. I have to speak to her in person. I'll write to her tomorrow."

Chandramohan stood up, satisfied: "I must go to Pondicherry tomorrow. It will take a couple of days to return. I'll come speak to you then . . . "

"Give me a call before you come," Kamala said, and gave him her phone number.

23

Chennai, India

TIME ISN'T THE EROSION of moments. It's something that moves with those moments. Time can also leap outside of moments and move along. Similarly, time may lag and seem out of sync with a moment. These movements back and forth are corollaries. The movement can only be distinguished in a moment. Life is like time. It can seem to move faster or slower than those moments.

Kamala moved within time. How easily . . . naturally . . . she had a grasp on life. Her life progressed along with the times. Chandramohan admired her openness.

Chandramohan went to Porur the day after he returned from Pondicherry. Kamala compelled him to stay for lunch. The two of them talked for a long time that day. He pulled a chair up to the entrance of the kitchen and talked to her while she cooked.

She told him that Raji had called her as soon as she got the letter, and that she planned to visit on the Saturday and stay until Sunday afternoon. They made small talk for a while. It was she who brought up Yogesh again. She thought that she couldn't leave these things unsaid, and mentioned some of what she knew to him.

As he was leaving after lunch, she said, "There's an old judge called Rajanayagam . . . he's from Chavakacheri . . . lives in Anna Nagar now. He's one of the more important people in Raji's life; someone she respects. Raji will listen to anything he says. It would be good to meet him. And you can be open with him, no need to hide anything. Raji usually goes there before she comes here, so she might do that this time too."

After he had spoken more to Kamala about Raji that day, Chandramohan felt he had a more complete picture of her character.

He wasn't sure if he had anything to discuss with Rajanayagam. But since the name sounded familiar, he thought he would go visit him. Not only that. Now that he had a good sense of Raji's character, he felt he needed to include anyone who could influence her in his efforts. So, he made up his mind to meet with Rajanayagam the next day.

He stuck to his plan and went to Rajanayagam's house the next morning. The lawn, the garden the sense of calm that pervaded everything, they all delighted Chandramohan. Seeing a new face at his doorstep, Rajanayagam arose from his seat in the hall and came outside.

Chandramohan introduced himself. He told Rajanayagam that Kamala had asked him to come meet him.

"Come inside," the old judge said and invited him to sit down. He asked a woman who looked like she might be a servant, to make them some tea. It was only after he had drunk his tea that Chandramohan introduced the matter he had come to discuss with Rajanayagam.

He told him that Suthan was his friend and had lived with him when he first arrived in France. He stressed that Suthan had lived with him for four years, so he would understand that they were close friends.

"Sheila came with him too, didn't she?"

"Yes. But Sheila isn't with Suthan anymore."

Rajanayagam turned to him in surprise. Chandramohan explained everything in detail. Then he said, "I've come here to find out about Raji."

"Why, are you concerned that she might be living with someone as well?" he said quietly. If he had smiled it might not have felt so harsh.

Chandramohan was taken aback.

The old man continued, "She's in the refugee camp. She does what she can for the thousand refugees there. Everybody is in such a hurry to get 'asylum' overseas nowadays, who cares about helping the refugees in the camps here? Only one or two people like Raji have that kind of concern. Can't stand even that, is that it?"

Chandramohan pacified him and explained why he had inquired about her. Rajanayagam seemed to calm down. But it was clear that he was not quite himself.

"Raji is coming to Madras tomorrow. Kamala akka said she would come here first. If she does, you must talk to her and help us with our efforts," Chandramohan pressed on.

"Mm," Rajanayagam mumbled reluctantly, though his sternness was gone. "I can't do much myself. I can't pressure her. I'll let her know. If she listens, fine. Because it's the kind of thing that slips out of your hands when you force it. Even if, and I mean if, she agrees, I still don't think she'll go to France."

"That's not important. It's enough that she agrees."

"Look here, thambi, you can't transplant a tea bush in Jaffna. You can't grow the long drumsticks of Jaffna in the hill country. The relationship between soil and person is very much like that."

"That's true, aiyya," Chandramohan agreed. "There's more than fifty thousand Tamils in France now. Many of them are quite happy with their houses . . . cars . . . and getting an education for their kids. Some really enjoy themselves. Grand birthdays, saamathiya celebrations, weddings . . . they're oblivious to everything beyond them. They're completely assimilated into the adopted land's cultures. They don't care at all that that there's a war going on back home about the anguish our people are experiencing in the refugee camps, the misery of the people stuck in Vanni, or even the erasure of language and traditions that's happening in these foreign lands."

Rajanayagam got worked up as he talked about it.

Rajanayagam understood that Chandramohan wasn't the average man he had taken him for. He was a thoughtful young man. He hadn't been assimilated. And he seemed not to want others to be lost to assimilation either. He cared about his language and his culture. He may have been forced to go overseas, but he hadn't lost a sense of who he was.

Rajanayagam asked if they could go sit outside for a while. Chandramohan stood up. The old judge took his pipe and walked out to the verandah. He switched on the outside fan to high and sat down. Chandramohan sat beside him.

It was beautiful outside. Lightbulbs glittered in the silent darkness of the monsoon. The sky was covered in dark clouds that hid the stars. There was cold in the air. The gusts of air from the fan made the air even colder, but he had realized from his time there that a fan was needed to keep away the mosquitoes.

Though it was in the city, the house felt like it was somehow separate. Houses surrounded it on three sides, and Chandramohan was surprised that it gave off that feeling. His own house in Nantes was very much like that too. He stayed for a while, immersed in its beauty. Then he expressed his wonder openly to the older man.

He was puffing puck . . . puck . . . on his pipe. He nodded

deliberately. "It's true. It's nothing else. This feeling wouldn't exist without the margosa tree beside the eastern wall, and the rain tree on the street just outside the gate."

Chandramohan looked at the time. He gestured as if to say it was time he left.

"It looks like it's going to rain, aiyya. I have an auto waiting too . . ."

"You didn't send your auto away? Go send him away and come back. We haven't talked about half the things we should . . . stay here, you can leave in the morning."

Chandramohan tried to demur. The other wouldn't allow it. Then Chandramohan thought it was for the best. If he went to Mala's house the next morning, he could meet Viswalingam too. Raji would be coming up from the camp. It could turn out to be an important day. He went out and sent off the auto.

When he sat back in his chair, the old judge asked him if he'd like some food, or more tea. Just tea, Chandramohan said, and the older man went in to ask for more tea, then returned and began, "Thambi, you were telling me about our people's selfish behaviour. Look here . . . the court case around Rajiv Ghandi's assassination just ended. The ruling, and the way the ruling was delivered has amazed the legal world. Our people don't seem to care. Tamil Nadu was a great source of support for us. Now we're destitute, orphans. Our people's disinterest is a whole problem on its own. If this lack of interest continues . . . there's no use in appealing the decision either. Somehow, we gather the funds we can and run around and do what we need to do . . . whatever happens, happens."

Chandramohan couldn't accept his old-fashioned politics based on ethnic feeling. It was the ideology that struck him the most, more than the antiquatedness. The most he could respect in this issue was Tamil nationalism. It had the potential to expand until its drew in all of humanity. But the old man was speaking of ethnic feeling. So Chandramohan stayed silent and didn't express his dissent. He saw no point in hurting the judge's feelings.

Rajanayagam quickly grasped the meaning of his silence and discreetly changed the subject. He was starved for conversation. He didn't have many friends either. One day he had met a young lawyer named Satkunam opposite the Shastri Bhavan, and that young man visited him occasionally. He only talked about court cases. He spoke eagerly about the Special Court inquiry into Rajiv Ghandi's death, the ruling, and the precedents. Raji would come. She couldn't speak expansively on things, but she could get to the heart of things and speak to the hearts of other people. Mala . . . Kamala . . . none of them examined issues with any depth.

He saw that Chandramohan thought of the common good and seemed to have an internal life as well. The common good seemed to encompass current politics, social, economic, and cultural issues, and his internal life revolved around literature.

He had spoken of something that affected Rajanayagam directly. "Language is for speaking. It's utilitarian. But literature proves that it is also meant for pleasure. We speak a common language. But literature has a special language. When you give it that special attention, language alone can work all kinds of wonders and generate pleasure. I love that. About three or four years ago I read a work called 'Theeva.' I only got the third installment, but I felt that I journeyed along with it."

Rajanayagam perked up. He was right to think it was just a strategy to speak the thoughts that erupted in his mind cryptically. That's what the young man was saying too.

"I had believed that only poetry could reveal the possibilities and flavour of language until then. 'Theeva' showed me that prose could achieve the same thing."

Rajanayagam realized very clearly that this young man wasn't like the many others who came from France; he had a sense of the sophistications of the French language after his time over there; he was contemplative, and firm in his opinions.

His excessive praise of "Theeva" made Rajanayagam slightly uncomfortable. But this didn't last for long. He took it for a true critique from someone who didn't know who the author was. "I saw it in a magazine too. It was good. But the title . . . what was it . . . what is Theeva? I don't understand," he said.

The young man replied, "The name is a marker. It could have been X. It tells us that there are reasons why extremism arises. The philosopher who gives out commands must have the discipline to abide by them. Or the consequences can be terrible . . . this was the primary focus of the story, or at least that's how I read it."

So, he understood it. And that, too, from a part he had grasped the whole. He didn't have to know exactly what the title was meant to convey. Each person would read it differently.

"What's the form of the story?"

"It's a short story. A sophisticated short story. And it's a story that narrates itself in a new way."

"Thank you."

The young man turned to him in question.

"For your praise of 'Theeva.' I wrote it."

Chandramohan was stunned. He had thought the work was by some youngblood.

As they ate, the judge pointed to a picture frame on the wall and said, "My granddaughter."

The garland and pottu on the picture indicated that the subject was dead. He narrated her story. It was tragic. He told his own story. It was compelling.

24

Chennai, India

RAJANAYAGAM WAS AN EARLY riser. Sunshine, mist, or rain, he woke up at five and walked over to the Thirumangalam junction, bought the newspaper and returned. He did it to get a walk early in the morning. There was no other way of experiencing the city's atmosphere without dust or exhaust fumes.

Chandramohan was awake when Rajanayagam set out to get his newspaper. He was ready to leave when Rajanayagam returned.

"Are you setting off?" he asked.

"Yes. I must go to Mala's place and then straight to Besant Nagar. I have a couple of urgent things to get done. I'll give you a call when I'm finished."

"Okay. I'll speak to Raji at length when she comes by."

Chandramohan walked leisurely to Viswalingam's house.

Viswalingam had gone to sleep on the verandah and was just sitting up looking at the doorway when Chandramohan arrived. He had gone away somewhere the previous week and returned feeling weak and sick after being drenched in the rain. He had recovered somewhat, after two days of rest.

Viswalingam had been happy from the first day back home.

Senan had called Sheila, and they said that she had asked how he was, whether he still went off on his wanderings, and whether his appetite and sleep had returned to normal. She said she really wanted to talk to him and asked if he would come to the phone to talk to her. His eyes welled up when he heard this. People do come around eventually.

He would talk. He would love to talk. It had been ten years since he had seen or spoken to her. But he couldn't say when. He would only be able to talk when he had something definite to say. He could say whatever he wanted to anyone else. But with Sheila, things had to be concrete. She was his daughter . . . but when it came to speaking to her, it never occurred to him to ask those loving questions, give that affectionate cautioning. If it occurred to him, it felt fake. "Let's see," he had thought. Then Chandramohan arrived.

Vishwalingam sat upright to see who it was. He didn't ask. From the familiar way he entered, he could see the young man had been there before. It seemed he knew who Viswalingam was, too. Chandramohan smiled lightly. "I've come from France. I was here a week ago."

Vishwalingam smiled back. "Come inside."

The young man sat across from him on the ledge, looking into the hall. "I don't see anyone . . . ," he began.

"Only Saraswathi is here. I think she's washing clothes. The rest of them have gone to the temple. Some special ceremony. Shall I call Saraswathi?" He began to rise.

"No, don't. Please wait. Let her come in her own time."

Viswalingam realized that he wanted to discuss something with him. Chandramohan didn't let the opportunity slip and told him about Sheila and Suthan parting ways.

Viswalingam was stunned. Just the previous day she had asked about him over the phone. He had thought about it when he woke up and been in a happy state. He held back his emotions, "The wrong they did to Raji . . . it wasn't going to go away," he said, getting to the root of the situation.

Chandramohan told him that Suthan felt the same way too. With things as they were, he asked what he thought of the idea of bringing about a reconciliation between Raji and Suthan.

Viswalingam pondered on an answer. The question was irrelevant. He needed to think. But his surprise made Chandramohan wonder if he had only just heard about all this. He asked him: "Didn't anyone in your house mention this to you? I had told them about it when I came last week."

He shook his head: "They were whispering among themselves. But they're always like that. So, I didn't think much of it. Even if they knew, what would they care about it? She's sending them money every month, isn't she? Or . . . They're the kind of people who might think it's a good thing. If she's alone she can send them money whenever she wishes."

Chandramohan was shocked. Could people as close as your own family be so selfish?

"Fakeness has spread, thambi," Viswalingam said, as if he had read his mind. "It feels like these relationships exist for money. Love is fake. Whose love can you take to be pure? This is most true of the Lankans living outside the camps."

Just then Siva, Mala, Poobathy, Senan and the three little ones returned from the temple. Chandramohan went into the hall with them.

When Saraswathi realized he had come, she too joined them. "I heard someone talking. I thought it was someone on the road."

None of them seemed affected anymore by what Chandramohan had told them about Sheila. He realized in amazement that Viswalingam was probably right in what he had said of them.

It was clear that Siva was going through the travails of being a man living with his in-laws.

Chandramohan didn't stay long after he had his tea. Viswalingam was heading out with a yellow cloth bag on his shoulder at the same time, so the two of them walked slowly toward the bus stop.

Everything he said was saddening. But . . . Chandramohan could see that Viswalingam was not only affected by sorrow.

Viswalingam was going to Adaiyaaru. As soon as he heard this, Chandramohan called an auto and offered to drop him off there.

"Do you need to see someone in Adaiyaaru?" he asked.

"Mm."

"Will you come back in the afternoon?"

"It might be the evening. Or maybe tomorrow."

"Just wandering around . . . ?"

Vishwalingam smiled.

Then his face darkened, and he said, "This is some fate. If I ask myself why I should live like this, my heart will burst. Not because I can't deal with difficulties. I'm speaking about the state of my family. I can't remember when I last spoke comfortably to my children. I've forgotten the days when I could sit quietly with my wife and talk without a care. Ten years . . . maybe twelve? Can you believe it? Are we really living? Is this called a life?" The words poured out of him in a torrent.

Chandramohan stared straight ahead at the street. He didn't turn to look at the man. He knew he must be in tears.

It was fourteen years since he last came here! Two circles! He had lost his country. But he had not forgotten. He was a splattering of the nation's grief. Some of its effects were hidden, the loss of relationships and love. To love young and lose your mind . . . was this what they meant? He was not a young man. But he was human. He might have passed his prime, his body was worn out and wounded, but who could say he didn't still need love?

The auto was passing Ghandi Mandapam.

Chandramohan began, as if to remind him of what they were discussing at home: "Raji is coming up from the camp today. She might be staying here tomorrow. If you see her . . . , could you talk to her about what I said. I know it may be hard to bring up . . . because of Sheila . . . "

"There's nothing for Sheila to be upset about here. I will certainly talk to Raji about this."

Vishwalingam got out at the Adaiyaaru bus station. Chandramohan sat in the auto watching Viswalingam walk across the pedestrian crossing and hurry towards Indira Nagar.

"Are we really living? Is this called a life?"

25

Chennai, India

WHEN HE GOT TO Besant Nagar, Chandramohan washed, ate, and got dressed to go back out again in Satha's auto. He stopped along the way and made a phone call to Porur. Kamala told him that Raji had come that afternoon. She had come straight to her place without going to Rajanayagam's because Kamala had asked her in the letter to come quickly. Raji would leave for Anna Nagar the next morning and then return to the refugee camp.

"Well, akka . . . did you talk to her about it? Did it work?" Chandramohan asked eagerly.

"I just brought up the topic lightly. Don't jump to the idea that you can get her consent at once and head back. Why, we may get an answer we aren't expecting. What?" she said realistically.

"Okay, akka."

"First you need to be introduced to her. Raji will be going to Rajanayagam's house tomorrow at ten o'clock. If you go there, you can meet her."

Chandramohan agreed to her plan and hung up.

That afternoon, everyone in the house went to the Ashtalakshmi temple in Besant Nagar. They asked Chandramohan to join them, and he went along as well.

Like with a shawl in cold weather, it was comforting to be bound by these practices. But the shell only offers protection until the fledglings are fully grown. Beyond that was the grave. All these protective coverings need to be shed at some time.

Perunthevi looked very beautiful that day. The atmosphere at the temple stirred Chandramohan as well. But did the atmosphere seem beautiful because of Perunthevi? Or did Perunthevi seem beautiful because of the atmosphere?

When he got back from the temple, he called Rajanayagam, who told him that Raji had arrived.

"Kamala just called to tell me."

"I'll get there by ten o clock."

"Do you have something to do now?"

"I was going to have dinner and go to bed."

"You can come here and do that."

"Now?"

"Why . . . what's the delay?"

"No. There's no need for you to trouble yourself . . . "

"This is no trouble. Besides, next time I go to London, I'm thinking of visiting France. Then, I'll need a place to stay for a couple of days . . . "

"By all means, you can come to my house."

"So, you hesitate to come to my house. But I can 'by all means' come to yours . . . ?"

"I'll be there before ten," Chandramohan said laughing quietly.

When he got to Rajanayagam's place, he sent the auto away and walked in. Rajanayagam was seated on the verandah as though waiting for him.

As if by design, the clouds that had been gathering overhead dissolved and poured. The rain looked like silver streaks against the distant light. The black clouds dissolving into silver seemed like a magical feat. The rain poured down in a heavy shush-shush. The wind blew, and a spray of rain fell over them.

But neither of them wanted to go inside.

Chandramohan had not seen such rain in a long time.

Rajanayagam brought out a bottle and two glasses and put them down on the low table. "Are you in the habit of imbibing, thambi?" he asked.

"A little."

In the horizon the lightning flashed like rivers intermittently and the thunder resounded. The weather station had predicted heavy thunderstorms in Kadalur and Pondicherry for the next forty-eight hours. There had been a warning of rain and storms in the southern coast of Tamil Nadu.

"Will Raji come tomorrow if it rains like this?"

To Chandramohan, Raji was still just a character portrait. She was a woman who had refused to leave her land . . . she had fled from luxuries in a world that chased after them . . . as a result she was destroying her life . . . these were not characteristics you encountered every day. They were anomalies.

He remembered that Prabu's father had a similar love of his homeland. He knew not only every road and lane in his village, but the measure of every cornerstone. He knew which houses had coconut leaf fences and which had stone walls and metal gates. Was there a temple in the north whose history he didn't know? But he too had been pulled up by the roots and brought overseas. She was not like that.

"What is it . . . what are you thinking so hard?"

Chandramohan smiled and brushed the thought off. "Thinking about my village. And the people who care about the village. I was thinking about Raji."

It was three o'clock by the time Raji arrived at Rajanayagam's house.

The rain had eased off in the morning. But it kept drizzling. There had been some flooding, and travelling had been difficult. When there was no sign of Raji, Chandramohan had called Porur and inquired; he was preparing to leave for Besant Nagar when she arrived. She said she was leaving for Kilapudur the next day.

The flashing smiles that were part of her nature once were slowly returning. But Rajanayagam noticed with a shock that her face was withdrawn. He introduced Chandramohan to her and she barely smiled, making him wonder if Chandramohan was the reason for her reserve.

She joined in their conversation. At one point she casually asked: "And in France . . . Sheila and Suthan are okay?"

"They're fine," he said, and prompted her with, "Did Kamala akka say anything special to you?" bringing the topic to his chief concern.

"No," she replied.

"Do you have to go back to the camp tomorrow?"

She replied that she needed to be at the camp the next afternoon. She had been expected back that day but could justify staying a day longer because of the storm. He asked her when she'd be able to come back to Chennai. When she asked why, he replied that he needed to speak with her.

Kamala akka had written asking her to come in a hurry, and now he was saying he needed to talk to her. Her brow furrowed with the suspicion that something was afoot. So far, he seemed likeable enough as an acquaintance. So, she calmly explained that it was difficult for her to come often. This was due to the regulations of the camp, she explained. But if it was urgent, she could come.

"We must meet again," he urged.

"Okay, then I'll come. I'll come next Saturday and leave on Sunday."

She understood that he wanted to talk to her about something that Kamala akka hadn't disclosed yet. She wondered what it might be.

26

Chennai, India

CHANDRAMOHAN WRAPPED UP MOST of his work before Raji returned to Chennai.

She had weighed on his mind. When asked himself why, he realized that she was not one to look for outside assurance but to on take things for herself. Hers wasn't a superficial beauty. If you looked at her that way, she wasn't anything at all. But she was everything. Her unprejudiced, and yet fearless gaze, her smile, her assured womanhood, all inspired that feeling. It was a beauty unique to the north of Lanka. The women do not become diamond-hardened and sinewy. But they have a force that moves them through their actions. Her complexion had darkened with the sun and the salt air. He saw the tan lines at the edge of her sleeves, the neckline and shoulders revealed her natural complexion. She had an ascetic quality that took in all she observed as information. She possessed an elegance. The posture of a temple statue. She did laugh occasionally. It was a cautious laugh. Was it a caution that her laughter must not be seen as her norm, or an encouragement to familiarity?

She could be the right person for Suthan.

One by one he contemplated all that people had told him she had been through. What she was going through now was also much. She had said so herself. It could be that all these experiences had made her stubborn. They would need to break through her stubbornness.

"You can break through a person's stance with an argument and change their mind. But what argument can get through someone's stubbornness?" Chandramohan asked himself as he lay in bed that Friday night.

While he waited for Raji's return he frequently spoke to Prabu over the phone. He was concerned that he shouldn't forget any of his tasks as his departure approached.

Prabu had told him that the Stockholm branch of the Cultural Assembly was eager to host the ninth anniversary following January during Pongal. He had also told him to bring back some good news about Suthan and Raji. Chandramohan was about to say that it was a complicated issue, and anyone who was not directly involved with it would not understand but held his tongue and reassured him that he would try his best. Prabu urged him to go visit Suthan's mother in Madurai. Chandramohan said he would try.

Chandramohan went back to Rajanayagam's house on the Saturday. Raji was there, talking to the old judge. She told Chandramohan she'd just arrived. Her indifferent expression told him that she had come because only she had to. He went in and brought out a chair and sat down.

"I was just talking to her about you," Rajanayagam said.

Why should her face look so pale because of that?

Raji had bowed her head.

It was important to respect people's feelings. These were sensitive issues that could not be coerced or forced. Had Kamala put pressure on her? He turned to Rajanayagam with a questioning look. He understood his expression and nodded slightly in assent. Right, there was no point in hesitating or holding back anymore. Chandramohan waded into the problem directly.

He spoke to her very clearly about Suthan and Sheila's split. He explained the condition Suthan was in. He insisted that this was not because of his split from Sheila. No matter how you looked at it, he finished, if she came to an understanding with Suthan, time would heal them.

Afraid that Chandramohan might overstep his limits, Rajanayagam said, "You don't need to worry about it, thambi. She's an intelligent person. She can figure it out and come to the right decision on her own."

Like a firecracker going off, Jasmine's mother Theresa came to Raji's mind. She would start talking, with no sense of the other's feelings, or the delicacy of the issue, content that she was qualified to give advice. She was always convinced everyone else was ignorant. She had especially thought of Raji as "that island girl" and pitied her. But Rajanayagam considered her a capable person. He liked to give advice, but he left the decision to the individual. No matter who they were, no one had permission to invade her mind.

She heard a voice in her head that took a different tone: "Who do you have but these people? Girl, you only have this circle of friends and acquaintances. Amma, thangachi, thambi . . . who do you have left? You had Yogesh. He did as you wished. He wanted to be yours and you cast him somewhere out there. Now he's not around either. Whom else do you have? You had a friend called Selvamani. A garland-maker's daughter. She was lost to the sea. Another friend, Jasmine. Your best friend. She ran away to Australia without even telling you. Did she contact you after that? Did she even think about you? You didn't think about her either, did you? You have a relative called Arasi. She lives in a tiny village on the shore in the north of Lanka. Years since you wrote to each other. Then . . . shouldn't these folks at least speak? How old are you; are you still young? Over thirty-five. How are you going to live out your life? You may not want to think about all these things. But those who love you, who show some concern for you, will think about these things, won't they? And this man is like a grandfather to you . . . the other one didn't come here looking to profit from anything either. He was thinking about the hearts of two people when he came rushing to help. What's the point of you getting angry?"

The silence spread out around them.

Rajanayagam broke the thick silence by saying, "Think about it and give Chandramohan a good answer when he returns to France, Raji."

She was gazing elsewhere.

There was a black screen in her mind. She saw the gentle glitter of waves . . . their furious roars . . . the people swallowed up into the heaving, swirling belly of the ocean . . . the sacrifices it still demanded . . . Suthan had not wet his feet in it. He had run away.

Rajanayagam and Chandramohan looked at each other. Was she crying? Was she numb, unable to cry? "Raji . . . !" Rajanayagam uttered. She turned slowly. Smiled. She seemed to unwind from a tight coil. Neither of them could fathom her emotions beyond that. She said: "I'll never think of what Suthan did as a great crime. The problem is . . . this was not Suthan's only crime. You may or may not know about it, but I know. Those are the things I can't forget. I don't think I'll be able to make peace with them in this lifetime."

She let things go quiet for a while and continued, "You're all asking me to think and think. As if I have not been thinking before and only started thinking now. Whether directly or indirectly, who could have thought more about Suthan than I have? Now the situation is different. I can feel sorry for Suthan, but I can't change my mind."

"Don't talk this crazy talk, Raji," Rajanayagam said, a little sternly. "You don't need to be so stubborn and rush your reply this way. You can say you'll think about it, at least. He has come her with good intentions. There's nothing worse than wounding a kind-hearted person."

Suntharalingam used to say the same thing.

She smiled. Her smile didn't reveal whether she would or wouldn't think about the proposal.

They heard the gate opening. Two women entered. Mala was one. The older man arose to see who it was but couldn't identify her.

From inside the verandah, Raji stood up, crying out "Arasiii . . . !"

27

Chennai, India

RAJI AND ARASI COULD not speak from the emotions that
rose up like waves inside them. It wasn't a measure of their joy.
Nor their sorrow. They forgot everything else as memories of their
village, and their days there reverberated like shockwaves through
them.

It was only when Rajanayagam, who had learned who it was
from Mala, intervened, that they came back to the present.

Raji and Arasi smiled lightly.

"Come in, let's sit in the hall," Rajanayagam said and took
everyone inside.

"Arasi, this is Chandramohan. A friend of your thambi's. He's
come from France," Raji said and introduced them.

Chandramohan welcomed the introduction and asked, "Did
you just get here today?"

Arasi nodded, yes.

It seemed that it would take a while before she could recover
fully from the deluge of memories that had overwhelmed her.

Mala, who had gone to the airport, told them what time the
Raji arrived.

Rajanayagam asked, "Who else went to the airport, Mala?"

"Just me, Siva, and Senan. We went by bus and came back by auto."

Tea arrived. They sipped it and made polite inquiries of each other.

Chandramohan got up slowly and went out to the verandah. He wondered why not a word of "How is thambi doing?" had escaped Arasi's mouth. When he thought of how Raji had introduced him, as though he were a friend of some third party, his heart fell. Was this woman going to relent and agree to start a life with Suthan?

Until that minute he had thought of Raji's stubbornness as stemming from some recklessness. But when Suthan's own sister didn't inquire about him, Chandramohan realized that there must be some strong reasons behind these two rejections and was too shocked to think beyond it.

What reasons? Even if his attempt to bring Raji and Suthan together failed, he felt he needed to know that aspect of his friend's life before he left. It seemed that Rajanayagam had sensed his unease. He too rose and came outside. "The sister didn't ask about her brother . . . is that what you're thinking about? Be patient. This is like a knot in a ball of yarn. When you loosen one knot the rest of them come loose on their own. I was thinking that it's a good thing Arasi arrived at this time. Arasi can apply more pressure on this matter," he said, easing Chandramohan's mind and drawing him back inside.

Raji kept looking at Arasi. How war wrings out a person! She recalled their last meeting back home. In eighty-five. Velayutham is alive then. She has gone with Maheswari to say goodbye to them before she leaves for India. He's delayed getting home. He had said he'd be home for lunch, but it was getting to be evening and he was not home yet. Raji notices Arasi's anxiety. She talks to them; she makes them eat . . . but she is on edge inside. The whole town suffered. But it's love that stirs this suffering. Suffering is measured by the extent of one's love.

That relationship had been snatched from Arasi. She had lost her father while he was here. But she had sent her mother in search of her father and herself stayed behind. She had such love for her motherland. As strong as her own. Raji could relate to it.

"Arasi, haven't you gone to see your mother?" Rajanayagam asked.

"I must go. I'll go tomorrow . . . or the day after," she replied.

"Are you planning to go back to the village? Or stay . . . ?"

"No, no. Maami is planning to come here in two or three months. I'll wait to see her, then I'll take amma. I'll be going back."

A lot of this was unclear to Chandramohan, so Rajanayagam explained it to him. When he heard all the details, that Suntharalingam had died and his wife and daughter hadn't known about it; that Valambikai had come to India in search of him, lost the address of his friend and ended up in a refugee camp until Suntharalingam's friend heard of it and went with Raji to get her; that Arasi had suffered back home not knowing what had happened to either of her parents until she received a letter from Maheswari recently, Chandramohan was stunned.

"We say that the shortest distance between India and Lanka is eighteen miles. But really . . . it seems further away than Canada. How many years it took to for news of a death to travel from here to there!"

Rajanayagam's soft murmur reached his ears and stayed there.

Grief upon grief . . . only in Lanka.

28

Chennai, India

RAJI FELT NO DESIRE to eat. For her part, Mala had steamed some pittu for dinner, knowing that she was partial to it. At her insistence, Raji ate a little. When Raji usually visited Chennai, she would stay up until midnight, eagerly watching the cartoon channel on TV, keeping Kamala awake as well. Around eight-thirty that night, she brought out the mat and pillow and lay down. Her eyes closed almost immediately, as if from exhaustion.

She had planned to go to Anna Nagar and from there to the Organization for Eelam Refugee Rehabilitation in Egmore. She'd had to cancel those plans. She thought perhaps she could stay the next day and go on to Egmore on Monday and take the bus from there to Kilapudur. But until the bus arrived in Porur, she had still not made any firm plans.

Perhaps it was the stress weighing on her, or something else, she awoke in the middle of the night. Her eyes opened into darkness. She had been covered with a sheet. Kamala akka must have covered her.

It was cold in the room. The back window was open. The sounds around her told her it was raining. Though the door was closed, a faint light seemed to spread through.

She got up silently, so as not to disturb the silence, opened the door and looked out. Kamala akka was asleep on the sofa. The streetlamp shed its light through the glass-paned windows, and she noticed the time was nearing two-thirty. There would be no more sleep for her. Whenever she awoke at this time, she spent the rest of the night in troubled thoughts. It was the same on the island too.

She realized she was heading into a crisis. She went back to her mat, pulled the cover up and closed her eyes, but all the faces of the people who had created this crisis passed through the screen in her mind. First, Chandramohan, whose arrival had created the dilemma. He seemed a different kind of person, with his careful speech and firmly furrowed brow that proclaimed a fiercely active mind.

Rajanayagam appeared as the next threatening figure. She could not resist if he compelled her. She still called him sir, as she had from the beginning. As far as she was concerned it was another way of calling him thaatha. He too treated her as he might his granddaughter Laxo and showered her with affection. It was a bond that had grown stronger after Laxo's death. He was also a friend to her. He would talk to her, and understand her as a friend, but compel her like a grandfather. Then she found it hard to say no to him.

She didn't think Arasi would apply any pressure on her. She knew that Arasi had no great faith in her brother. But what could she do about amma? She was arriving from Canada in the next month or so. The pressure would tighten then.

Amma!

Did she still melt? At one time her skin tingled at the thought of her mother, was it still the same?

It was. As soon as she heard her mother was coming, she felt the yearning of a calf. Every hair on her, every artery trembled for the "mother who feeds her child milk before it cries out."

But she knew her mother was not the same person she was before. Whether she was justified or not, she no longer thought of Raji as her child. How many years it had been since she'd gone to Canada! She hadn't written to her once in all that time. She suspected that her mother didn't even resent Rajendran as much. She had told Raji that she was born to destroy the Ponnusamy name. Her birth had always been a portent of destruction.

She loved her sister Vijayalakshmi. She wasn't only her sister. She had grown up crawling after Raji, like a baby chick chasing cheep . . . cheep around a hen's legs. Who would have thought that lame child would have got married? She hadn't believed it possible herself. It was the only reason she had left her homeland. Whom did she have to look out for now? What kin did she have left on that soil? They had all migrated. It was just the soil left after an uprooting. Why shouldn't she move as she wished to now?

But if amma got back and heard of Chandramohan's efforts, there would be trouble. She might not want to see or hear about Raji. But Rajanayagam, Viswalingam, Kamala akka, and Arasi would let her know. Then amma herself might well come running in search of her. She might beg: "Just agree and write the letter, you fool." She might even threaten her: "Look, I will climb up the Anna Nagar tower and fall and kill myself if you don't." She would want it resolved before she left for Canada again.

Raji hadn't yet calmly sat with Arasi to discuss all that happened. There was so much. The village, the state of the country, maami, immigrations, the war, the teacher Sankarapillai, and Kanthasamy appa, Thiraviyam, his short and plump friend, Thiyagu, the sudden disappearance of the teacher Nesamalar from Chennai . . . maybe even Yogesh.

Pictures of the Khajuraho statues still rose and swept over her like waves. They appeared in her dreams and disturbed her with pleasure. She was still a woman.

More light streamed in through the window.

She sat up and leaned against the wall. Though it had been a sleepless night, her eyes were not irritated. Raji got up after a while and came outside. Kamala had woken up by then too. She was in the bathroom.

There was kolam powder in a vessel at the entrance. The kolam, lamp, turmeric water, temple bells all reminded her of auspiciousness. Suddenly, she felt the blessings of Nagabooshani spring to her ears.

29

Chennai, India

IT WAS PAST LUNCHTIME, close to three o clock, when Raji and Kamala left for Anna Nagar. When they got to Rajanayagam's house, Chandramohan was already there. He smiled when he saw them. He told them Arasi would be there soon. Kamala turned to leave saying that she had people to visit in the next street, and she would be back soon. Raji left with her. She ran like a child running after its mother after throwing a tantrum, he thought to himself. He knew the reason.

Arasi arrived then. She had a few magazines and the Sunday editions of the Virakesari and Thinakaran newspapers, and a letter in a long envelope clutched in her hands. The envelope was not sealed. She seemed to be much more clearheaded today.

"Is the Judge aiyya not here today?" she asked.

"I think he's asleep. I didn't ask them to wake him. Shall I?"

"No, no need."

"Why don't you sit down?"

She sat.

She seemed to have taken on a different aspect than that of the pitiable victim. He now noticed that there was a fierce gleam in her eyes that transcended village innocence or modesty. It was the gleam that often sparked the fire, he knew. In the poet it was poetry, and with other artists it took whatever form their art took.

"The letter . . . where do you want to send it . . . shall I send it through someone?" He was referring to the envelope in her hands.

"No," she said, unfolding the sheaf of paper that was in it. "Poetry. I thought I could send it to one of the newspapers for publication . . . I must get an address from aiyya," she said as she handed it over to him.

"The Last War, for you and for me, Krishanthi," he read.

She had detailed the sexual assault and murder of a young student in fiery letters in poetic form. But "Last War" seemed not quite right.

"Last War . . . I don't understand."

"What's going on now should be the final war. All the problems will be solved this time. I don't think we can bear another war," she said and quickly turned away. She turned away to hold back her tears somewhat. She smiled.

"How is the poem?" she asked after a while.

He was moved. It was condemnation by someone who had emerged from the warring earth. He smelled the blood, flesh, and death in it. When he came to himself, he told her that the poem was good. "Do you want to send it to any Indian newspapers?"

"I'm not sure . . . "

"Then, give it to me., I'll have it printed in a magazine I know in France."

She gave him the envelope as well, to show her consent.

"When did you come?" They heard Rajanayagam's voice from the room. He had just woken up.

"Just now," Chandramohan said.

"Arasi, come here. I need to ask you a few things about back home," he said. Arasi walked over to him.

"Chandramohan, you come in too."

"You two talk. I'll come soon."

He opened the newspaper Arasi had left behind.

Arasi told Rajanayagam the story of hatred—shell blasts, devastation by Kfir bombers, buildings and trees broken and crushed, a palmyra grove decimated into a clearing, and the great human tragedy of the mass exodus.

Then she spoke of the quiet displacement of people from Thenmaradchi. The Movement had expected a heavy attack on the area and had announced on their radio station that all the civilians should evacuate the place. She said the massive migration of nineteen ninety-six, which happened without any resistance, and with no information from the outside, was referred to as the quiet displacement.

Chandramohan spotted a long poem on one side of the page to which the newspaper was opened.

*Kaandavanam! **
This Kaandavanam erupted in a fierce flame.
Fire woven with fire giving birth to fire.
The burning sun
The gusts of red sand dust
The hot breath of the smallest leaves
Of the trees in the forest
And a thirst that cannot be quenched
By pitchers and pitchers of water drunk . . .

In the other room, Arasi continued, "It was at the time the Iyakkam had struck the Mullaitivu army base. The Sri Lankan government had lost a cache of weapons and a large number of soldiers. The people in those areas were furious that the real scale of destruction had not been released in the newspapers. It was to retaliate for this defeat that the army intensified its efforts to capture Kilinochchi. The army moved its troops from Poonakary and Elephant Pass. To keep it covert . . . and to create a screen . . . they attacked Thenmaradchi. Until then, there had been no great impact on Thenmaradchi. But that time, it was a heavy blow . . . "

Rajanayagam heard the sound of his house collapsing. The clay roof tiles, curved crossbeams, crossbars . . . all scattered to across distances. The mango trees in the front yard, the jackfruit trees by the fences beside the house . . . branch by branch they broke and fell apart.

Did he weep? A faint light shimmered in his brimming eyes.

The shepherd
Set fire to Kaandavanam,
And the animals fled
The fire gathering like a cloud . . .

Chandramohan's gaze swam in the lines of poetry on the page.

"You could say that the migration into the Vanni began then. It happened without a murmur of protest. You could even say it was a journey to take the sick and the injured to a place that had some medical facilities. But then . . . they should have gone towards Vavuniya, shouldn't they? But the others who joined them couldn't think of what to do in their fear, either. Most of the people walked . . . carrying their belongings and their pots on their heads."

He read on:

Bodies shattered, hands lost, legs lost
Crumpled on beds
With open bed sores
Tired and suffering
The young, vital soil

Stretched out before their eyes.

Raji and Kamala arrived. Chandramohan went inside with them. What was the alternative to Kaandavanam? he wondered.

The three women left shortly after. They needed to speak of important things among themselves too.

Rajanayagam and Chandramohan sat in silence in the room. After a while, Rajanayagam stirred himself and said, "I don't think we'll get Raji to agree to anything in a hurry."

"I agree."

"The camp is a great help to the refugees. It provides a temporary home . . . a temporary country . . . temporary relatives. So, it's important to get Raji out of the camp first. She can only realize that she needs a life for herself away from the power the camp holds over her. So let's try that first."

Chandramohan knew that this was the turning point of his trip. He was overwhelmed by a sudden feeling that his journey had ended in failure. But not complete failure.

"Will Suthan come the next time?"

"He could."

"Her mother will be here by then too. It would be easier to push the decision when everyone is here."

"I'll talk to Prabu tonight. I'll leave on the first flight that has a seat. Raji is your responsibility now. Anyhow, I'll come by one more time to say goodbye to everyone before I leave."

He stood up to go.

30

Gonagala, Sri Lanka

You who are merciful, have you heard / crows are cawing/ the rooster is crowing / in the forest, trees are swaying / deaths are occurring . . .

DEATH IS ONLY NATURAL when it comes after living and aging. It should be the fruit that ripens well and falls in due time. But Lanka had become a nation where premature deaths were normal. They turned into poetry and floated in the air. Sankarananda was saddened when he heard it.

When he heard it, his soul rushed to Gonagala. He could only follow behind.

A great injustice had shattered those forty-four lives, striking as hard as airplane bombings and rockets. These murders were carried out with knives and sickles. Was this in retaliation for the twenty-two people sacrificed in the blind bombing of the Puthukudiyiruppu market in Mullaitivu District a few days before, on September eighteenth? The question arose in his mind the moment he heard the news. How could war justify war? How could cruelty justify cruelty? The bhikkhu had already been preaching Stop the war! War only births atrocities.

First Krishanthi's murder, then Koneswari's, and the nation trembled. There had been such an atrocious murder in the seventies too. Premawathie Manamperi had been her name. She had not been Tamil. But she too had been tortured and killed. He saw the thread running through those murders.

He realized his helplessness. With the weights and sorrows heaped upon him, he saw the reason he had stumbled. He was vulnerable because he didn't belong to an institution. He had felt some sadness over this. But he thought of the advantage it gave him and comforted himself. There was no need for him to change his stand, or to give in.

'The people understand. It is only you who need to understand!' He had called out to government organizations and religious organizations. He had written an open letter to the president. It had been widely published the previous year.

> The people have appointed you the country's leader to stop the war. Your devolution package was a fraud. Even your Tamil allies washed their hands of it. Your slogan seems to be war for peace. There has been no peace even after the fall of Jaffna; what do you have to say about that? There must be talks for a resolution even after a war. What you promised has not been fulfilled. In countries that follow democratic rule, it is the custom to resign in these circumstances. What are you going to do? —Sankarananda

The war continued.

Who would pay attention to a pilgrim bhikkhu? It was only the opposition party papers that ran the letter on their front pages for a few days. Then it was all quiet again.

Sankarananda reached Gonagala.

Forty-four corpses—children, women, and men. They had

been set out covered in long white sheets, witnesses to a protracted disaster.

Sorrow squeezed his heart.

Later, the sight he saw filled him with fear. He saw how people could forget themselves in their rage, how they could act. People came from all the neighbouring towns. Many hundreds of them were from Sinhala racist organizations. Was it grief that was demonstrated there? Or was grief being deliberately multiplied?

That evening, he accepted a doctor's offer of alms at his house, which also served as a hospital.

The town's vihara was just outside the town, beside a bo tree that seemed to touch the sky, its white branches covered in green vines. He walked over to it and sat on the ledge beside it. He thought he would spend the night here. Though he could not sleep, he lay down to rest his weary body.

Darkness covered the village. The lamps flickered in the weight of that darkness. Spots of light in the distant houses. In a little while they began to go out, one by one. For a while, the bhikkhu heard nothing but the susurration of the bo leaves.

He may have dozed off. He woke with a start when he heard a sudden noise. He listened closely.

Some movement in the dark. Four or five men. More men joined them. He heard something garbled about the Menik forest settlements. The shadowy figures moved on.

Though the bhikkhu did not know what was happening, he felt a twinge of fear in his soul. The lights that moved towards the village vihara now, in ones, threes, fives, tens and more . . . confirmed his fears. They were torches. The men who had retreated as shadows had returned as wild animals with lights.

The bhikkhu sat up.

The crowd saw the bhikkhu, who was so still he appeared to be meditating, and were taken aback. While some recognized him as the bhikkhu they had seen at the funeral in the evening, a few said pointedly that this was the preaching bhikkhu. The crowd tried to move away quickly when they heard he was the preaching bhikkhu.

"Come here!" the bhikkhu called them, and they returned, slowly. "May your hearts be at peace. That is happiness. Immeasurable happiness. Sit down. I must speak with you."

They sat in a semicircle around him, silently.

The tree swayed slightly. It made the silence even more dense.

The bhikkhu broke the silence gently: "No matter what sickness we feel, we hope to live. What justice is there in denying to others what we desire? Truly, life is suffering. We must redeem ourselves. You must not commit more sins and submerge yourself further in suffering. There is no sin greater than to take the life of another and torture another. Truly I say to you, listen: He who murders will himself be killed violently. This is what the Bodhisattva meant in the story of the goat."

The leaves on the trees stopped whispering. Had the breeze grown silent to hear the bhikkhu's sermon?

"The great city of Kasi had become the heart of the faith. It grew wealthy. At the time that the King Brahmathatha reigned, there was a great Brahmin pundit who lived there. When he wished to make a sacrifice for his dead parents according to the scriptures, he had a goat brought to him. He commanded his disciples to bathe it in the river, garland it, tie a piece of cloth washed in sacred water around its neck, and bring it to him.

"The disciples took the goat to the riverbank. They did all that the teacher had asked of them. The goat, who understood the cycle of birth and death, and the good and bad of deeds, laughed, then cried. The disciples were astounded. 'Why do you laugh and cry?' they asked. To that the goat said that he would answer their question after they had taken him to their teacher.

"When they were back with their teacher, the disciples asked the goat the question again. The Brahmin too, having heard the story thus far eagerly awaited the reply. The goat said, 'Once, in a previous life, I too had been a pundit like you. I too had sacrificed a goat according to the rituals. Because of that, I have been reborn as a goat four hundred and ninety-nine times. My head has been cut off in every one of them. This is my five hundredth birth. With this sacrifice I will finally be released from my sin. That's why I laughed. But by cutting me, you will be reborn as a goat five hundred times, and when I thought about that I cried.'

"Did you hear the words of justice? He who cuts once is cut five hundred times. So turn your hearts away from sin.

"Mountain and sea, sun, moon, and the earth are real. Human beings are insignificant. For every suffering you cause you will suffer five hundred times . . . for one murder five hundred times murdered . . . let us not do violence to living beings and bring on suffering in life."

"What happened to the goat in the end, Thero?" they all asked.

"The Brahmin released the goat. But one morning, the goat climbed the ledge of a mountain that had been shattered by thunder and scaled the peak, trying to eat the grass that sprouted there. It slipped and fell and died, and thus redeemed itself. The Brahmin avoided the sin. Then the divine being who had been born as a sacred tree in that place, witnessed these happenings and smiled, saying, 'Change your hearts! Reform your hearts!' That is what I say to you today: Change your hearts! Reform your hearts!"

When the next day dawned, content that no mischief had taken place in the Menik forest, Sankarananda calmly turned toward Colombo and began his journey again.

31

GUNANANDA ARRIVED EARLY IN the morning on the second day after he heard the news of Gonagala. His eyes red, anger in his heart, fury burned his skin. Anyone could see the height of his rage.

The funeral was to happen that morning and the crowd was enormous. The two young men from the Seven Seas media group watched with dismay. It was a political decision to have the funeral that morning, even though television journalists, foreign organizations, politicians, and many members of racist Sinhala organizations had arrived to say their condolences and left the previous day. "Look over there—it's Gunananda," Siva said softly. Thiravi straightened up and looked. "Yes, . . . I see him. We don't need to stay any longer. Let's go," he said and walked on. "We have not come here to give our condolences. Just to document the news."

Gunananda left the cemetery grounds and went straight to the vihara. There he saw a farmer walking past and summoning him gave him the names of two men, instructing him to tell them that he had arrived and would be waiting for them in the vihara.

When they heard the bhikkhu had arrived, the two men came

rushing. The three huddled together, speaking secretively. The bhikkhu scolded them in hushed tones.

"We were ready, Thero. But the others heard the sermon about the goat and changed their minds and went back," the two declared.

"Who gave the sermon?"

"The preaching bhikkhu."

"Him? He came here too?"

Any talk of that great man was anathema to Gunananda. Sasanka the king had cut down the bo tree in Gaya and burned it with the forest. He felt the same hate for Sankarananda that he had felt for the ancient king.

Gunananda was determined to confront him. He thought the meeting should happen quickly. Not a respectful meeting of disciple and teacher. Enough of the delays the man had caused to the Sinhala uprising. He was partly to blame for the A-9 highway not being opened yet. He'd only get a warning this time. Let him run back to the Walawe Ganga. Or the Mahaweli Ganga. Or let him run all the way back to Naga Vihara. Gunananda would not let him get in the way of the uprising. He would not hesitate to wipe him out. For some reason Sankarananda kept slipping from his grasp. Wherever Gunananda went, it seemed Sankarananda had left just a few hours before. The last time, in Vavuniya he had heard that Sankarananda had returned from Vanni, and he had gone to meet him. There he heard that the bhikkhu had left only a few hours before for Trincomalee. The same thing had happened in Anuradhapura. The thought made him feel exhausted. Was it a divine favour of Buddha's that helped the monk slip his grasp, he wondered.

He strengthened his resolve. Warrior bhikkhus like him shouldn't grow weary like this. His two companions were encouraged by the bhikkhu's revival.

"Why don't we try again tonight, Thero?"

That was a challenge. It didn't seem to be of any use trying to stir people up for violence again after Sankarananda had preached to them. But the two men would not let it go.

A few villagers were gathered up that evening under the bo tree.

"Tooth for a tooth; blood for blood. We must never forget we are a united people . . . a people who can rise up. Let us prepare for our revenge tonight," Gunananda said.

Silence took hold for a few moments before someone in the crowd piped up, "One murder . . . is a sin multiplied five hundred times, Thero!"

"Who said so?" Gunananda demanded: "Our race has a magnificent history. The purity of our race, the superiority of our language, and the sanctity of our religion have all been built through careful attention. If we get careless, or lose our passion, it will pave the path for our downfall . . . ."

There wasn't the usual echo of assent this time. Gunananda felt a burning in his chest.

Sankarananda was doing exactly what he said he would the last time they had met. "Do what you will," he had said. "I will go to the people. I will go village by village. I will preach justice and righteousness." It was all happening as he had said. Sankarananda was winning.

"The preaching bhikkhu is an evil spirit who is going to destroy the nation and the Sinhala race. He should be destroyed. You can disregard his words as garbage and brush them away . . . "

Another voice from the crowd piped up, "That is not the opinion of the preaching bhikkhu. Those are the words of the Bodhisattva. He bore witness to all this in his incarnation as a sacred tree."

Gunananda was shattered. The goats were beginning to follow behind the shepherd. What more could he do here? When he left the village, Gunananda felt as if he had been through a storm.

He wished he could go away to Meen Villu and fall and roll upon the lush grass of the beautiful gardens his friend Devapriya owned beside the riverbank. The next night he asked his five friends to meet him there. But he had to go to Kegalle before that. He rented a car and set off.

'It is time to be possessed by the spirit of war,' he thought to himself.

The spirit of revolution had entered the east as well, and here and there a few camps emerged. As hostilities grew, with an increase in arrests without inquiry and disappearances, the intensity of oppositional views increased as well. That was a noticeable change. The east was important because it was inhabited by a large population of Muslims. Many spoke of the need for unity between Sinhalese, Tamils, and Muslims. The most powerful language of the east was its poetry. They spoke of revolution through the language of poetry. But there was no one to hear it.

They planned to meet in Devapriya's place to think about how they could further prevent the people in the east from uniting. There was no special reason for him to choose the village of Meen Villu. Like Unupitiya, which was on the banks of the Kelani River, the fertile lands of Meen Villu were situated at the point where the Mahaweli river met the forest. There was a robustness to the people there too. Trincomalee to the north and beside it Batticaloa. There was pleasure and feasting to be had there. It was easy to keep his activities secret there.

He was in Kegalle in the early morning, got where he needed to go, and left in the afternoon for Meen Villu, where he reached before eight o' clock. His friends had already reached Devapriya's house and were eating when he got there.

Gunananda ate as well. After dinner, he asked, "Will it be very cold outside?"

"It will be moderate," the rich man replied.

"Okay, you all go ahead and sleep if you want to. I can't say when our planning might end. But after it's done, I will need your Land Rover," Gunananda said.

"By all means, take it. The driver will be sleeping outside."

"I won't need a driver," Gunananda said as he walked away.

His group of friends, which included two bhikkhus and three members of different organizations, followed him. They sat on a plateau on the banks of the Mahaweli.

The elder bhikkhu said, "What is the situation in Gonagala?"

"The funeral is finished."

"That's not what I asked."

"I don't mean their funeral; I meant the funeral of the golden age of Sinhala."

"I don't understand."

"What can I say? Should I tell you the story of the murder of forty-four Sinhala civilians? Or should I tell you the story of those who rose up in fury to take their revenge and were stopped and turned into paragons of truth? Then . . . even as I gathered them and called on them to 'finish this battle,' they dared preach the story of the goat to me, shall I tell you about that? What can I say to explain all this, Somarama Thero?"

"Did all this happen there? Who . . . oh . . . has the preaching bhikkhu gone there?"

"Yes. This is all the work of that vile spirit."

"You had said that he needed watching when you spoke of him before. Have you still spared him, bhikkhu?" Munesinghe demanded angrily.

"He should have been taken care of by now. Why are you putting this off?" Silva asked.

"I tried to avoid it. But . . . I came to a decision about him yesterday. I will give him one more chance. The bhikkhu must

leave his political work and disappear somewhere. Or else . . . "
Gunananda murmured.

"Kill him and be done with it. Why should we hesitate? The
Brahmin was only born as a goat because he killed a goat."

"Five hundred times!"

"Yes, five hundred times. But aren't we going to kill a bhikkhu?
So, we will be born as bhikkhus five hundred times," the older
bhikkhu said and laughed uproariously.

"Why the explanation now? Even if we're born as bhikkhus,
we'll be killed in those five hundred births," the ragged bhikkhu
said and chuckled.

Gunananda was silent.

Rajapakse, who was listening quietly to all this, spoke up: "We
can commit murder, it's true. Because we do it in the name of the
democracy. Anything done in the name of democracy is justifi-
able. The enemy does it in the name of revolution, freedom, struggle . . . and equal rights."

"We had talked about it the last time we met in Colombo, but
we left without coming to a decision. At the time we didn't even
know that parliament was going to be dissolved. So, we need to
come to a decision today. Which party are we going to support
in the next election? What do you think, Rajapakse?" Gunananda
inquired.

"It's not as easy this time to predict the outcome of the presidential election as it was last time. It looks as though both parties
are equally powerful."

"You're right. What do the others think? The same? Or do you
have other opinions?"

"The same. Rajapakse is exactly right," the older bhikkhu spoke
for all of them.

"Okay, let's leave this issue aside for now, and tell me the answer
to my next question. Does the SLFP's direction align with ours or

not?"

"They weren't in the beginning. That is . . . when the president first came into power the situation seemed to head towards unity. She appeared to be going along with the Tamil separatists' demands. Then she suddenly switched from her neutral position and leaned to our side. I think the situation remains the same now," replied Somarama Thero.

"Hm," Gunananda said, his head bent as though he was sunk deep in thought. Then he straightened, "Rajapakse, you must remember that we met five years ago by the Kelani Ganga before we left for the Kandy Perahera. That was a few days before Premadasa's assassination. I told you then that Madam Chandrika, who had taken the leadership of the Sri Lanka Mahajana Party after the death of her husband, was going to throw it all away and align with the SLFP. She immediately became the Chief Minister for the Western province. Then she became President. She made some overtures towards equality for Tamils at that time, as Somarama said. But that changed. Equal rights became just rights. That was the result of a small political shift. This is still a Sinhala nation. We are prepared to kill not just one but a hundred Bandaranaikes if we have to, to establish it. Is that not so, Somarama Thero?"

"Then she said that Tamils are not indigenous to this land," the young bhikkhu said.

"Did she say that?" Silva asked.

The young bhikkhu replied, "Yes. She said it in a television interview when she went to South Africa."

"So, she is going along . . . ?" Silva asked.

"Yes."

"Then, we'll support her," Somarama Thero added.

"And if she loses the election?" Rajapakse raised a doubt.

Gunananda was pleased with the direction the conversation

was taking. He turned calmly toward Rajapakse and smiled quietly. Then he spoke levelly: "We are not politicians, Rajapakse. Just
bhikkhus. You could go as far as to say we are warrior-minded
bhikkhus. Are we trying to gain something for ourselves when
we lean towards a political party? We do it all for the good of the
Sinhala nation. Therefore, it's our responsibility to ensure that she
wins. But we're not going to get on the political stage and preach
there. We are going to do it strategically. That's all. Understood,
Rajapakse?"

"Understood, Thero."

Gunananda checked the watch chained at his hip. "Hm . . . I
need to go out for a while. That one—where's the ragged bhikkhu?"

"Over here—he's asleep at the back here."

Gunananda roused the ragged bhikkhu and headed with him
toward the Land Rover.

When the vehicle had left, Silva turned to the elder bhikkhu.
"Thero, why is Gunananda Thero going out at this time?"

The older bhikkhu laughed menacingly. "The fish in the river of
the western shore are very tasty. And the bodies of those who eat
them are also very tasty. So, the ragged bhikkhu is taking him to
the sweetheart of the western shore."

"Who is this sweetheart of the western shore?"

"The daughter of the tuberose goddess," the older bhikkhu
replied and chuckled again.

When his laughter died down, Silva said, "Thero, you must tell
me the story of the tuberose goddess if you know it."

As they all wished to hear it, the bhikkhu began to narrate the
story.

32

THIRAVI HAD GONE TO Nainativu for Pongal the previous January. A loss, a grief that all was lost took him back there as though in search of roots.

He had stood in the doorway of his house in tears. He didn't even walk in. The conch store was in ruins, overgrown with weeds and roots. Of the coconut trees that surrounded his house, two had rotted, probably having been infested with coconut bugs.

He stood grieving alone like a stranger in his own land. With his beard and overgrown hair, it was not easy for anyone to recognize him. He rode pillion on a passerby's bicycle and got to Arasi's house. He planned to go to the Cultural Assembly's conference in Chennai the next January and it seemed like a good idea to go by Arasi's house and see her once. He should have gone to Kachai. But all he wanted to do was roam the island.

The mango tree was still strong. The mango leaves had fallen during the dry seasons and now covered the ground. As he stood in the doorway, he saw Kanthasamy appa lying on his easy chair in his front yard. The man squinted at him and called out, "Who is it?"

"That is . . . I'm Thiraviyam, appu."

"Oh, it's you? Come, come in . . . what's the news?"

"Nothing, I just came for a visit."

"To see me?"

"To see you too."

He seemed to understand that Thiravi had only come to see his old friends. He said, "Who's in town anymore, son? They're all running away; some new folks are coming in. Never mind that, have you seen your parents?"

He said he hadn't. "I can't seem to go there now that Santhi is gone, appu."

"What nonsense is this? Go visit them, son. Have some pity."

"I'm planning to see them on my way back . . . "

"Hm. You heard about Suntharam?"

"I know. I met Arasi once in Colombo and she told me."

"She told me too when she came here. Do you see how things are eroding around us, son?"

The old man seemed unable to extricate himself from the silence he fell into. Thiravi said goodbye and left.

Ariyalai was not the town he had once known. From Chetty Street on, the place was in ruins. You could see the Nallur Kandasamy Temple from the front yard of the house. Which street was where? Did they still have the correct names? There had been so many beautifully designed houses in that area. The bombs had reduced them to nothing. It was like being lost in a forest without directions. He kept going until he arrived at the house where his parents lived.

His father didn't invite him in. He was visibly shrunken. He must have thought, "Siva came by twice, and even though I sent for you, you never came." Did he know that it was Thiravi who had sent Siva?

There was an emptiness to the place without Santhi. But the loss of her was written in their faces, and in the air clinging to the house.

His mother stood across from him, crying. Every time she thought about Santhi she tormented herself, wondering, "Should I not have brought my children to this place?" She had left her hometown, a captive to her desires. Now she didn't have the home she was born in, nor the home she had gone to.

Sankarapillai had stopped by on his way back from Colombo a few years before, to visit his family and leave them some money. He was thunderstruck by what he saw. The house looked like a kiln. Clay walls. A roof of woven palmyra leaves. If the door was shut, it shut out both light and breeze. The door was about four feet high. When he got there, mother and daughter were lying down on mats inside the house. The door was open. He peered inside. All he saw was darkness. He called out to them. His wife came out. He never asked "Where are your brothers? You came back here saying you would live a great life, what's happened to it?" But it showed in his eyes. What could she have said? She wept. Sankarapillai decided to stay there that very moment.

The civilians in the north migrated to Vanni the year after he got there. What did they take with them? A box of clothing . . . a bucket . . . a few pots . . . plates, cups . . . There was no direction to their flight either. No clear path.

When they were fleeing through the Semmani paddy fields, he had slipped and torn a ligament in his calf. There were some people they knew in Navatkuli. But perhaps they too had fled? They wailed and lamented in the dark, fleeing with all the others. There was just one place left to go. Kachai. TULF Suntharam's daughter lived there. But how would they find the house without an address? When they turned around at Koyya Thottam beside the Vairava Temple and went to Madduvil east, they found a place where they could take refuge.

Hearing about the families that were travelling down the Kandy Road, his wife came and asked him, "What shall we do? It seems that people are all heading down to Paranthan and Kilinochchi . . . "

He shook his head vehemently, the pain searing his leg. "No . . . no . . . I can't anymore."

Six months later the army directed them to return to their homes. Sankarapillai decided that they could return. "What do the Tigers say?" his wife and daughter had wondered.

"No one can say anything. The house is important . . . we can't leave the house plot . . . let's go to Ariyalai now; once the situation improves, we might be able to go back to the island," he had replied.

They received ten thousand rupees to help with their return and repairs to their house. They built a shelter near the clay shack and settled down.

Then Santhi began to go to school in Nallur. They couldn't deny her an education. But they were afraid. They let her study, even though they lived in fear.

One day, Santhi went to school and never returned. When they went in search of her, they heard that the girls cycling home had been stopped by the railway pass by an army corporal, and two of them had been taken for questioning. Who knew which base the soldier belonged to? Or where he could have taken her? Sankarapillai searched all over. Kanmani's father went along with him, in search of his own daughter.

Two and a half years passed. Where did they not search? What did they not do? They reported it to the Missing Persons Bureau . . . wrote a petition to the provincial members . . . went to Colombo to speak to a member of parliament . . .

It was at that time that the inquiry into Krishanthi's murder had taken place. The case was closely followed by the parents of disappeared children. Even though they were reeling under the thought that their children might have suffered a similar fate, they felt comforted that at least such atrocities would not be allowed to happen again. It was an important sign that six soldiers were arrested on that charge. Hearing that a door was opening into the inquiry, Kanmani's father and Sankarapillai were overjoyed.

The news that came out of the inquiry only shattered them. There were around four hundred bodies buried in Semmani, one of the six soldiers had revealed. The judge had ordered that Semmani be dug up. The soldier revealed the location of the buried bodies himself.

Sankarapillai ran. Kanmani's father ran with him.

People lined up to look.

Bones . . . bones . . . bones . . .

Commotion everywhere.

Off to one side, weeping, laments . . .

Even now, whenever he thought of her, he walked over to the Semmani burial grounds. His leg never healed, and he was crippled permanently.

Thiravi's mother interrupted the silence. "Can you live without fear in Colombo?"

"You can, amma. There are three hundred thousand Tamils there now."

"Still, it would be good if you could move here?"

"What do I do with my job?"

"The children are still in Thunukkai?"

"Hm."

"Will they take good care of them?"

"They will."

"How are their studies going?"

He hesitated to reply.

Studies? Even now, she could still think of their studies?

"It's here and there. If there's fighting, they close the school. They open again when it's done. It keeps on like that."

"Why, you could bring them here. We can take care of them."

He told them he would think about it and left.

33

Colombo, Sri Lanka

THAT NIGHT, THIRAVI WOKE up suddenly. A confusing dream had left him disturbed. Swarna dangled from the rope she had slung through the crossbeam . . . Skeletons were being dug up in the Semmani mass grave . . . Abayan was running somewhere, the sweat pouring off him . . . The dreams were enough to disrupt his peace.

Light crept in through the window. He got up thinking he'd turn on the light but sat down again.

Birds squabbled in the temple tree and went quiet.

Silence spread its wings everywhere.

He heard a couple of vehicles roar by.

The sound of their engines told him they were army vehicles.

There was movement again, after four years of quiet.

Though the broadcasting service seemed aligned with his own position and gave him a sense of stability, he could envision nothing when he thought about the future. An antiterrorist group was terrorizing the town. Who could sleep peacefully at this time?

Thiravi had returned to Colombo shattered by the true faces of war that he had now witnessed. While you couldn't say that life in

Colombo had returned to normal, there was no sense that they were as affected by the war. The war was planned and mobilized from here, yet it was not a place that grasped its scope. There was a fear of martial law, but no fear of riots anymore.

Thiravi wasn't engaged in his work that day. Anil was to return to Colombo that evening, or the next. He would feel uneasy until then. He had not sent anything in the way of political news to RSS after Gonagala. He had last written a dance review of Vasantha Gugathasan's arangetram and sent it off. The fan whirled above him. Anil's wife had gone out. A few people walked about on the street. Still, the place looked deserted. He shut the door behind him and set off to have a tea at the bakery at the top of the street. It looked busy.

As he sat drinking his tea, his gaze fell upon three youths standing outside; one of them drew his attention. Those eyes looked very familiar to him. Where had he met him? Where did he know him from? Wellawatte? Kochikade? Kotahena? Maradana? Where? He might have seen him at the Poobalasingham Bookstore. The face looked like a Tamil face. It was only as he thought more about it that he remembered seeing him in Vavuniya. It was an unexpected encounter, but he couldn't forget it. He kept thinking about it even when he returned to the office. It was the sound of the telephone that finally disrupted his thoughts. The person on the other line wasn't someone he knew personally. It was the friend of a friend. He had come down from Batticaloa and called because he had got his number. He said that he had heard the Seven Seas World Tamil Service broadcast of him reading an editorial titled "The Face of Tyranny," and had been shaken by the emotional description.

The murder of Koneswari had been the height of the army's acts of hatred. It had stunned all of Sri Lanka one morning, when the news leaked out. Thiravi had taken down the news himself from his representative in Trincomalee. He could barely write the news report. A middle-aged woman raped by six soldiers in front of her children, and then murdered with a grenade placed on her abdomen. Everyone was surprised when the case wasn't buried like the other atrocities but was taken to court. The murderers were arrested and taken in for questioning. The coroner's report revealed the brutality of the event. The grenade had exploded and torn out her body from her pelvis to her chest cavity. He had described it without sensationalizing it. It was Anil who had told him to leave out the graphic descriptions, deleted some lines, turned it into a news item and sent it off by telegraph. Seeing the edited version, Thiravi had turned on him: "Do you see the different ways racial loyalty operates now, Anil aiyya? There's a face behind your outside face." Anil laughed. He liked Thiravi's anger. He knew it was stirred by unselfish causes. He said mockingly, "You have to be lucky to have an inner face." When Thiravi tried to respond, he pressed his hand. "You and I are working in this institution. You collect the news. I turn it into news reports. Your work is just to give the news. You cannot add your opinions to it, not even an inch. I will intervene. Though the radio influences public opinion, our job here is to report the truth. No event happens in isolation. Neither does it end abruptly. It emerges from a context, creates some shockwaves, gives rise to other events, and then subsides. You can't write the news as propaganda, with an aim to bring about one thing or another. Do you understand?" "Then, what is investigative journalism? That has a place in the news too, doesn't it?" Anil smiled. "That's one way to get the complete story. It's not meant to be a trial," he explained. Thiravi went silent. Though he felt like arguing further, he agreed with some of what Anil said, and Anil knew what his silence meant. He never argued just for the sake of it. Atrocities like the murder of Koneswari were being carried out in many parts of the country.

The troops were an arm of the government. They had no opinions. They had to obey the government; or more accurately, their leadership. If they were in the military, they had to abide by special military justice. They were allowed some brutality, some exceptions. The military moved through violence. It was possible that the blood and death it sowed came with mental distress. Death is not the only outcome of war. War brings about the destruction of lands, psychological wounds, disruption of education, and it shaped future generations. If twenty-five thousand people flee the nation's troops, it is easy to understand the breadth of fear that had spread. That is why trauma is considered a normal result of war. War is the sign of destruction, and destruction is the sign of war.

Thiravi understood that. He knew that it was a powerful thing that his writing could have an impact in people. It made him happy too.

34

Colombo, Sri Lanka

THE GOVERNMENT COMPLETELY DENIED the veracity of the newspaper reports and complaints from the rebel group that the people in the north, especially people in Vanni, were not receiving food or medical supplies and people were dying from starvation and lack of medical care. The TULF had the same complaint. Anil contacted the Sri Lankan branch of the Red Cross to learn the truth. He heard back that both the complaints and the denial were true. It was only when he asked for an explanation for this unusual answer, that he was told that even though food was being distributed, it was only relegated to the areas under army control. He was also informed that the news that people were suffering from malnutrition and deteriorating hygiene in the Vanni region was true. When Thiravi pointed out that the conversation had the essentials of a short interview, Anil gave him the task of formatting it into one for broadcasting.

Thiravi began writing at three that afternoon but could not finish it even by nine that night and had to dedicate two more hours to it the next morning. Anil heard the fifteen-minute audiotape, which was a combination of interview and report, praised him, and had him send it immediately to Radio Seven Seas. It was one o' clock when he returned to the office.

When Thiravi arrived at work, Siva and Thisayan were waiting for him.

Anil had been at pains to be a good host to them.

They didn't have any pressing work that day. It was Saturday, though the day of the week never mattered there. They only had one day off. As the only two employees, Anil and Thiravi could decide on which day. Still, Saturdays and Sundays were special. Anil's friends would usually drop by on Sundays. So that was special. Munadasa, a Sinhala English newspaperman, would come by on Saturdays. A film, art, and literary critic, Sumithra Abeysekara would visit as well. Every weekend that they were in Colombo, the dramatist Wimalasekara would come by too. They would all drink a little and talk enthusiastically on subjects ranging from politics to theatre, cinema, literature, and art. Tamil artists found this a welcoming space as well. The place was called RSS by their friends. It stood for Radio Seven Seas.

There was still time before the RSS would converge.

Thisayan had a half-bottle of Mendis in his bag.

Sankarananda arrived at the door just then.

Thiravi got up to welcome him. Siva already knew him well. Thisayan had heard of him. Thiravi asked him to sit down and went in to call Anil.

Anil came out to welcome the monk as well.

The monk barely waited for Anil to sit across from him before getting to the point of his visit. He said he had read Anil's recent book. He had immediately thought that Anil was the best person to write the introduction to his historical treatise. Anil was surprised. His second book had just come out without much fanfare. Thiravi was translating it into Tamil. It was important to him that a bhikkhu had sought out the book and read it so quickly. Thiravi had spoken to him occasionally about the bhikkhu's historical treatise. Such a work needed a furious reader and ceaseless intellectual thought. He felt it was appropriate that his book had fallen into the monk's hands.

"Thiravi has spoken to me about your great historical work. I am glad to hear that it's ready for publication. If all you need is a foreword from me, I'm ready to write it. But . . . "

Seeing his hesitation, the monk urged, "Tell me."

"It will take me a while to read it. I am a measured reader. We may need to talk about the book afterwards as well. If there are any issues, we will need to make corrections before I begin the foreword. So it makes sense to read your book in its manuscript form. It's not my practice to write an introduction after the book is printed."

"No need. You can read the original manuscript and write the introduction."

"Wonderful. Have you made the arrangements for printing, Thero?"

"I have. I am going to print it myself. I can make arrangements for distribution later. A donor friend will bear the printing expenses."

Anil, Thiravi, and Siva all understood the reason the bhikkhu wished to publish the book himself. "Did it take you a long time to write your treatise, Thero?"

"A very long time. I have planned it in five instalments. I have been writing for six years. I composed it in my mind and tested it before I wrote anything down. There won't be any need for edits. My handwriting is very clear. There won't be any difficulty in reading it."

"Did you make notes before you wrote it?"

"I wrote the book on my journeys. So, I didn't make notes to work on. It is a documentation of the layers that arose in my mind. But I read a lot during my journeys. There was research I had to do. That was useful in helping me get to know different authors perspectives. But my book isn't based on events."

"I don't understand."

"It's a new form of writing that is sourced in hypotheses. My teacher, the Walawe Ganga bhikkhu believed that the events of the present can help us predict the future very precisely. I have seen some of his hypotheses come true myself. But it's difficult for someone who hasn't experienced it themselves to believe. But through dialectical reasoning, you can see a thread running through all these events. What a privilege for a country to have two thousand years of history! But my work tells of ten thousand years of history. I have titled the first section Koneswaram. A destroyed city. When my book comes out, it will shake the foundations of Lanka's history."

Anil sat up looking at him.

The others stayed frozen.

"Was Koneswaram built on hypotheses too?"

He noticed the slight pause before the other replied.

Though the question wasn't intended to be a trap, it was one.

The bhikkhu said, "Yes. There is no history without hypothesis."

The bhikkhu smiled slightly, as though embarrassed. How many wrinkles there were in his face. How tired his muscles seemed. How grey, wrinkled, and aged his body. And yet, when he smiled shyly it was as if a flower blossomed . . . it was like a child smiling . . . it drew you in with a serene glow that calmed the ripples of a troubled mind.

The bhikkhu continued, breaking the silence. "Every event has causes. Any event . . . any lack of movement . . . happens for a reason. The reason can arise from speculation. For instance . . . it's a historical event that King Gajabahu participated in the festival to bring a stone marker for Kannagi. If he attended because he was invited, that means sea travel between India and Lanka was possible then. If sea travel was not possible at the time, how could we believe this event happened?" He stopped and looked around at them to see if they were following him. There was a searching fierceness in his eyes. A lightning flash of amazement.

"Lanka's ancient history is remarkable. Adam's Peak is the place where Adam and Eve were banished after they tasted the forbidden fruit in the garden of Eden. It was a land as heavenly as the Garden of Eden. Though the Gautama Buddha was incarnated in India, several Buddhas appeared on the island of Lanka before his time. The coming of those Buddhas happened approximately at the times that the Mayans and Incas appeared and flourished in South America, and the Aboriginal tribes flourished in Australia. The reign of Raavana was not imaginary. It is a symbol of an attack on the dominance of the Naga tribe over the Yakka tribe. Only Tamils lived on the shores of the island of Lanka. They were mixed with the Naga people. The proof of the Tamil settlements is in the Hindu temples in those areas. This is the result of my hypothesis."

Anil was shaken. But his awe was exceeded by his disbelief. He realized right then that this wasn't going to be research based on an academic discipline. But he also saw that it could be a new form of history from a dialectical perspective.

Sankarananda prepared to leave. "I've given the original manuscript to a friend. I'll send it through someone."

"I will write the foreword. But if you think of someone else qualified to do it, don't worry about having asked me already; please go ahead and have them write it, Thero," Anil said.

"I see many changes in you. Do you worry a lot? Could be. But you must live too. Where are your children? Still in Vanni?" the bhikkhu asked Thiravi as he was leaving.

Thiravi answered all his questions.

"You're in a good place. Your suffering will ease. I don't know if you remember, in the island they used to say that the lizards around a great tree come to no harm. Don't abandon Anil. He is a source of strength for you."

He said his goodbye to Anil.

He peered closely at Siva and said, "Come," and took him outside with him.

"Thiravi hasn't yet recovered from his grief," he said.

Siva told him what had happened to Thiravi's sister. "But he absorbs himself deeply in his work to forget all his miseries," he finished.

"Good. He may become overwhelmed by his grief sometime. You must take care of him."

The bhikkhu left.

35

Colombo, Sri Lanka

IT WAS LATE AFTERNOON, and the city was in a confusion. Siva looked out from the doorway. The bhikkhu dissolved into the crowd like an illusion.

Siva realized then that if the body was essential to the movement of man, the mind was even more so. The bhikkhu's body had grown tired. It was the purity of his thought that kept him firm and still wandering. Even if he collapsed from exhaustion, if he got up from his bed, he had the capacity to work furiously again.

Siva returned to the office.

Thiravi was looking through the window at the sea beyond the railway tracks.

Anil was lost in thought.

Thisayan had opened up one of the daily newspapers, not wishing to interrupt their thoughts, and was reading. The vacuum left by the monk was palpable. Slowly, the talk of Sankarananda's new history arose among them. Thiravi teased Thisayan that he had not asked the monk any questions. No one apart from Anil aiyya had asked anything. Thisayan replied, trying to slip out of the topic. Thiravi didn't let go. Thisayan finally said, "I don't have any issues around this book and its pre-nineteenth-century history. I only care about how the bhikkhu views the Indian descendants here. I can only praise or criticize the work after I have read that section."

He turned around and smiled gently at Thiravi. Then he turned away and stared straight ahead. He could see the railway track through the window. He watched a train pass. His smile had vanished, and his face became clouded. But his eyes showed a fierceness that surpassed great stretches of time and distance. "You may have heard of the Daathu*-year famine. I feel it. I can still feel it. I don't know if there has been such a famine in any other country in the world. But the famine that occurred in Tamil Nadu in eighteen seventy-six was devastating. Its ravages were so terrible, family women sold their virtue to save their lives. There were corpses on the streets, deaths in every house. Do you know how many people died from it? Four million. Just try to imagine what kind of famine that was. Though it began in the Daathu year, it lasted for fifteen years. My ancestors came here to survive that famine. I will never forget it. When I think of all that suffering, I feel like I'm not one of you. My politics are different . . . even my culture, my arts and literature are different."

Anil understood the tension and tried to diffuse it by calling Siva aside, giving him some money and asking him to get some rice parcels, for their lunch there.

Siva got on his motorcycle and sped to Maradana. They all liked the non-vegetarian food from an island shop there.

They ate together when he got back.

As Thisayan prepared to leave, they heard the hum of a motorcycle near the entrance. Thiravi peered outside. It was the young men he had seen outside the bakery the previous day, riding 'double'* on the motorcycle. He gestured to Siva to go see what they wanted.

Siva went up to the entrance. "Whom are you looking for?"

"We need to see Sankarananda Thero."

"He's left."

"Can you tell us where he went?"

"I don't know."

"When will he come back?"

"I can't say."

"Has it been long since he left?"

"About two hours."

After the motorcycle had left, Thiravi asked what they had wanted. Siva told him. For the first time, Thiravi realized that they needed to keep an eye on the safety of Sankarananda Thero.

36

THAT SATURDAY NIGHT, THE sea crashed in terrifying sheets of spray on the eastern shores of Sri Lanka. The ocean roared and hurled water from the depths of its belly like a drunkard wo . . . ack . . . wo..ack hacking and vomiting as it rolled.

Darkness stretched out in all directions. One or two stars showed themselves in the cloud covered sky. This was a village of Muslim agricultural labourers. Silence had fallen. But the quiet was not a sign that the village was asleep. It was how things were. Many villages were similarly hushed during the nights.

Some hearts may have lain awake with sorrow, yearning, and desire, forgetting the next day. They lived in silence, unable to disturb the great silence.

Even when the stars do not glitter, nor the moon cast its glow, or the breeze dance, there are hearts that burn as if they did, in every age. Their skin burns with tongues of blazing fire when stroked.

They say that fish sing in the lagoons of Batticaloa. Their song would have sounded like weeping that night.

Yasin lay awake. The heat of her body was rising. He had been with her in the iluppai groves this time last month, at around this time of the night. The night had been a dance of the senses. She had lain curled inside the length of his body.

Religion . . . beliefs . . . she knew all the reasons this was wrong. But time had plucked her husband away from her. Perhaps not time, but war. Her husband had gone to the next town in search of work, unable to bear the sight of his children's hungry faces. He had gone by bus and was shattered before he even crossed the border of the town. The Iyakkam said it was the army who had set the landmine. What did it matter whose crime it was, so many women of the town had lost their husbands, so many children lost their parents . . . the devastation that falls, falls all the same.

It had changed the direction of her life. He had become her strength. The sanctuary of all her feeling. When he left, he said he would return on the twenty-eighth, that was two days ago. He worked in Eravur. Then it was the twenty-ninth . . . the thirtieth . . . and he didn't come. For the past six months, he had kept his trysts with her. He was not a man who would forget. He had sworn it on Amman. But he hadn't come that day for some reason. She slept in the verandah and stared out through the porch at the foot of the iluppai tree. She did not see the ember of his cigarette, the flare of a match . . . none of it. Even until midnight. Then Yasin got up, went over to the tree, looked around and went inside to lie down.

She would have stayed awake until dawn. But somehow, she felt angry that he hadn't come. She was surprised that she felt this resentment without any sense of the dangers that might have befallen him.

She heard a dog bark in the distance. Could it be him the animal was barking at? But she lay there, with no will to get up and wait for him. The barking ceased. She heard a stifled hum like the sound of an oththu* rise very close to her ear. It was a terrifying sound that broke the silence or created it. Though she was used to it by now it never ceased to frighten her.

She fell asleep after a long time.

A mob of about a dozen disturbed the heavy quiet, with the thumping of their feet and their thin murmurs. The mob spread out into the town.

Dogs barked.

The town stirred.

But it kept sleeping.

The clouds had dispersed, and by the light of the sky it was possible to see that these were Muslim youth.

The mob, which had picked up its pace, paused in front of Yasin's house. Then it declared its fury by tearing open the woven gate and storming in. The next moment . . . thumping, as though someone was kicking at the door. The two children, Yasin, and her old mother were startled awake and started wailing.

"Open the door!"

Yasin slowly opened the door a crack.

"Are you Yasin?"

She said yes.

The next moment two men pushed her aside and leapt into the house.

One of them grabbed her firmly by the hair.

The children screamed. The old woman threw herself at their feet, pleading in her choking voice. Who would listen?

Rip . . . one of them tore at her dress. Another ran over and pulled away the rest of her clothing.

One man stood outside and shone a flashlight directly at her.

Why this excitement?

At her bared breasts?

Who could be excited at the sight of a mother's breasts?

But vicious hands grasp at her. When she tried to stop them, her hands were twisted behind her. Only then did she understand what was happening to her.

She pleaded . . . prayed . . . howled . . . shouted . . . "Someone help me!"

The town had closed its ears.

They said it was a time of war. No one could help anybody else. They had enough difficulties taking care of themselves.

Her torn voice passed the ponds . . . passed the lagoons . . . passed the paddy fields . . . and flew to the eastern shore.

As their rage grew to its height she was dragged outside. Her clothing all gone. She huddled, trying to cover her body with her hands and legs in her misery.

One man, who had come prepared for their project cut off her long hair . . . sarak . . . sarak . . . and threw it to the ground.

Yasin begins to lose consciousness in her agony. The mob leaves her in her front yard, bald . . . naked.

The "judges" did not forget to tell her that this was the punishment meted out to her by the Jihad Committee for her immoral behaviour as a Muslim woman.

The moon shed its glow.

Through the length of the village streets, the dogs barked . . . whimpered . . . and went silent.

37

Chennai, India

MAHESWARI HAD WRITTEN THAT she would only be able to come next year, since Viji was in her confinement. Raji was not in a hurry to leave the camp. But Rajanayagam was in a hurry to get her out of there. He had written to the Tahsildar, saying that she was having constant abdominal pain and that she needed permission to stay in Chennai to get medical attention and to be cared for by her relatives. He had to go back and forth to the office, but he managed it.

Raji did not say her goodbyes to anyone when she left the refugee camp. She simply told them she was leaving. She had given away everything except her basic clothing. She had forced Malar to accept a saree of hers. Malar had liked the sea-blue saree with its floral embroidery. As she left with the tall older man, now grown thin and white-haired, her one regret was that she wouldn't be able to say goodbye to Malar and her mother. She told him about it too. He asked where they were. When she said they were in Trichy, he said they didn't have time to travel around now, she would have to write to them from Chennai.

It was evening. Darkness was beginning to spread, with a mist covering the area.

The camp crowd was unshaken.

They would sense her departure soon enough.

It may be true that there is no vacuum left by a single person that cannot be filled, but some vacuums take a long time to fill, some vacuums are never filled.

No matter how hard he tried to convince her, Raji refused to stay at Rajanayagam's house. It wounded his feelings. "Why, Raji?" There was a break in his voice.

"I don't want to."

He turned his gaze toward the vehicles flying by.

"Sir!"

"Mm."

"There are around two hundred women in the camp."

" . . . "

"All of us go to the toilet by the sea . . . only after dark . . . or before the dawn. It's a place where you can't ease your discomfort whenever you feel like it."

He turned to look at her face, lit by the headlights of the cars as they sped past.

"The fear that a man might suddenly come outside . . . it doesn't ever allow us to fully empty our bowels. We have to run out in a hurry and run back in a hurry. During the hotter months, the afternoon breeze blows softly. If it blows from the forest toward the camp . . . you'll be sick to your stomach. The stench is so strong. I have borne it all and stayed there. Your house is like a palace to me. It's too luxurious for me. Kamala akka's house is excessive too. But I have no choice. Let me stay there."

She said she would visit often. But as the months went by, she came once a week, and later once a month. Even that happened on a random day and time. If he asked: "Why don't you give me a phone call before you come?" She'd reply, "If I call you then I must come. This way, if I'm not in the mood, I can stay back." She would get out at the Thirumangalam Junction and visit Arasi, Mala, and Saraswathi before coming to see Rajanayagam. Then she would leave, saying that she had to catch the bus as soon as it turned to dusk.

Viswalingam had been at home the last time she had visited Anna Nagar.

Her life was a great sorrow to him. He sensed that it was heading to a point of no return. Chandramohan had come down from France two years before and tried to enlist Kamala and Rajanayagam to help turn her life around. He had discussed it with him too. But he had not returned. He had overheard Mala tell somebody that he had written to Kamala. He might have been delayed because Maheswari's trip had been postponed. And before you knew it, the years had circled by, and this one was almost over. It would have to be next year if anything. There was no certainty that next year wouldn't end like this one. What certainty did they have that the Indian High Commission wouldn't deny Maheswari a visa as it had the previous time? Everything was uncertain and remained to be seen.

"What is it Raji, we haven't seen you this way in a long time?"

"I didn't come the last month, maama. I need at least twenty rupees to come and go. It's a strain on Kamala akka. But I'll soon visit regularly. I'm arranging for some work . . . I think it will come through next week or so. What's going to stop me going back and forth if I get it?"

It was only then that he saw another side of her. The public reality was one thing. Her private reality was another. That her mother, sister, and family were in Canada was the public reality. Her brother had a good situation in Mumbai as well. But she? This was her private reality.

She had been a shelter to his family in the beginning. Now he must be her shelter.

A thought occurred to him.

Ten days after Raji visited them, Viswalingam took the train to Mumbai, with the hope of arranging some money for her.

Mumbai, India

He was not a stranger to Mumbai. He had been there five years before. Mumbai had not changed at all. He took the bus to Mathunga and inquired at Rajendran's address, only to learn that he had left the place a long time ago. He returned to Sempur and made arrangements to stay overnight and left for VT station. He scoured the streets around there for a group of boys who had paid money to an agency to go to Dubai and been cheated. He asked about Rajendran. It was useless. There was a group that would hang out drunk at the shops on the street across from the Mumbai-1 post office. When he inquired among them, he got some news. He waited at the Queen's Restaurant entrance that evening and saw Rajendran arrive at around seven.

It didn't take long for Rajendran to recognize Viswalingam. "What's this? When did you arrive in Bombay?" he asked with genuine joyfulness.

Viswalingam told him.

"To see me?" Rajendran replied in surprise. He wondered if the man had come to send off someone abroad.

"Chi chi . . . nothing like that. I need to discuss some family matters with you."

Rajendran stood for a while with his brows furrowed. "In that case, wait a moment," he said and went inside. "I need to get to Nariman Point in a hurry. But never mind. Come with me, we can talk along the way." He hailed a taxi.

Though he said they could talk as they went, Rajendran didn't create an opening for him. He didn't speak to the driver either. Viswalingam resisted the urge to speak.

As the taxi stopped at the Gateway to India by the sea, Rajendran said, "Gajen, you go ahead, I'll wait here," and turned to Viswalingam. "Aiyya, come, let's get out here," he said and got out of the vehicle.

Viswalingam got out as well.

The beach was not crowded. A few groups of three or four people dotted the shore. A few sat alone staring at the sea. The ships that waited to head into the Mumbai harbour swayed gently on the waves.

Rajendran went and sat on one of the concrete water breakers. Viswalingam sat beside him.

It had grown dark. It was misty too. There were yellow lights flickering in the distance. The breeze was heavy with salt and damp. The waves splashed against the rocks in bright flashes. The foamy edges of the ocean stretched out in white lines over a long distance.

"Aiyya, it's getting misty. Are you okay?"

"It's okay, thambi."

Silence drifted between them for a while.

Rajendran couldn't guess what Viswalingam had meant by family matters. Could it be . . . had he come because there was some problem between Suthan and Sheila, he wondered, and felt a little afraid to ask.

He broke the extended silence himself. "Tell me, aiyya."

"What do I say, thambi? We lived side by side on the island. We were as close as children of the same mother. That's why I came to talk to you. It's an internal matter regarding your family, yet I have to say it. I think you won't take it the wrong way either . . ."

Rajendran was listening very attentively. He remembered that he hadn't been that way back in their hometown. He loafed about, went to the cinema, drank, got into all kinds of unnecessary trouble. He used to be skinny. Dark, too. Now he seemed to gleam. He had grown stout. He had an air of wealth. Money was power, he knew. He had experienced the powerlessness that came from the lack of money.

"What is it, aiyya, you're quiet?"

"It's only," he hesitated: "Akka is not in the camp anymore."

Rajendran looked at him, unspeaking.

"She's with Kamala now."

Rajendran vaguely remembered the name.

Viswalingam continued, "At least when she was in the camp, she got refugee funds. Now I hear she's looking for a job somewhere near the house in Porur! Why should she deserve such a fate? Think about it, thambi."

"What's there to think about here?" Rajendiran replied abruptly: "She brought about all her problems by her own stubbornness. If it was something someone else had heaped on her, you could feel sorry about it. You could try to do something about it . . . if it was possible. But she chose this life on purpose, saying this made her happy, this satisfied her. What can we do, aiyya? You tell me."

"Even if that's true, you can't just walk away from her, thambi. You're her brother, no?"

"I haven't forgotten it, aiyya. I do think about her occasionally. Thangachi is in Canada, amma is in Canada. Even I am fairly comfortable here in Bombay. Every time I think about why she has to suffer in a refugee camp, my chest hurts. No one will believe it if I say it. I have cried thinking about her . . . cried tears. If you ask Amba, she'll tell you how much I have been tortured by the thought of it." He stumbled for words. "That's all I can do," he said, as he found his calm again.

"No, thambi. Maybe you're saying this because she didn't go when Suthan tried to take her with him . . . ?"

"That too. It's been around ten, twelve years since that happened. Viji wrote to her this past year, asking her to write if she wanted to come to Canada. She has the means to go even now. But akka said she wouldn't . . . "

"There's some justice in her position, Rasa."

Rajendran peered deep into his eyes, in the yellow lamplight. There was a glow of entrancement in them. An integrity.

Viswalingam spoke calmly, "Within a few years of getting out of Sri Lanka, we have forgotten our circumstances, the war, the destruction. It's only a few people like Raji who don't forget and still worry about it. A lot of people have benefitted from Raji's work; people who are not related to her, or even from the same village. Isn't it important that at least a few people don't forget? They can do these things only by sacrificing themselves. Its only we who think, 'my family, my child,' and fall into selfishness. As things are . . . who are we to call these few good people stubborn?"

Rajan felt he had to object.

This is a natural reaction of most people whenever something burns their conscience. It's easier to despise something thoughtlessly, rather than think about it and change one's ways. But as he thought about it, he found some clarity.

"I didn't know Suthan's father had died. It was a comfort to me that at least Raji had been there to take care of him during those final days," Rajan said, with a twinge in his heart when he thought about these relationships.

Viswalingam seized upon his softening mood.

"Thambi, this is how some matters can get delayed in ways we cannot foresee. We must think of Raji's decision as something of that nature and make peace with it." He went on, "The child was like that in the island too. Always in a rush . . . always a hurry.

When did she ever give up a struggle . . . ?"

That slightly forward-leaning walk . . . always in a hurry . . . always the drive to get ahead . . . always that gurgling laughter . . . she had taken on life's burdens so easily even at that early age. Rajan had never thought about what they had been like when they had been a family. Now that they were scattered, each in a different direction, he thought about it. Though akka was in a different place, she was not too far away. In what birth would they ever return to that land, that house, that life together?

His eyes filled with tears when he thought about it.

When he came back to himself, Viswalingam had stopped talking. He was waiting, as though he sensed him melting. He waited a while before he said "Thambi . . . !"

"Hm . . . !" He grumbled and then asked: "How is akka doing now?"

"She's okay. But what of that? What a great curse it is to wither at the time she should have lived her life! She looks like an old person . . . her hair has started going grey . . . "

"Akka's?"

"Mm . . . how old is she now, thirty-five, thirty-six?"

He remained silent.

"What's she doing for her expenses?"

"Kamala takes care of her. It's a good thing that Kamala's husband went to Canada, by God's grace. Or . . . do you know how much your akka would have suffered?"

"I want to help her. But akka, she won't accept it."

"If you show up suddenly and say you're going to help them, anyone will hesitate to accept it. Go see her . . . talk . . . there must be some connection between the two of you again, don't you think?"

"You're right in what you say. Akka was in the camp all this time and I didn't feel up to going to visit her there. Now . . . now that she's out I'll definitely come and see her."

"Yes, you do that."

"It seems like amma's trip was postponed for a year, then another year, now it looks like she won't be coming this year either . . . "

"That's what I heard too. Your younger sister is in confinement, they said. She wants to see the grandchild. And you know that Arasi is here too?"

"Arasi? I didn't know. When did she come?"

"It's going to be two years soon . . . "

"Is that so?" Rajan was amazed.

They were getting closer and closer. It was only he who had not seen any of it happen.

"I want to go right now . . . see Arasi, akka . . . I want to see everyone. If I go straight after seeing you, it will be like seeing our small island again . . . " His eagerness overflowed into the pauses between his words.

"Thambi!" Viswalingam said. "I need to ask you one more thing . . . "

"Go ahead."

"How is your connection with Suthan these days?"

"Connection . . . ? It's been a while since that dropped. I don't even know why. I wrote to him a few times. No reply. I let it go."

"Mm. Suthan is not with Sheila anymore either."

"What are you saying, aiyya?"

"It's true."

"What happened between them?"

"I don't know, Rasa, don't know. She doesn't talk to me. She only chitchats with her mother and sisters. They didn't know about this for a long time either. Someone came down from France. That's when it all came out."

"So, the problem has been there for a while, then?"

"Over four years, it seems."

"Then . . . Sheila is on her own there?"

"Mm . . . "

"She's sending money for the house expenses?"

"That's the only way the house is still a house, thambi. Or this lot would have eaten each other up by now . . . Mala got married. You know that, right?"

"When was that?" Rajan was surprised.

"Three years ago. A boy from the village."

"You could have got hold of Sheila and had her send your son-in-law overseas somewhere, couldn't you?"

Viswalingam told him about all their efforts.

Things that he'd heard of happening to strangers had happened within his own inner circle. It was just he who had been untouched by it.

Viswalingam said, "Thambi, I had no idea that my plans would be fulfilled so smoothly. I made an offering at the Vadapalaniyar temple before I came. Murugan has not abandoned me. When will you come there?"

"Soon. When are you planning to head back?"

"I'll leave tomorrow . . . "

"Then stay at my place tonight, before leaving."

He didn't object. There was another urgent matter he wanted to discuss with him. He could talk about it right there. But Rajan needed time.

"Thambi, are you in a rush?"

"Why, aiyya?"

"I still need to discuss another important matter with you."

Rajan turned to look at him in surprise.

"It's true, thambi. All this is just a roundabout way of getting to what I wanted to say," Viswalingam said and paused for a while, looking outward. He continued: "I hear that Suthan isn't in good shape either. A boy called Chandramohan visited from France a year ago. We only found out all this through him. He mainly came to find out what Raji's frame of mind was, and how she was doing."

"I don't get it, aiyya," Rajan replied.

"He had come to see if he could try and reunite Suthan and Raji."

"You think that can happen, aiyya?"

"Why not?"

"It could. Did he talk to akka?"

"He did. Not only him. The old judge Rajanayagam, Kamala, Arasi, me . . . we all tried talking to her. She didn't agree. At the same time . . . she didn't refuse either. No one pushed her beyond that point. We thought amma would be coming soon, and we could think about it then. Now it looks like amma isn't coming. But Chandramohan is coming back at the end of this year . . . "

Rajendran said nothing.

He thought this was an opportunity for Raji to have a good future. He recognized that they were right to place these responsibilities on him. It touched his heart that there was always someone somewhere who would come forward to suggest a good deed.

They both got up when Gajen arrived.

They climbed into the taxi, Rajendran with his new burden, and Viswalingam ecstatic that the burden had been taken off his shoulders.

38

THE TAXI FLOATED IN a flood of people and vehicles. It crawled all the way to Bandra. Rajendran lived in an apartment building there. It was difficult for ordinary people to get a ground floor apartment there. When they rang the bell, a woman opened the door and peered out. She brightened at the sight of Rajan, and let them in.

Viswalingam sat on the sofa and observed the woman, who was standing off to a side, thinking that she looked like she might be Chinese.

Who was she? Was she the maid? It didn't look like it. She seemed polished and had a glow about her, which led him to think that she had a different role here. He could see a baby sleeping through the open bedroom door. He recalled Rajan mentioning Amba, and his guess seemed to be confirmed.

Though she stood aside demurely, there was an air in her manner and her gaze. It was a sense of comfort in the home. A confidence that came from having authority in the house. Rajan watched the range of emotions that flickered across Viswalingam's face, a smile mingled with shyness. He turned and called out to her, "Amba!" As she approached, he described Viswalingam as someone from his village . . . like a relative . . . maybe even closer than that . . . and introduced him to her.

Viswalingam wasn't shocked when Rajan introduced her. He had already worked it out.

She clasped her hands and said, "Vanakkam!" in beautiful Tamil.

He looked at her in surprise and smiled.

"We don't need any tea. We'll eat in a while. What have you made for dinner?"

"Idiyappam."

"Okay. Set it out. We'll come. Gajen, eat before you head out."

The three of them washed their hands and ate.

Idiyappam and a spicy pepper sothi. There was a meat curry from the afternoon as well. The food had the aroma of Jaffna cooking. Viswalingam thought that Rajan must have taught it to her. But to have captured this flavour must have taken a lot of time and effort.

Later Rajan and Gajen went outside. Through the window Viswalingam saw the flare of a match as Rajan lit a cigarette.

Amba was of a different race, it was true. She could be from Nepal, Assam, Manipur, or Nagaland. He couldn't tell the fine distinctions of features between all these groups. But no matter where she was from, she was a beauty. Golden skin. A slender frame. Long black hair. Small dark eyes. Bright even teeth. He could see there was a kind of sensibility in her that had a Tamil element. She had every desirable quality. But would Maheswari accept her? What would Raji say to this? Even if Rajan hadn't thought of these questions when he married her, Viswalingam thought of them now.

Would the woman who had left refusing to see her daughter again because she turned down a marriage, now reject her son for having married? Their relationship had already eroded somewhat.

He had heard of Lankan Tamil girls and boys who went overseas and married people from their host countries. Some of them
out of love, others out of necessity. He could understand them. It
was the last weapon available to those who were not accepted by
the countries where they sought refuge: to marry a citizen of that
country. It stopped them from being deported right away.

But what was the reason behind Rajan and Amba getting married? Wasn't this for love?

Rajan came in after sending Gajen off. He sat beside him on
the large sofa. He leaned back comfortably and said, "You were
good friends with aiyya, I know. Taking care of you would be like
taking care of aiyya, in my mind, and that's why I brought you
to my home today. The situation in my home isn't ideal to bring
people from the island over and welcome them. I think you might
have guessed why by now. Don't let akka, amma or anyone else
there know about it for now. When the time is right, I'll tell them
myself."

"You don't need to tell me that, thambi. I understand the situation. Never mind . . . where's the girl from?"

"Assam. I married her after six months of knowing her. It'll be
four years now. One child. A boy. He's exactly the image of aiyya.
You can see him in the morning when you wake up."

"That's fine. Your wife speaks some Tamil?"

"She started to learn after we got married. At first, I used to talk
to her in Hindi. Now she has learned Tamil. The child only speaks
Tamil. I have taught her how to cook our food . . . "

"I thought so when we were eating. It was really good."

His admission came easily.

They spoke for a long time about the island and about the state
of the country. When they were done, the conversation turned
to the Sri Lankan refugees in India. When he realized how tired
Viswalingam was, Rajan set him up in the front room and went

into his own. Amba was still awake. He told her to go to sleep, opened the door to the bedroom balcony and stepped out. He sat on a wicker chair, smoking a cigarette.

A small blue light burned on in the bedroom.

He saw that Amba tossed and turned, unable to sleep. She always felt stressed whenever any Sri Lankans came to stay with them. She tossed and turned and stayed up thinking. Rajan had noticed this many times.

Rajendran turned to look outside. His heart was overflowing with emotions. They didn't sour the inner feelings like culture-stiffened yogurt. Instead, they fermented inside him . . . filling him.

His thoughts were stirred by akka. Then amma. Even Suthan. Then the situation in their village. He had many friends on the island, like Soruban and Nallathamby. But he had rarely thought of them. He did now. What had happened to them? Had they stayed and been killed? Or gone off to Germany, France, Canada, or Australia, living happily? Many of them must be married and have families by now.

Whenever he thought of his circle of relationships, Amba appeared in his mind. Would amma at least accept her for the Tamil she spoke?

39

Chennai, India

RAJI WAS ABSORBED IN a thick book, seated on the entrance steps to have better light. She was unaware of him opening the gate quietly and standing in front of her. Her head was bowed in concentration.

It was akka. It looked as though Kamala was not at home. How akka had changed, Rajendran thought. She hadn't grown taller. She hadn't put on weight . . . but there was a change. Her face was not lined with age or wrinkles, but he could see the threads of grey in the front of her head. She had misplaced her life . . . and was unconscious of it . . . were those who were swept along by the tides of life so unaware of it themselves?

The great river of time springs up and flows along. Even the weak swayed and danced along on that journey. Only a few, like Raji . . . or Arasi . . . tried to turn the tides in their lives and got swept away by the current to end up far away, swept into the hollows and bushes somewhere.

"Akka!"

She sat up with a start.

Tall . . . broad . . . flashy . . . "Who is it?"

Her hesitation felt like a blow to him.

"It's me, akka, Rajendran . . . "

He could have wept. His voice broke. What were tears, after all, but the breaking of a heart?

How many years had it been since he had seen her? Twelve years. The years the Pandavas had spent in exile in the forest! Oh . . . !

She closed the book and stood up. As she stood on the step, they were able to see each other face to face. She peered deep into his face, his eyes. The resentment he had borne toward her was gone. This was not the old Rajendran. He never knew to call her akka so lovingly. She looked to see if anyone had accompanied him and said, "Come in."

He took off his shoes and left them on the step before going in. He slowly sat in a chair across from her. His eyes were misty.

Seeing his emotion, she began the conversation herself. "When did you come from Bombay?"

"Last night."

"Did you come especially to see me? Or . . . did you come and hear that I was here . . . " As he stiffened in denial, she said "No, Rajan, you were in Bombay I was wondering how you heard that I have left the camp and am living in Porur now, that's why I asked."

"I came to see you."

"How did you know?"

"I knew," he said firmly.

She didn't push him. She wasn't going to ask him why he had come, either. He had to arrive at it on his own. She waited.

After a while, he said, "Amma was supposed to come. Then I heard she wrote saying she wasn't coming. When is she expected to come?"

"She's written saying she'll only come next year, apparently."

"Written to whom?"

"To Arasi, and Mala."

"Doesn't amma write to you?"

After a short pause, "No. It's been twelve years since amma wrote to me."

"It's been longer than that for me," he said.

She didn't reply to that. She stayed silent. The silence she had allowed to weave its way between them implied that perhaps amma was justified in not writing to her.

"Why did amma become that way?" she wondered out loud. Her amma . . . their amma . . . she had been extraordinary. She had gone through so many difficulties to raise them. She had thought of them at every moment. How could she then cast them off like that? There was no doubt that her son becoming a wastrel and Raji refusing to join Suthan were wrongs in her eyes. But what had hurt her beyond that?

Raji had thought long about it. At first, she couldn't figure it out. But eventually she did. She knew her mother, so she knew the reason.

The loss of her father had a lasting effect on her mother. She never had an event where she didn't somehow include his memory. She saw any help they received in their village as due to him, and therefore coming from him. She never rushed into saying or doing anything important. She would hesitate. She said aiyya would tell her what to do. She had devoted herself to her husband. She had only stayed alive for her three children. She would need no effort to kill herself. She could make any breath her last if she wished.

To someone so single-minded, everything Raji did seemed to be in defiance of aiyya's wishes. She had already made up her mind that Suntharam had come rushing to arrange a marriage between her daughter and his son because "someone" had told him to. It wasn't a pretense on amma's part; it was her reality.

A reality devoted to aiyya. Who was Raji to refuse his initiative? Maheswari's son could not stop Raji from going against her father's wishes. It was enough for her to be poisoned against him too.

"Akka!"

"Mm . . . " she emerged from her reminiscence.

"I hear Arasi is here!"

"Who told you? You may be in Bombay, but you seem to know everything!"

He blurted out, "Will you come? Let's go and see her."

"I've been meaning to. But I can't today. Kamala akka has gone to Mangadu. It'll be seven or eight when she gets back. When are you going back to Bombay? First, tell me where you're staying."

"In a lodge. It's near Central Railway Station. I can only stay for two more days, akka."

The way he said it revealed that he didn't think it was enough time.

It was true. He had amended his ways, and it gave her joy to hear him speak like this.

"Who knows when you'll come back if you go now? You'll only come again when amma comes, isn't that so?"

"No, akka. I will come to see you now, too."

She made some tea and brought it out to him.

Then as she went into the kitchen to cook, he followed her and stood there talking to her. He had his lunch there and prepared to leave at four o'clock.

"Come to Anna Nagar tomorrow to see Arasi, will you? I'll go straight there," he said as he was leaving.

Her strained circumstances prompted her to say no. But she didn't want to hurt him, "Okay, let's see."

The answer was enough for him. But he still stood there. "What is it, Rajan?" she asked, seeing his hesitation.

"Akka!"

"What?"

"You shouldn't say no."

She lifted a blank gaze to him.

He took out a wad of notes from his trouser pocket and stretched it out to her.

Her eyes turned cloudy in a flash.

He was standing before her as a brother, as someone who understood his family obligations and care. What more could she ask for? What could money give her, more than the satisfaction, or the joy she felt in that moment?

Yet she gently turned it down. "No need, Rajan. I'm happy enough that you asked me, like this. If I need anything, anytime, I will ask you myself."

It was a punishment. But she hadn't stabbed him to the heart, either.

"Don't forget, I'm still alive. Call me, that's enough. I'll happily come."

"Okay," she said.

He walked away.

40

Chennai, India

RAJI HAD ARRIVED FROM Porur when Rajan went to Mala's house the next day. Raji and Arasi were seated on the balcony talking.

It was June. The season of the fire star was beginning. The body had not cooled from the previous day's heat before it began to warm up again the next day. It was easier to be outside than to be indoors during this season. The rapidly spreading heat had been the harbinger of the fire star season. The balcony was sheltered by the margosa tree and the two coconut trees next door. The tall asoka trees gently fanned the breeze. The sun would only pass over that side after eleven or twelve o'clock.

Though Rajan could see Raji and Arasi upstairs on the balcony, he stopped to speak to Viswalingam, who was on the verandah, preparing to leave.

Viswalingam spoke kindly, asking him how he was.

Mala and Saraswathi learned he had arrived and came out to ask him how he was as well. When he asked about Senan, they said he had not woken up yet. Poobathy stood behind them and smiled. Why did she smile? Did she recognize him? He hadn't recognized her. "Poobathy, go back inside," Mala scolded, before he realized who she was. She had been a scrawny child in short skirts the last time he saw her.

Since they could not speak at length, Viswalingam got him to write down the name and address of the lodge where he was staying before he left.

Rajendran went upstairs.

They made some small talk and exchanged what news occurred to them.

All three were cautious, so as not to cause rifts during this long-delayed reunion. Raji went downstairs for a while to talk to Saraswathi and Mala.

Rajan came to the point immediately. "Arasi akka, I came here in a hurry from Bombay to speak about akka. I hear that Kamala akka and this Chandramohan from France had spoken to you about this matter . . . "

"Yes, they spoke. I have brought this up with Raji many times myself. I don't think she'll listen."

He thought for a while. "She didn't counter with anything, did she?"

"No. That's what we're thinking about now. If there was someone who could speak firmly to her, I think Raji might consent."

"I hear Chandramohan will be coming back soon. Aiyya says that Suthan might come as well. At that time, it would help to bring akka around a little, wouldn't it?"

"It would help. But who's going to do it?"

"Can't you, akka?"

"Rajan, I have pushed this issue as far as I can."

"Then who else is there, akka?"

"The old judge Rajanayagam is there. The man is going back and forth between London and Chennai. There's going to be a decision in the Rajiv Gandhi appeal case, that's why."

"What can he do about it?"

"They need money for this and that. And the judge is busy with that. The Q Branch already has an eye on him. God only knows what will happen."

"You think there might be some trouble?"

"That won't happen. He has three children in London. He has studied there himself. Also, he won't have any big issues, he used to be a Supreme Court judge in Sri Lanka. But they've got their eye on him. That's not good."

"So . . . is there nothing we can do for akka?"

She could see the concern that had rooted so deeply in him. She was thrilled that he was no longer the boy he used to be in the village, or the boy Raji and Maheswari used to write about.

"There is."

"What is it?"

"We need to bring maami here. The sooner we can do that, the better. If maami comes, we can do it."

Yes. If amma came, Raji could be moved. She would be an immovable pestle to anyone else. Her hard stubbornness wouldn't give. "And you have to do that too."

"That's what I've planned. And you should write too."

"Me?"

"Why? What's wrong with a child writing to their mother?"

"Amma won't come if I write."

His eyes clouded over immediately.

Arasi reassured him. "That will never happen, Rajan. She feels you have committed an unbearable wrong against her. You can't say that you're not at fault either. So, she might have put off writing letters to you. Look here, you haven't written to her either; she must be the same. Think of it that way. If you write, she will definitely write back. And another thing, your letter will affect her more than any letters the rest of us would write. Only your letter has the power to make her come here. If you want—wait and see."

He didn't speak. She didn't try to force an assent out of him either. Something in her told her that he would write.

Mala called them both downstairs.

They came down. It looked like Senan had just woken up. His hair looked like a crow's nest. Siva was on the verandah drinking tea, absorbed in the day's newspaper.

41

Mumbai, India

WHOSE MISTAKE WAS IT that he had become a wastrel? Rajan wondered. Was it all his own fault? Were there no outside influences that had shaped him? Time after time there was a scattering of people like him. But his mother wouldn't acknowledge that. Singaravelan, Kutti, Siri . . . they were such a scattering. Suthan on the other hand was an ejection. Circumstances had sucked him in and spat him out. It was Viswalingam who had explained the difference to him.

The thought troubled him for many days after he returned to Bombay.

That was when Arasi had called him. "So, have you written yet? It's been three days since I wrote. Don't think about it, just write. Haven't you heard the saying that even the pestle will budge?"

It had been a week since he had decided he would write. But not one line came to him. Two days after Amba had left for Assam, it happened. He had gone out with Gajen and had just one beer. He had come back and had a pav bhaji at Pandyan's food truck. He had not felt like eating for a few days. No appetite.

As soon as he got home, he washed his face and sat down.

The solitude of the evening was conducive to thought.

Through the open window he saw one side of Bandra. It was dark and lit up. It was awake and asleep. Moving and still. Separation and desire quenched. He knew Bombay like the back of his hand.

He had a travel agency for his income. Something came in regularly. Though it wasn't in the hundreds of thousands, as before, he still earned in the thousands. He had a savings account in the bank that accumulated a thousand or two every month.

A sense of fatigue . . . boredom . . . had crept into his life. He had lost track of many people who had been close to him. He still spotted a few acquaintances on the street. Soma was still under that pipal tree. He never left the roots of that tree. The wedding hall was just across. It got crowded during the wedding seasons. Then everybody would leave. But Soma alone would not budge from the foot of that tree. He did have a time when he'd move. But only he decided when. The liquor store was just past that. Whenever someone called him for a drink, or whenever he got some money, he'd go drink.

Everyone knew that Soma had been there for twenty-five years. The Mumbai VT police station was nearby. The police there knew him too. There used to be a Marathi family, a man, woman, and a child, who lived under that tree. That family had somehow disappeared from there. Only he remained. Everyone knew him only as Soma. Whether he was Somasuntharam or Somapala*, who knew? He had come there with the wave of migrants who had come to work on the ships in the seventies. Some people said that some vengeance was tying him to that place. They said he had killed a rival for a place on a ship. It was an impulsive murder. He had broken the bottle that was in his hand and stabbed the man in anger. The man was dead on the spot. How would he escape? There was a bucket of blood flowing on the street. It twisted around his leg in accusation, like a lotus vine. He himself had forgotten that he was a Lankan. He had been telling people that he was Tamil. Many heard from him that it was possible to forget your mother tongue. He once spoke to a Sinhala man in Marathi in the Seamen's Club, saying that he was born in Monaragala and that he knew neither Sinhala nor Tamil.

Rajendran had escaped such a fate. He had gone in search of his relationships with a fervour for his roots because of this. He had been terrified of emulating Soma's rootless life. He thought akka seemed to understand that somewhat. She had come to be quite normal by his last day there. She had said, "Come by whenever you can," as she sent him off.

It had grown dark by the time he left. It seemed that her eyes had grown misty. Perhaps she too had succumbed to that fear of loneliness?

Arasi, Mala, and Siva had accompanied him to the railway station. Arasi had not spoken much. She had frowned in thought as she waved to him that day when they saw him off. It was a sign that she had easily understood him. But it was the thought that akka had understood him that made him happiest. For as long as Arasi was a poet, she could find a way to understanding, even in these difficulties.

If amma understood him too . . .

He had got everything together to write.

The first line fell into place.

Dear amma,

Then he stumbled, as if he had forgotten his language. What else could he write?

The thought of Soma came to mind.

A slow smile rose in his heart.

He thought over each word before he wrote it. He scratched

words out but kept writing. How long it had been since he had written a letter! The Tamil didn't seem to come to him at times. Finally, he signed it and began to read it over, calmly.

I'm writing this letter to you after a long time. I often felt sad that I was not able to write to you when you were in the island. I wanted to write to you when I heard that you had gone to Canada. I had too much work. So many problems got in the way because of all my work rivalries and jealousies. Finally, I was not able to write.

You could have written to me. Even if you didn't write separately to me, you could have sent a message in the letters you wrote to others. I looked to see if you had, many times, and was disappointed. Let it be. I have faith in the mercy of our Nainativu Amman that the opportunity will come some day.

I am somehow okay here. I have my own home in Bombay. I run a travel agency. As long as Suthan stayed in touch with me, I had some hope that one day I would go overseas too. Not anymore.

Now I remember, I heard you had said to someone, "Why does he hold on to a friendship with a man who abandoned Raji and dragged another woman off with him." It's true. I never thought of it at the time. I thought at the time that akka was in the wrong for refusing to go with him. And I was furious when I heard that she had gone off with Yogesh.

I don't know anything about Suthan anymore. He doesn't call me either. He doesn't write. I thought let him go, it doesn't matter. But I got to know something that drew my attention. Sheila and Suthan have split up. Viswalingam came here once and told me about it. That was when I also heard that akka had left the camp and was staying with Kamala akka.

I went to Chennai to see akka. I spoke to her. Akka spoke to me strangely at first. But when she realized that I wasn't who I used to be, she was very affectionate with me. I thought she might have some money difficulties and gave her some money. She told me she didn't want it. I was very sad. But I understand that I had done wrong. I had neglected her for so long. Akka had been in the camp for twelve years. I had never gone to see her. Never wrote a single letter. If I suddenly go visit her and claim our relationship and give her money, her self-respect won't allow her to accept it. I am not angry with her anymore. I feel bad with all my heart that she is in this situation. Her hair is turning grey. I wanted to cry when I saw it.

That was the first time I felt angry with Suthan. But I think that it's time to put away all the anger and to think things through. I don't want us to get into a situation we regret, by acting thoughtlessly. With Suthan being alone now, I wonder if we can try to rekindle her broken relationship with Suthan. Suthan's friend Prabu had made some attempt through another friend of theirs, Chandramohan, who had come to India from France the year before last. Arasi akka, Kamala akka, Rajanayagam and Viswalingam all tried talking to akka. She didn't agree to it.

Now, this is the important part. An organization called the Global Tamil Cultural Assembly is celebrating its twelfth anniversary in Chennai at the end of next year. Chandramohan is coming soon from France to organize it. It looks like Suthan might come with him as well. We can try again to change akka's mind. It would be good if you came to India as well at this time. Akka won't be able *to deny your wishes. Everyone thinks that things will work out if you come here yourself. I believe the same.*

Nowadays it's normal for married folks to get divorced and marry others, even among our people. I hear that this is most common in Canada. You may have seen a lot of this kind of thing yourself there. We should think of the relationship between Suthan and Sheila as not unusual. What does it say when they don't even have a single child to show for their past relationship? Doesn't it show that there's a possibility for a relationship between Suthan and akka? Besides . . . we're not even in a situation where we must accept everything that has happened just because the woman is from our home and we have to be the ones to reach out to Suthan. The attempt is being made from their side. We shouldn't let it go. Even Viswalingam told me the same.

I eagerly look forward to your arrival. When is Viji due? You will come, won't you?

Forget all the past feelings and please write. Aren't we your children? Even now. Always.

Give Viji, her husband, and her children my love. I will write to them separately later.

Send me a good reply, amma.

Your loving son,
Rajendran

When he finished reading it, he was surprised at himself. It wasn't just full of words. It was full of feelings that would stir his mother's heart.

42

SUDDENLY ONE DAY, THERE was a message from Maheswari, saying that she would be coming on the ninth of the following month. Kamala had received the phone call. But it wasn't a conversation. She had simply made her announcement and said they would speak about all the rest in person and left it at that.

Kamala called Raji immediately and told her.

Raji had been sitting outside reading. Recently, her voracious reading had become a source of strength for her. When she heard the news the novel she was reading stopped moving. Her face hardened. It was news that held a little joy and a lot of sorrow for her. Raji knew why her mother was coming in such a hurry. Though no one had said anything to her, from their movements she had been able to tell what they were up to. Now Arasi would push. Rajanayagam would push. Even thambi would push. The phalanx had formed, and the knowledge spread a sadness within her. How would she stand up to this problem? The question filled her whole mind.

"What is it, Raji, you haven't said anything?" But what could she say to Kamala? She smiled lightly. She closed the book and set it down beside her. Her face looked like despair taken form.

Kamala grasped her frame of mind and walked away without waiting for a reply. Was that the reason Rajendran had come? Would he have written a letter to amma so soon to drag her into this? Would amma have rushed to come here without even waiting for Viji's delivery? Truly, thambi had changed a lot. She couldn't remember him calling her akka much when they were back home. But now, it was akka . . . akka . . . once every beat whenever he spoke. It was his affectionate speech that helped her see it. He would have written out all his thoughts from that changed perspective. So just like her, her mother understood the change and was rushing to them.

It was confirmed that amma would come. She got a visa at lightning speed and booked her plane ticket as well. There was no going back on this now. Would amma roll her eyes and glare at her like before? Would she look at her the way she had eighteen years ago when she asked her "With whom did you go to Colombo?" Would she be beaten like she had been with the ladle, or with something else that came to amma's hand?

She wouldn't. So many years had passed. She would have seen and heard so many things. Living in that wintery country where the younger generation didn't have the same reverence for their elders, life would have taught her a few things. She had grown old too. She had been forty then. She must be around sixty now. Raji had grown old herself. She used to be called a girl, now people referred to her as a woman. Was she still the age where she could be beaten, even in caution? She was too old to be scolded, too. But amma had one last weapon. She would cry, she would threaten to kill herself. What could she do then?

All the same . . . if she came, Arasi would join forces with her. Arasi had an authoritative kind of love. Don't do that . . . do this . . . she was the only one who could give Raji commands. And she had used her authority over her. Arasi had been resentful when she arrived. Could none of these people write her a single line? But when she saw them in person, the confused circumstances and the strange environment had pacified her. Raji was intimidated by correspondence between Arasi and Chandramohan. Though she knew it was only about literature . . . poetry . . . a feeling that they were aligned somehow ate away at her. Chandramohan was getting delayed. But, without a doubt, he was coming. There was talk that Suthan would come with him too. Someone called Prabu, a friend of his from Germany, was also supposed to come. It was going to be an awkward situation.

She knew Suthan very well. He didn't stand upright anymore. He had done, back when he was at the university. He had had the magnificence of a hermit. Not anymore. When he deluded himself, he lost all of it. Including the magnificence. Even now, if the discussion didn't go in his favour, he would bow out. When he bowed, that was it. He seemed pitiable. To anyone. She had felt sorry for him too, many times. If the man who came stood up straight, she could face him and argue with him. But if he was bent and cowed . . . it would stab her in that old wound. Then she too would bend, forgetting all his faults. Forgetting all her own faults too.

There were nights when, caught up in her emotions, she lost sleep. Flesh close to flesh . . . pressed . . . entwined . . . the painful urges of life. But she had no desire to expand this to husband, child, and family. She didn't hold that a woman's life only found completion through childbearing. Even Arasi had agreed. It shouldn't be predetermined for women but be a matter of choice. True. Motherhood wasn't an ideal she held.

Everyday she heard a cry from the life that war had snatched from them. Ruin wherever she looked. Philomi had suddenly disappeared from the Keelapudur refugee camp. Early the next morning they found her corpse on a distant beach. She had hidden in the sea the day she had been found out for enjoying those forbidden bodily pleasures. These too were symbols of ruin. She didn't have to yearn for a family. She was weighed already with her obligations. It was a mercy to her that she couldn't see the sea here. Had she been listening for a voice from the other shore day after day, in the camp?

Raji stood up.

From inside the house, Kamala watched her as she broke down.

43

Peliyagoda, Sri Lanka

THE KELANI LEAPT. ITS sound, *sala sala!* had spread into the quiet of the shores. The moon had risen to its height and glimmered silver. In the distance, cars drove by, points of light on the bridge across the river before they disappeared. Behind the vehicular bridge, was the railway bridge, like a woven black braid. A boat dance on the riverbank. The waves explored the rope that tethered it to a small tree on the bank.

Gunananda sat with his head bowed. A range of emotions moved across his thoughts in layers. His friends sat in a semicircle facing him. This was an assembly.

After a long moment, Gunananda nodded his head deliberately, up and down, and straightened; he had come to a firm decision. The small group that had assembled around him grew excited. "No other way . . . there's no other way," he said over and over again, like someone who had lost their sense, before he stopped. "We will have to meet with the President. We have no choice but to put the problem before her."

"Which problem?" said the young bhikkhu, a member of the Sinhala Bala Mandalaya.

Gunananda turned to him. He said: "It has been four years since Jaffna town fell to the army. But there is still no main highway to the north. Don't you find that surprising? This question has been plaguing my mind for the past little while. I thought of all kinds of things . . . the soldiers deserting, the mental strain, the inadequate training, the shortage of modern weapons. But I have only now discovered the true answer."

The faces of the five before him shone. "What is it? . . . What?"

"I moved from speculation to closely examining the causes and outcomes of the events and figured it out."

"This sounds like something someone else said before, doesn't it, Thero?" It was the fearless young bhikkhu.

"True. It's the foundation on which Sankarananda built his new history. Speculation can help determine specific decisions too."

"Okay. What's the great discovery you made from that?"

"Thousands of soldiers deserted during Operation Jayasikuru, it's true. We can also admit there is a shortage of up-to-date weapons. But I figured out the greater reason behind it all. It's the double-dealing of the man who oversaw the Vanni war!"

"Are you talking about the military leader in the Vanni war?"

"Yes."

"Can it be?"

"Why not?"

His friends must have thought his answer aggressive. They glanced at each other. They had expected a solid answer. But the bhikkhu was insisting that practicality was the reason. Recently, even they had found the bhikkhu tended towards impatient speech and a tendency to ferociously enforce his decisions on them. But his ability to gain audience with high-ranking political and religious leaders whenever he felt like it kept them clinging to him and admitting to his superiority.

The old monk said, "We need to make an important decision

about another thing today."

"What?"

"We have to come to a firm decision about the voices in the capital that support the militants."

"True. There was a voice in the hill country that was echoing in their favour from inside the government circles too. It's not there now," the younger bhikkhu said. But Gunananda interrupted him: "No need for that now. We'll see after I speak to the president."

The old monk laughed at that. Munesinghe went on cackling. The old monk quietened when Gunananda raised his eyes, but Munesinghe trumpeted his laughter like an unleashed elephant in heat. "The bhikkhu has grown weak, my friends. He's getting old. He can't do things like he used to. If you go hunting after women all the time, your pulse will stop throbbing. I hear that the ragged bhikkhu has to finish up his feasts, because he can't even . . . " He roared.

"What do you say, Munesinghe?" Silva asked with a giggle.

"Let it be. His throbbing pulse is not relevant now," the older monk interjected.

"First, let the bhikkhu give up his laziness, and the excessive copulation that is bringing him to this state and re-energize himself. No more empty talk. The future is in darkness. We need to be able to cast light on it. We are still looking to him for more leadership," the young bhikkhu finished.

"I don't care whether you people have faith or not, I have absolutely no faith in him anymore!" Munesinghe said, striking the ground in his rage.

The old monk struggled to bring the atmosphere back to normal. "Don't make any hasty decisions. It's important that we stay together now."

"How else do you expect me to say it? The ragged monk has made him a degenerate. But it's the loss of his edge that's bothering me now."

"What do you mean by that?"

"The bhikkhu had a great opportunity to destroy Sankarananda in Gonagala. He let it slip because he was off pleasure-seeking, Thero."

"No! I had to go to Kegalle on a different matter!" Gunananda shouted.

"He had a chance in Colombo . . . on Marine Drive in Wellawatte. Sankarananda was just ten or fifteen yards ahead of the bhikkhu, he couldn't even touch his shadow. What is that old man's physical capacity, and what is the bhikkhu's strength?"

"You're drunk, Muna," the old monk said.

"True. When am I *not* drunk, that you want to make an issue of it now?"

"You have some resentment against Gunananda Thero . . . "

"Resentment? Me? Against the bhikkhu?" Munesinghe laughed again, darkly. "He doesn't care what comes to hand to quench his heat. I am very selective about what I consume. Why do I need to resent the bhikkhu?"

Though he had raised his voice in agitation, Gunananda had grown quiet again. He watched them all in silence. He stopped trying to deny anything. "You want to talk about my bodily needs any way you like to satisfy your selfish needs. I'm happy with that. Go wherever you want. But I am going to dedicate my services to the nation as fiercely as before. I won't talk about it anymore. You'll hear about it," he said very calmly.

Quiet descended around them again. They clearly heard the *sala sala* of the Kelani. The full moon had disappeared. The city would soon awake into dawn.

The young bhikkhu disturbed the quiet. "Thero, I meant to ask you earlier and forgot."

"What is it?"

"So, you're going to express your suspicions to the president and ask for action to be taken against the military leaders, okay. Will she take action?"

"She will. I can force her to, if needed."

"How, Thero?"

"I'll remind her that her chances of winning in the next election are growing slim. I can help save her from that slide, I'll say."

"Can you?"

"I can."

"How will you do it?"

"If I have to kill a thousand people . . . I can give her that victory."

His five companions shivered.

The only person who was still unafraid was the sleeping ragged bhikkhu.

Suddenly, as if by magic, Gunananda stood up, his fatigue and weakness gone.

"When will we meet again, Thero?" the older bhikkhu asked.

"Next Poya day. If it's urgent, you'll get a message. Until then, don't waste your time eating, drinking and sleeping all day. Some Sinhala artists are using the slogan of ethnic unity as a foundation to create plays and films, and distributing them saying that they are the people's art. I want all the details about them next time we meet here. Keep an eye on these feminists who say they're beyond ethnic differences as well. They too can corrupt some of our plans," Gunananda said as he walked away in a hurry.

The ragged bhikkhu woke up and looked attentively at Gunananda, as if expecting to be called.

But Gunananda did not slow his pace, and quickly disappeared.

44

Colombo, Sri Lanka

ONE SIDE OF THE Galle Face Hotel was awash in a yellow glow. Across it, the metal statue of the late Bandaranaike stood as if expecting some news. Nearby was the old parliament. The Holiday Inn, Hotel Samudra, Central Bank, and Ceylinco House . . . a cluster of large buildings. Beyond that, the nucleus of political administration and authority. Though the heavy darkness had lifted, it still looked somber and imposing. Even in that early morning, all the surrounding streets had been subjected to intense searches. There were rumblings of military vehicles from all sides. There were watchtowers everywhere. And in them were sharp-eyed soldiers with machine guns. In the street that cut between the fort and the harbour stood the Presidential Palace, with the Central Bank building straight across from it. Two jeeps drove in opposite directions all the time around the Presidential Palace.

These were unusual circumstances. The newspapers that morning explained somewhat the unusual situation.

The president leaves for London tonight!

It was an important day.

Some of the more important ministers had been invited at ten o'clock to meet with the president to discuss details of administrative activities and receive instructions on urgent security issues. That was customary. But the weight of this dawn had nothing to do with that custom. Instead, it seemed that there had been a rushed meeting with a select few before that. This was revealed shortly after.

The car of the Minister of Home Affairs arrived first, sirens blaring. Shortly after, several other cars arrived, carrying the heads of the three branches of the military and the Dean of Malwatte. They realized that the parliamentary secretary for the Department of Defence had arrived already.

The president had a closed meeting with the five, excluding the dean, at eight o'clock.

Had she not slept that night? Why the red lines in her eyes? This observation increased the urgency of the meeting. But they all said their ayubowans*.

The president sat at the head of the table. She began her preamble. "Thank you all for accepting this invitation and coming to see me without any delay. The battle to capture the A-9 highway has been going on for the past year and a half. We have only captured a few kilometers of it so far. We have paid a high cost for this, economically and militarily. From the ordinary Sinhala citizen to the Buddhist monks, no one can believe this."

The president's gaze took them all in in one circle.

They all looked puzzled, still unaware why they had been called.

The president continued, "I keep getting report after report that the Liberation Tigers have prepared for conventional war, and their military maneuvers and strategies seem to exceed the predictions of the Tamil rebel groups that have come over to our side. I am compelled to believe this. But I have just found out that this may not in fact be true. Just yesterday afternoon, a bhikkhu from the Kelani vihara came to see me and pointed out that there is a terrible plot behind all this."

Her audience then guessed the cause of the emergency meeting. They shifted in their seats in satisfaction.

"The problem the bhikkhu has brought to my attention is very important. It reveals a betrayal. Anything done against the country is the same as treason. The mystery of why there hasn't been a road opened up to Jaffna by the military commander in charge of the Vanni war, in spite of all these losses, is solved now."

"What mystery?"

"Mystery—how?"

"What is that mystery?"

"There is reason to fear that a treacherous link exists between the military command in charge of the Vanni operation and the Tigers, or some southern parties or organizations that are willing to align with their terrorism."

"Is that true?"

"Is it possible?"

"Are you sure?"

The murmurs lapsed into silence again.

The army chief broke the silence. "Has there been any evidence submitted to the honourable president to support this accusation?"

"If there had been any evidence, I would have called it a crime."

"Your excellency, forgive me . . . but I must condemn in the strongest terms these irresponsible accusations made against the brave soldiers who sacrifice themselves on the battlefield for the good of the country. Until now, in the past fifteen years, we have lost twenty-five thousand brave warriors . . . "

"That is true. I understand the delicacy of the situation. But when someone puts forward a logical argument, you can't afford to ignore it . . . "

"We have suffered so many setbacks up to now, because we have ignored such possibilities . . . " Deshapriya, the parliamentary secretary for the Department of Defence spoke up.

Who had given the parliamentary secretary the authority to speak? Apart from organizing meetings, taking minutes, and informing the ministers or ministries about the decisions in a timely manner, what other role or right did they traditionally have? The question blazed through many minds, and sensing this, the president turned her gaze toward Deshapriya. Deshapriya lowered his reddened eyes.

"Though he spoke out of turn, Deshapriya's words are correct. We have not been given a suitable explanation for all our reversals." The president stopped and looked at the minister of home affairs: "How do you think we should solve this problem?"

"I have nothing more to say on this matter. I am ready to do whatever the president thinks is right."

"An action?" the chief commander of the army asked.

The president thought for a while and said, "I think we don't need any action. But because we can't afford to ignore anything, I will recommend a transfer. We have quite a number of young commanders who have just trained in Pakistan."

"They won't all want to go to Jaffna."

"There's no room for debate here; no meeting. If my London trip hadn't interfered, we could have talked about this tomorrow or the day after. This is a time that calls for urgent action. Don't talk as if there aren't commanders who are willing to go to Jaffna."

"There are those who want to go. But they are not suitable."

It was clear the army chief didn't want a change of commanders. There was some justice to his objection too. Even a transfer would be considered an action. These kinds of unselfish objections appealed to the president. But she didn't reveal her feelings and stayed firm.

"Why don't you appoint a suitable person from those who would like to go? Make it happen quickly."

When Deshapriya looked at the president with an expression that asked if that was all, the president nodded.

"That's it," she said, and the group said their farewells and dispersed. In two minutes, the Dean of Malwatte was ushered into the room.

The president stood up, bowed her respects, and waited for the monk to sit before sitting down herself, wondering what the reason was for the urgent meeting.

The Maha Thero said, "I shouldn't ask the reason for your London trip. The leadership of the Sangha are opposed to the Norway government's peace talks. We are concerned that the president's trip may have something to do with that. There is no more reconciling with terrorists. War is the final solution. It is, in a way, the appropriate solution to this problem!"

The president understood the purpose of his visit.

It was a visit that inspired fear. Because they didn't show any concern in matters other rather religion, language, or race. Even in these matters, they tended only to observe the government's actions closely. If they were rushing to interfere now, it was a frightening sign.

But it was her country too? And her position made her even more concerned for the country. She spoke in a measured voice. "It's been a long time since the ethnic conflict has been an internal affair for Sri Lanka, Thero. We can't claim to be an independent country and disregard the opinions of other countries across the world and our neighbours. This London trip is for personal reasons, in a way. But I can't refuse any organization's attempts to meet as a result of Norway's attempts to bring about a reconciliation. We need to bring forward our reasoning on the reconciliation through that process."

"Okay, let the reconciliation process happen," the dean acquiesced. "But why do we need Norway? We can ask India to mediate."

"These have all been decided already, Thero."

The monk looked at a point across from the president and said: "The election isn't far away. You shouldn't forget that/"

A hardness had entered his tone.

"You haven't forgotten it either, have you? Good. Thero, there were Tamil votes that also counted toward my victory in the last election. I had promised then that I would bring about a solution to the ethnic problem; and if I don't fulfill that promise, how do I face the next election?"

The Malwatte dean had grown quiet. It wasn't containment, it was the tumult of agony. The words didn't come to him.

"We have to accept Norway's mediation and at least announce some kind of peace talks," the president continued. Though she said it gently, she said it firmly.

"The Buddhists don't like your reconciliation attempts . . . "

"This is not a government for them alone."

"The consequences will be tragic."

"What are you going to do?"

"Madam . . . !" the bhikkhu roared. Then he calmed his anger, "The leadership will call out for protests that will engulf the country!" he said.

The bhikkhu was threatening. Whom? The president of Sri Lanka. She couldn't accept it.

There were issues that could not be compromised on, and she had paid the price for them. First, through her father. Then her husband. Now a danger to her children.

"The position of the president is not a Buddhist Sangha position. It's not even a party position. It's the leadership of the country. If it is the same country from Point Pedro in the north to

Devinuvara in the south, then it includes the welfare of the Tamil people, just like everyone else."

He refused to give in to this reasoning. "I will make you answer to the people for this," the Thero thundered.

"That is up to you, Thero."

The Malwatte dean's eyes narrowed. He glared at her until they turned red. It recalled to her mind, as though in warning, the events of more than thirty years ago . . .

She stood up. "You must understand my position."

Her appeasing tone calmed the Thero somewhat. "I want you to reconsider your decision. Go on your trip to London and return. May you be guided on your journey. I will meet you after . . . "

The Thero walked away briskly.

The president stood there, staring after him.

45

Chennai, India

KULASEKARAM HAD WOKEN EARLY that morning, as always. He drank tea at the shop and returned. Thavamani was still not awake. Or Vasanthi. Or Param. Shouldn't Thavamani have woken them up too? To sleep when they felt sleepy, and wake up whenever they felt like it—what kind of life was this?

He came in and sat on the shiny black rock set inside the front gate.

Blub . . . blub . . . he heard the sound of water rushing though the water pump here and there.

The people downstairs had woken up too. It didn't look like anyone on the second floor in his home had woken up yet. He grew more and more irritated. 'It looks like they'll only get up when I go make a noise,' he thought as a rolled-up newspaper landed in the front yard. He picked it up and looked through it. Then he folded it and left it on the steps of the house downstairs and sat back again on the rock.

Whenever he thought of the place, and their living quarters, sharing a house with another family, he couldn't help remembering his village and his home there. It was as if this time of day was meant for such thoughts, the way they leapt to him and took over his mind. The rock was his seat then.

His thoughts rose in a wave and built his house in his memory. Eighteen stretches of land in the front and a tile-roofed house. Cross beams made from dense, mature palm trees they had chiselled to build that house. A front door and pillars of margosa wood, naaval tree windows. They had not been purchased at a timber yard. He had roamed the village searching for the right tree, bought it, cut it down, and carved out the columns and planks. He had built the walls with thick concrete blocks. The heat could not so much as peep inside the house. He had turned his garden into an oasis. Plantain, pomegranate, lemon, mango, jackfruit, coconut, murunga . . . what didn't he have?

To have land and a house meant a way of living. He was the symbol of a unique culture. So, he kept on about his own house . . . his own house even here. But this was the only house he could get for the rent and deposit he had. His family lived on the upper level of the house. But he felt that someone lived above him. Whenever he heard a thump . . . thump . . . he felt as anxious as though someone were stomping on his chest. Life had turned upside down for him in this land.

When he thought of all his suffering, he felt furious at Siva.

If Siva hadn't joined the Iyakkam and come running here, he would never have come here himself. He had come here first. But who could go off to a safe country and leave his wife and children in a war-torn place? So, he brought his wife and children there. Not only did he extract Siva from the Movement, but he also tried his hardest to get that boy, with his heart problems, sent overseas. That was why he had hung around one of those men who made fake passports and spent thousands as time dragged on. Nothing worked. As the net tightened around the criminal classes in India, they all escaped, every man for himself. He had not known what to do and felt helpless, when he heard that their neighbour across the street, Mala's sister, had gone to France. He took advantage of Mala's lingering feelings for Siva.

Those people did as they said they would, too. Who was unlucky here? He, or Siva? The boy got ready to leave the country but got caught with his fake papers at the airport . . . it was all defeat upon defeat. Now, he couldn't pressure them anymore. It was only his desire that still twitched and poked at him. He couldn't be unreasonable with them just because he had his ambitions. Besides, what could he talk to that Viswalingam about? He had a soul that couldn't act unjustly even if it brought him suffering.

Even before the first trip was planned, Kulasekaram had crushed their hearts. Now he had changed houses and moved further away from them.

Time kept passing.

It was all they could do to survive here. The children of some of their close relatives and some of their distant relatives lived overseas. He wrote to them and occasionally received small sums of money. Thavamani still didn't know about the money he had in his bag. She might never know. Her job was to take whatever she was given and cook it. Once they had had meat, fish, everything. Now it was just one curry. He was only glad that she didn't make sambar. Their family had lost all other luxuries. What kind of work could an agricultural farmer like Kulasekaram find in Chennai? If he didn't earn a living, they had to suffer through these difficulties. But writing letters was a job too, wasn't it? He couldn't write to his relatives only to ask for money, he needed to stay in touch with them afterwards. It wasn't easy to maintain that correspondence.

Could they go back . . . could they go back . . . he had spoken to his wife about it a thousand times. Thavamani had decisively said that they could go back. But it was hard to put it into action.

Going back wasn't as easy as tying up a bundle and walking. It was a journey they had to make without a bundle . . . even now. They had to make several arrangements, and it all took a lot of money and effort.

He didn't know how to run his household. Even if he kept the matter of money closed, all to himself, he needed to discuss out-side matters. He could only discuss them with Thavamani. He had spoken to her the previous day.

"What do you say, Thavam? What shall we do? Siva doesn't look like he's taking care of this business of going overseas!"

"That's what I've been thinking too. There's no temple I haven't prayed at. Even God refuses to open his eyes . . . "

"If Siva leaves and calls Param there, I could happily die the next day. The two boys will take care of the burden of the older sister . . . "

"Why are you blabbering on like this? With the shift in Saturn coming up, something good will happen for sure, just wait and see."

"That's what I think, too. If Siva comes, talk to him about this."

He had said the same thing so many times. She had brought it up too. But nothing was within their control, and the situation didn't budge.

He saw some movement upstairs. They must have woken up, finally!

Saba came in search of Param just after ten o'clock. "Is Param here?"

"Where are you dragging him off to at this time, thambi?" Kulasekaram asked.

"We're going to play cricket."

"It's good to play cricket. No cost involved in the game. But the heat keeps rising and will split your scalp."

"You don't feel the heat so much on the lakeshore side."

He called out to Param.

Param came out, asking, "Why Saba, didn't Senan come today?"

"No. There are some relatives coming from Canada to visit them. He's going to the airport," Saba replied.

After Siva and Param left, Kulasekarám, who had been leaning on the wall of the verandah, turned inside and called out, "Thavam!"

"What is it?"

"You know that Maheswari maami that Mala talks about?"

"Yes . . . "

"It looks like she's arriving from Canada today."

"Tchoo," Thavamani sighed, as if to say who cared if Maheswari maami came from Canada.

Kulasekaram closed his eyes and leaned his head against the wall. Why should he be the only one dreaming?

46

Chennai, India

THE MOMENT SHE HEARD Maheswari was on her way, Arasi telephoned Rajendran. He came from Mumbai to Chennai. Amma would stay at Mala's house, so, he hurriedly rented a house in Arumbakkam and moved Arasi there. He went to Madurai and picked up Valambikai himself and delivered her to the house as well. He threw out the worn-out mattress at Mala's house and bought a new one to replace it.

Arasi tried telling him that she didn't need her own house. She was prepared to go back to Jaffna the week after maami returned to Canada, she said. He told her that he would then use the house himself.

Viswalingam was present. He looked meaningfully at Rajendran. How good it was that he wanted a house in Chennai. He, his wife, and child must move and live here from now on; the Tamil she had learned would be most useful here . . . all kinds of thoughts ran through his mind. Rajendran found it impossible to reveal that relationship, so someone else had to do it. Who would? Breaking the news could only help that Assamese girl, the child and him. Viswalingam pondered on these things as he prepared to head out.

Saraswathi's heart melted when she saw Rajan taking such pains over whether amma would need this, or amma would need that.

That afternoon, as they waited for amma to arrive by plane from Delhi to Chennai the following morning, Rajan said his goodbyes to Raji, Kamala, Arasi, Valambikai, Rajanayagam, Viswalingam, Saraswathi, and Mala. When Raji asked him to wait and see amma before he left, he replied that he had work to do, that he would return on his way to Trivandrum the next week and left for the railway station.

It was good for her to have the time to think . . . to give in. He had privately asked Mala to call him in a couple of days and let him know about amma's frame of mind, and whether she asked about him. "Don't forget, Mala," he repeated, over and over.

It was two days after Maheswari had arrived. She had gone to visit Rajanayagam and a few other Lankan people she knew. On the third day, when they had gone to Arumbakkam, Mala said that it would be easy to go to Porur from there, why didn't they go and see Raji while they were there? "Is there no road for her to come to Anna Nagar from there?" Maheswari had asked in reply. It took Mala some time to understand what she had meant. "She'll come. She probably hasn't come yet because she's afraid to see you face to face," Mala said.

When they got back to Anna Nagar, Mala went to a public call booth and telephoned Raji to say that if she didn't come to visit her soon, amma would be upset with her. She should at least drop by one evening for a quick visit.

The next morning, everyone was seated indoors. It was getting close to breakfast time, and they passed their time happily. Everyone was lightly aware that Siva and Mala were picking a quarrel with each other in their room. It was a family fight, and Maheswari didn't fail to notice it. The two little ones said goodbye and headed off for school, and the quarrel became harder to ignore.

Mala was the first to come out of the room. No one should have such an expression on their face. It was not that it looked hateful. It manifested hate.

Siva hovered inside the doorway. He needed to come out. He pulsed with the need to come outside and ask them for justice. But his embarrassment silenced him. Maheswari had already observed how he had shrunk into himself from repeatedly feeling his inadequacy.

Mala walked to the kitchen with an air that said, "I may have come after you, but that doesn't mean I'll stay and be trampled underfoot."

Why this declaration? Was it for him or for the rest of them there? What was her strength? What was his weakness? Wasn't it money?

That had to be the reason for his shrinking so much. Words soaked in so much unhappiness, he almost cried. "Amma told me back then that you'd say all this," he said.

"Then why didn't you all let it go? Why did your father come carrying a kavadi*?"

"This is all his fault."

"And he, he came to arrange a marriage out of pity. How insulting he was to me when he first found out! Didn't he open his door just because Sheila was overseas, and he wanted to send his son to France?"

Seeing their language flow without any boundaries, Maheswari wanted to check them and contain it. Seeing that Saraswathi was watching the whole thing without intervening, she felt it was urgent to step in. But that uncontrollable girl, the words spewed out of her mouth. "Your father spoke correctly. But he never breathed a word about us having to feed you the rest of your life, why was that?"

"Oh, you fool!" Maheswari was shocked. "Just because he lives with your family, is this the way you throw around your words . . . as if he were no more than a blade of grass . . . ?"

No one spoke.

The silence stretched out, despair all around them.

A short while later, Siva put on his shirt and came out. He seemed to gaze into Saraswathi's eyes for a minute. His tears stayed suspended on the edge of his eyelashes, as though afraid to flow. The next moment he turned away suddenly and wiped his eyes. Then he hurried out and into the street.

It could have been considered an abrupt separation. Maheswari understood what was happening. What did this generation take seriously anymore when they acted? But that blow would scar the soul.

Such scars did not heal easily.

Two days passed.

Though she knew Siva would not return on his own, Mala didn't attempt to send anyone to bring him back. Saraswathi was frozen with shock, saying it was all her ill fortune. Viswalingam never showed any sign that he knew what had happened. As usual, he came, slept, woke up. And went away somewhere in the morning.

Maheswari took Senan with her to Kulasekaram's house on the third day.

She didn't know anyone in that house, apart from Siva. But she put her faith in the good intentions of people and didn't think twice about trying to do something well-meaning.

When Maheswari arrived, Siva, Kulasekaram, Thavamani and Param were all at home. Everyone, apart from Vasanthi, was outside on the verandah.

Seeing Maheswari approach, Siva informed his parents. Kulasekaram looked up and couldn't believe his eyes. Was this the woman who had come from Canada? She had braided her hair at the back, and it was woven through with many white threads. She had a small line of holy ash on her forehead so as not to have it bare. She wore a dotted sky-blue saree and blouse. She had grown a little fairer. She had a slight sheen.

People her age living in Canada would be civilized.

Kulasekaram stood up to welcome her, "Come in, please." Siva stood up and moved aside.

It was only when he looked closer that he saw the gloss in her fair skin that seemed to form in that wintery country.

Though money had given her a certain amount of power, she wasn't used to approaching people she didn't know to address their private problems or make peace in a way that respected their way of doing things. She had only hoped that the urgency of the situation would give her the confidence to speak to them, so the family's little grievances didn't take root and turn into gaping wounds.

Kulasekaram spoke excitedly. It was only small talk. It was she who brought up the issue of Siva. "Who knows where these children get so much anger, so suddenly?"

"You give them some good advice too," Thavamani said. "I have talked and talked about it for two whole days, and I am exhausted. He's angry that his woman didn't come to take him back. How long can this anger last—between husband and wife? It sounds like she has said some harsh things . . . "

"I was there too when their argument started. People have so many problems in the world. They know nothing about trouble and squabble among themselves," Maheswari said.

Siva was not an obstinate sort. By nature, he was a man who heeded his elders' advice. "Put your shirt on and let's go, Siva. I'm here . . . what . . . let's see if she says anything now," Maheswari said. Siva got ready without another word.

Maheswari brought Siva back as dusk was falling. She brought Vasantha and Thavamani along as well, despite their protests. She couldn't stand the families linked by marriage being estranged like this.

Raji and Kamala arrived the next morning.

Seeing Raji enter, Maheswari was taken aback at her appearance.

How could she not have thought about Raji all this time? If she hadn't been immolating herself, how could she look so tired? Who was the cause of this misery? She? Rajendran had written: "It's hard to see akka in this condition," and it was true. She had wasted away . . . he could have written that she was destroyed. She wanted to run down and embrace her and wail, "What is this state?" She used to look like a statue from the Amman temple koburam.* She had lost her figure, like a woman whose body was worn out from giving birth to several children! But Maheswari contained herself. She didn't stay in the doorway but hurried upstairs.

Kamala brought Raji upstairs after they had had some tea. "You have changed a lot after going to Canada, akka," she began.

"It's twelve years since you've seen me! Maybe that's why I look different," Maheswari replied.

"Everyone changes over time. I'm talking about the changes in your habits."

"In mine?"

"No? It looks like you've given up chewing betel altogether. Your teeth are gleaming . . . isn't this a big change?"

"Oh . . . you mean that? It's not just betel. I have given up on thinking about some people too."

Kamala felt she shouldn't stay there any longer. Now it was up to the mother and daughter. Let them fight it out at least and come to some sort of clarity and peace. "You two talk. I'll be back," Kamala said and went downstairs.

The western sky had turned red. The sun was a half-hidden

circle, like a carved-out pumpkin.

Raji sat beside her, with her head bent. She became conscious of her mother staring intently at her. But she didn't raise her head.

"What is this state you're in, Raji?"

It was the only hint she gave of her heart shattering to pieces at the sight of her daughter.

Raji raised her head. When she met her mother's gaze she bent her head again, as if she wanted to run and hide. "I was in the camp for a long time . . . that's why."

Maheswari wanted to slap her hard. She kept her composure and said, "Not everyone in the camp could have let themselves go to ruin like you."

"How will my fate ever leave me?"

"You had a fate just like everyone else has."

"Only I could end up in such a useless condition . . . "

"It's all because of your own mistakes. From one mistake to another . . . then yet another. Your destruction is your own doing. I told you back then that if you went the way you did, you would end up like this way," Maheswari hissed through gritted teeth. It was the only way she could hold back the rage that was seething in her.

Raji had begun to cry. Her lips trembled in small bursts.

The light from the streetlamps and the lights from the back of the house next door fell dappled between them. The clouds furled and the sky quickly grew dark.

Seeing Raji's distress Maheswari's heart softened.

"How lovingly did I give birth to you . . . how lovingly did I raise you! When did I say no if you asked me for something? I have said no to the boy. But never to you! I thought you would raise up this family. The family has somehow raised itself thanks to the grace of Sannathiyan.* But you have fallen so low. It's one thing to be destroyed by fate. It's a crime to lose your judgement.

You are not only destroying yourself, but you're also destroying me. If Nalan was destroyed by fate, you have been destroyed by your bad judgment."

"Amma!"

She went on as if she didn't hear her. "You lost your father when you were small. But I raised you without any deprivation. Is this how you repay your debt of gratitude? Had I known you would act the way you did, I would have jumped into the well and died that day."

"That's not how it is, amma."

"'I won't let any blame fall on this family. No matter how much I have to suffer, I will save all of us,' you promised me that day. Did you forget? But now our family is in shame. So many people who knew Suntharam have asked me, 'Wasn't there a registration between Suntharam's son and your daughter? Apparently, the son is in France . . . why is your daughter in India?' Shame . . . shame . . . in Canada, India, in the island, wherever we go, shame . . . "

" . . . "

"I need you to answer me now."

Raji was startled. Amma had come straight to the point she had been so afraid of. No room for niceties, she had been thrust straight into it. Amma had come upstairs with a plan.

"I didn't come here to go sightseeing. I came here to see you. Even Viji told me: 'You go see about akka's matter; he's here to take care of me, that's enough.' When I go back, I have to go with a positive decision . . . I need your answer."

Someone came upstairs, and seeing the tension, dashed back down again.

Maheswari was very direct. "Suthan is not with Sheila anymore. They say it's been five years since they separated. Not even a child to remember that relationship by. Suthan wants to live with you.

It doesn't make any sense to refuse him at this point. I spoke to Chandramohan just yesterday. He's coming here soon. Suthan will come here after going to Germany. They said if we ask him to come, he'll come. They mean he'll come if you agree to this. Your answer will decide whether we are to have any relationship as mother and child from now on . . . "

"Amma . . . " Raji struggled to find the words.

No tears came to her then. Just terror. A trap . . . amma was a trap. 'Yogesh! Where on earth are you? Come running! Come running now! Take me away with you! When I needed to reject Suthan, I went away with you. Now, to save me from this trap, you must help me. Come running!'

Kamala came.

She quickly guessed what had happened. "How can she reply right now, akka? Give her ten days or so," she said.

"Chandramohan will be here by then. I can't keep waiting for her reply either. One week . . . I need a reply in seven days. If she doesn't come here, I will come to Porur, even if only to get an answer from her. I can see the Anna Nagar tower clearly, even at night. I will climb up there and jump . . . you know I can do it . . . remember that."

Maheswari stood up and scurried down the stairs.

The asoka tree rustled.

47

Chennai, India

IN ALL THE TIME Maheswari stayed there, even though she was in the same house, she never had a chance to speak openly with Viswalingam. He was always rushing around. Saraswathi had told her the reason when she had stayed with them a long time ago.

She still felt sorry for him, as she had before. It was a great misfortune to have to run around working, even at his age. It was true that their lives had shifted from its axis. But even in this state many managed to live without working so hard. Was his fate somehow different? Maheswari thought about it many times, even after she got here.

That day she had woken very early in the morning. When she got up and came out to the front yard, she saw that Viswalingam, who had slept on the balcony, had just woken up and was stretching his limbs. Seeing that he wasn't in a hurry, Maheswari went upstairs. "What is it anna, it looks like you're not going anywhere today? You're not in a hurry?"

"My body feels prickly all over. I feel like I'm getting a fever. So, I thought I'll wait and see."

She leaned against the wall. He stood across from her, smoking a beedi.

"What is Raji saying?" he raised the subject.

Her face showed a determination. A rigidity. It had the hardness of decisions that had already been made.

She knew the situation and wasn't worried. She said, "What's left for her to say? She has said all she wanted to say and is done. Now she must hear what we have to say."

"That's right. It's a relationship they started, isn't it? If she's consented to it, then I'm happy."

"Not yet. Raji knows that's the reason I came here. I won't let her go until she agrees to this. Let her think. I have told her I need to know the answer before Chandramohan gets here."

Viswalingam wondered: "Why don't I tell her about Rajendran at this point?"

Rajan had asked him not to say anything. But someone had to interfere and get this started. Rather than drag this on forever with "Later on . . . another time," if they told her now, Maheswari could meet her daughter-in-law and grandson as well. This might help quell her anger against Rajan as well. Why does this woman hate Rajan? In all the time she's been here, not one word? Can a mother be so hard-hearted? Then a thought occurred to him. Her antagonism towards her son was based on his old ne-er do well habits. If he was a family man now, and living well, didn't that show his old habits were a thing of the past? Does Maheswari have to make another trip from Canada to deal with this? If he said what had to be said calmly, thoughtfully, everything would be fine.

"What is it anna, are you feeling cold?"

"I feel like I need something to cover up with."

"It sounds like malaria. Don't leave it like this. We have to go to the doctor and get some medicine."

"Mm. I was thinking I might go at ten o'clock."

Perhaps because they were each absorbed in turning over their own thoughts, it was difficult to start an easy conversation.

The morning light drew the eye with its beauty.

Anna Nagar had changed a lot in ten years. Before, it would stretch out openly when they looked out at night! Now they were surrounded by multistorey houses that made this house look shrunken in comparison. But this rooftop balcony always had a special beauty about it.

Maheswari turned her gaze away from the skies. She smiled when she met his eyes. "Chennai is only gentle on the eyes in the morning," she said.

It was true. Later in the day, if it was summer, it was all dust, dirt, and blazing heat; in the winter it turned into mud and chaos. Deafening racket was common to both seasons.

"I need to ask you something."

"Tell me, anna."

"You mustn't get upset."

She laughed.

"It's been so many days since you arrived. You have not said a word . . . even once . . . about Rajendran—"

"Why do I need to say anything?"

"He can do a thousand wrongs, but he is your child, isn't he?"

"I have a grandchild to light my funeral pyre."

That's stubbornness, he thought. Raji had it too.

"You can't talk that way . . . and just throw away the child you gave birth to, thangachi. Even so . . . if it was only a matter of Rajendran, I wouldn't say anything beyond this. Now Rajendran is three people. It's not good for you to keep rejecting him."

"What are you saying, annai?"

He hadn't expected such an emotional reaction from her.

He spoke gently. "Back then . . . of the boys that went to Colombo in search of work, ten out of a hundred would marry someone they fell in love with. Five out of those would marry Sinhalese girls. This is a common situation when people travel from one town to another and has been happening for ages. It can also happen if you go from one country to another."

" . . . "

She remained silent. But a hole yawned out in the pit of her stomach. It felt like a ball of thorns rising up to her throat. She realized that somehow, she had become woven into this vague story he was telling, and trembled.

"You have moved to another country now, too. You can't be unaware of these kinds of things. Now, this is happening in your own family as well . . . "

"Rajendran?" she said, looking straight at him.

He nodded his head.

She struggled not to fall to pieces.

He felt sorry to see her in such a state. But he spoke with a clarity he had not planned . . . not expected. "If you don't think I'm interfering in your family matters . . . let me say something. You should not have neglected Raji and Rajendran for so long. You too are responsible for their lives turning out this way."

"Did I tell her to abandon the man she was registered to and to run away to a refugee camp? Did I tell him to drag some dog he found on the street and marry her and have a child?"

"You can say a thousand things, but I can't accept them. It's not only you . . . you can take it as a common problem among all parents. We want to see our expectations fulfilled in our children, but we don't think that they each have their own desires. I think both sides need to go together. Rajendran needs to come today or tomorrow . . . you need to speak to him . . . without berating him, or being hasty, or losing your patience. Thambi has changed so much. You will be amazed, and wonder if this is the same Rajendran, thangachi. He has married a northern girl. Assamese.

But she speaks Tamil. She's a good-natured girl. I saw her myself. They have a son. He's around three. And now, the best thing is to accept it, and everyone live together. Thambi had asked me not to say anything, he felt that he would find the right time to tell you himself. But someone must bring up this topic, don't they? That's why I told you."

He said he would return after he washed his face and went downstairs.

When he returned, she was still sitting in the same spot.

"Thangachi!"

She came back to herself at the sound of his voice.

"You saw all this in person yourself, didn't you?" Maheswari asked.

"Yes. Why?"

"No. It shouldn't be just gossip. That's why I asked."

He told her how it had come about.

"You made the right decision when it came to Raji, annai. But you made a mistake when it came to Rajendran. I have made the right decision."

"Why, thangachi, what is this decision you've made?"

"Though I mainly came here to sort out Raji's problem, Rajendran's problem is equally important, annai. I had wanted to come after Viji's delivery, and I only decided to come right away because of Rajendran's letter. Viji and my son-in-law have found three potential brides for him there. That girl sent me on my way, saying 'It doesn't matter how much it costs, find anna and bring him with you, amma.' How am I going to go there and tell her your annai is married and has a three-year-old already? And that . . . a northerner. When they find out, our race and our people won't include them in anything anymore. You're . . . what . . . going to the shop now? Don't be offended but ask Mala to bring me some tea. Bring me some betel leaf when you return from the shops as well. This will all only be sorted out if I turn back into the woman I used to be."

When Viswalingam returned after having had his tea, he brought her some betel leaf from the shop.

After a while, Maheswari came downstairs and went over to Viswalingam, who was seated on the verandah. "I need to go to Bombay, anna. It will be good if we can leave this evening. Can you come with me?"

He wanted to ask her what decision she had come to. But he had second thoughts and never asked. Why should he? She had changed form. Her form told him what kind of decision she had made.

Amba's face came to mind, and he felt his eyes tear up. His pity for the child was secondary to that. Still, he said, "Okay." She would do this, even if he didn't go along. If he went along, there might be some way in which he could lessen the blow.

48

Chennai, India

MAHESWARI HAD TAKEN OVER Viswalingam's spot on the verandah and from there she gave out her orders. Her mouth had turned frighteningly red. Her eyes had somehow transformed, and seemed lined with the same red. It was a good place for her to stretch out and spit out her betel juice. Not only that. She had no need to show people her face too often. This was a convenient place from which she could give her commands, and for others to remain hidden as they replied.

Siva came back after trying to call Rajendran. "Maami, Rajendran is not in Bombay right now. It's been four days since he left for Trivandrum. When he left, he said he was going to stop by Madras on his way back. That's what his wife said."

"Hmph . . . he's got himself a wife!" Maheswari muttered to herself. She picked up another betel leaf from the tray on her lap and began smearing the lime paste on it without turning to look at him. Then she said, "Hm . . . that's good too. What do I need to talk to her about, without seeing him first. He'll have to come here today or tomorrow. Isn't that so, Siva?"

"Yes, maami."

"Has maama returned? I had sent him to call Raji."

"When he left, he said he was going to visit the doctor on his way back," Mala said.

"Let him take his time."

Slowly the household began to relax again.

Though she had asked Raji to hurry, it was four o'clock before she arrived. She came alone. She kept asking Viswalingam what it was about, but he didn't tell her anything. He didn't think Maheswari was planning to discuss any solution with her. She was only calling Raji to announce her decision. So, Viswalingam simply said, "Come, and you'll find out," and hung up. Raji was anxious and fearful when she arrived. She had thought that Chandramohan would be there. She had no reply for her mother.

When she arrived, Maheswari told her everything abruptly. Her tone quickly revealed that she would not allow her son to remain with a foreign woman. Raji felt relieved by this situation. With Rajendran in trouble, Maheswari might forget about Raji for another four or five days.

It occurred wondered if Rajendran's situation was even a problem. She thought it was enough that Rajan had fallen in love with some woman. Amma had openly called her a northerner. But Raji remembered hearing about north Indians railing against the Assamese immigrants, saying they were nothing but estate workers. It was now clear to Raji that this was no more than prejudice.

It rained lightly that day. As soon as it stopped, the heat began to spread. It left the skin clammy, and there was no release from it. Most of them had come up to the rooftop balcony. The three little ones were running around squealing and playing with a neighbour's child. Viswalingam had not yet returned.

Suddenly, an auto stopped at the entrance. Kamala and Rajendran got out.

Seeing them, Maheswari stood up hurriedly and went inside.

Kamala came in and sat across from her, Rajendran sat beside Kamala, his head bowed.

He still felt apprehensive at meeting his mother. He guessed that his secret had been revealed to her, when he put together Maheswari's calling Raji urgently, Viswalingam's absence from the place, and Poobathy's deep frown.

Amma had got older. The climate of the country she lived in had lightened her skin and made her glow even more. But that didn't mean she had spent her days there happily either. She had dark circles around her eyes. He could see a few wrinkles. She kept squinting. He made a note to himself that she needed to get her eyes examined and get a pair of spectacles. Her mouth was red. This was the image he had held in his mind. Her eyes were red and withdrawn. This was the mother he had seen before. But there was a whirr behind her withdrawn eyes that held both a growl and treacherous claws; these were unusual to him. She stayed silent to maintain her composure. Someone else must break the silence.

"Did you get the letter I wrote, amma?" he asked.

She hesitated in her reply. "Mm," she said. "Why talk about a letter now? If you mail a letter it will come! Raji's matter is not as important to me now. It's your matter that has fallen like a heavy rock on my chest."

Rajendran was not taken aback. He had already known the stand she would take. There was nothing for him to say. If she asked, he would tell her the truth. He had to tell the truth. Lies would only make her angrier.

His silence irritated her even more. "Look, Kamala, he does what he does and he sits there with no shame."

Kamala tried to pacify her.

Though Maheswari calmed down a little she wouldn't move away from the topic. She said loud and clear, "My life is hanging on two marriages now, Kamala. One marriage needs to happen.

The other needs to be broken off."

There was no need for further explanation.

"Amma!"

"What, are you shocked? I felt the same way when I heard about your wedding."

His words came out tearfully. "It's been four years since it was all done, amma."

"If you were so in love with her, then the four years you have spent with her will have to do. If she has any such feelings . . . then the child can be her gift."

It fell like a hammer blow to the heart. He was shattered but pulled himself together. "She is a good woman, amma!"

"That may be. That's not the issue here. She could even be a woman from a northern country . . . but what is her caste . . . her background! If she's a low caste, you will create a low-born generation. We don't even accept marriage to a Sinhala woman . . . and you . . . to go marry some Hindi woman . . . we don't need this, Rasa, leave it."

His heart felt like a twisting hole. She was like a demoness; what was she saying,? But he couldn't find the strength to oppose her either. "Pity her, amma, isn't this a betrayal? Amma, how can I . . . .?"

"Aaah . . . ha . . . ha . . . ! A betrayal? What is that, Rasa?" She chewed her words as she stood up. She walked straight up to him. He had begun to bend, but now held up his head instead, his hand on his throbbing temple. She looked directly into his face, her eyes moving back and forth between his eyes, searching for a doorway in. "Do you even know the meaning of the word pity?" she asked. She seemed to slide as though she had lost all her strength when she suddenly pulled his hand away from his temple. She stood up again. She looked him up and down and then laughed again. She looked at Kamala. Then she went back to her chair and sat down, looking at him.

The tears gushed down her face. Saraswathi came downstairs and stood in the doorway. She turned toward Saraswathi. "Did you hear Saraswathi, what my child just said? I was full to the brim to hear it. When I hear that my child understands the meaning of conscience, betrayal, pity . . . I felt prouder now than I was when I gave birth to this one, after all the penance I did. Wouldn't your heart ne full if your child said something like this? Me too; my heart is just overflowing while I stand here."

Silence fell.

The three of them stayed there unmoving.

Maheswari turned to Rajan in a fury. "You dog . . . who do you think you're talking to, about betrayal? Didn't you betray me? You told me you were going to get on a ship in Bombay; that I should borrow money if I need to; that you would pay off principle and interest within the year, and I went and sold off my paddy field at a loss and heaped forty thousand rupees like jackfruit on you. You didn't so much as send me a letter, but spent all that money on food, and drink and whores, and had a good time . . . you didn't think you were betraying me? My boy has grown up, he has gone to India to get on a ship. I trusted you and thought I had nothing to fear anymore. I waited for seven years. You turned your own mother's hopes into disappointment . . . what do you call that, if not betrayal? In all this time, you would have fed fifty . . . a hundred people in Bombay. Did you even feed me a single meal, for giving birth to you? Tell me, Rajendra. You want to talk about betrayal now. Everything you have is a betrayal of me. I won't curse you . . . let me be the sinner for giving birth to you . . . let this womb rot for having carried you . . . " She said all this as she beat her stomach. Saraswathi ran up to her and pulled her hands away to stop her, crying: "Don't akka . . . don't!" Maheswari wailed and went into her room.

They heard her fall on her bed.

"Amma . . . amma!" Rajan's heart bled. He had passed the point of crying.

The silence refused to leave the room. A gloom fell over the place like a mother had dissolved into the air. Rajendran stood up after a long time. He walked slowly into Maheswari's room. Maheswari lay prone on her bed, like a coconut tree laid low by a storm.

The sight wrenched his heart. "Amma!" he said, through the dimness. When there was no answer, he called out again, "Amma!"

"What?"

"I'll do as you say, amma. Don't cry, amma."

There was a shadowy movement.

Rajendran walked back to get an auto with Kamala and Raji.

49

Chennai, India

CHANDRAMOHAN'S ARRIVAL CAME AS a surprise. He had come with his friends and said he would take a bus to Puducherry that night and to Thanjavur from there. He spoke to Rajanayagam over the phone, telling him that it would take him a week to return to Chennai. He almost asked about Raji's decision, but decided against it, thinking that it was better to speak of these issues in person. Rajanayagam sent his cook to tell Maheswari that Chandramohan had arrived.

Maheswari felt that all would be righted by the grace of Sannathi Murugan. A kind of joy began to bubble over in her, but she kept it concealed.

Maheswari left for Bombay the next day, with Viswalingam in tow. She hoped to sort out Raji's situation before Chandramohan returned.

Mumbai, India

Viswalingam did not approve of her intentions. But he couldn't refuse her. He was not obliged to her, but he agreed. He was not a man who could say no. He couldn't even find the words to say no to strangers. "Annai, I need to go to the Puzhal camp, can you quickly come with me?" or "Anna, I need to get someone out of the Mandapam camp. Come with me, we'll be back soon?" and he never refused. They were his people.

Maheswari knew that he was accompanying her reluctantly. But who else was there to accompany her? That night, he refused his dinner.

"Why, annai?"

"I'm not hungry. You eat."

"I know why you're saying you're not hungry."

"I wouldn't have come to do this kind of work for anyone else."

"I know."

"How can I go along with something like this, thangachi? I have gone and stayed in their home . . . eaten . . . picked up the child and played with him . . . "

"It's not that I haven't thought of it. You don't have to be there when I talk to her. It's her language . . . or if you can find some Tamil person who speaks this Bombay language or Hindi, send them to help me, you just show me the house and go away. I'll take care of the rest."

"She speaks good Tamil."

"Never mind. It will help to have someone on my side there."

He didn't object beyond that; but he didn't eat.

He rented a room in a hotel near the VT station, left her there, and went out, returning by afternoon with a Tamil Nadu man he knew, called Krishnan. Though Viswalingam had explained the matter already, Maheswari poured out all the details and her motherly lament in Jaffna Tamil.

Krishnan was very sympathetic towards the Lankan refugees. He had aligned himself politically with those who were support-ive of the Lankan Tamils after the demonstration condemning the massacre of Tamils in the pogroms in eighty-three. Maheswari's grief melted his heart. He agreed to go to Bandra with them and speak to the Assamese girl.

That evening, around seven, Maheswari spoke with Viji over the phone. "I just arrived in Bombay this morning, Viji. Viswalingam annai came with me."

"What's happened, amma? I have been worried about this situation ever since you told me about it."

"I haven't spoken to her yet. We're going tomorrow in the morning."

"Go see what she's like and everything . . . and hit her with a big number. I don't care if it's even two lakhs. She won't say no to that."

"That's what I think, too. But we'll need the money right away . . . "

"Give me the address of the hotel . . . " Viji took the address, phone number, and all the details from her mother, and said, "Stay in your room until ten or eleven o'clock. I'll transfer it through an undiyal*. Take the money with you when you go. She needs to see it."

"All right, Viji."

The next day, Maheswari awoke excited.

Bombay, released from its sleep by the first sound from the milkmen, was sweet to the eyes, and even the nose. Crows . . . doves . . . trucks . . . tugboats, all screeched as if to strengthen their claim on the city. In the east, the sunrise was spectacular. Now the engine of Bombay would begin as if by clockwork.

Krishnan arrived there before ten-thirty. They waited another hour for the money to come through and left around noon. "You must come too, annai. I'll only feel strong enough if you come. You don't need to say anything. I'll do all the talking. You can stand aside as if you're not connected to this," Maheswari said and dragged Viswalingam along too. He thought of the old saying, "If you marry a forest-dweller, you will have to roam the forests and hills." It wasn't hard after that.

They caught a taxi and arrived in Bandra past one o'clock.

Amba answered the doorbell and was surprised. Who were these people? But she knew the man who stood behind them. Rajan had introduced him as someone he respected as a father figure. But why did he look so dejected and stand apart? They had arrived at a time when Rajan wasn't at home. When someone called for him a few days before, she had told them that he had gone to Trivandrum and would go to Chennai before returning to Mumbai. Yet here they were. This woman was certainly not a stranger.

Before she could wonder any more, Krishnan explained who she was. "Vanakkam," Amba greeted her immediately. Then she fell at her feet hastily.

She was strikingly beautiful.

"Well, she needs that beauty to seduce people," Maheswari thought to herself pettily, though she herself had to admit that the girl's beauty wasn't intentionally seductive. She had a slightly Chinese cast to her face. Perhaps this is what Assamese people look like, Maheswari concluded.

"Come in," Amba welcomed them.

The three of them went in and sat down.

"Wait a minute," she said as she moved to go inside, but Maheswari stopped her with a gesture. "Do you speak Tamil?"

"Mm."

It didn't seem as though she was at all happy to hear it, Amba thought. Her husband's mother's face showed no trace of eagerness to see her daughter-in-law or her grandchild. Nothing good was going to come of this . . . a cry began in her heart.

"Sit here," Maheswari said. Amba sat across from her and

Maheswari spoke softly: "You know that Rajendran had some connections with a rebel group a while ago?"

She nodded her head, yes, she knew.

"Now . . . he has no more connections with them. But the group feels that he has betrayed them," Maheswari said, and stopped. She looked around at everyone. Then her gaze pierced Amba's confused face as she continued, "Rajendran is my only male child. The group that hates him is as terrifying as the group that killed Raji Gandhi with a suicide bomber. There's nothing to stop them doing what they like. We tried to give them some money to appease them . . . but they won't agree to it. We heard they have sent someone to shoot Rajendran . . . "

Amba's face tightened. As she suddenly realized it had been ten days since he had left home, "Where is he now? In Trivandrum? No . . . Has he come to Madras?" she asked anxiously.

"He is in Madras. We have left him somewhere in a secret place," Maheswari replied.

"Thank God!" she sighed in relief and seemed to calm down.

"Oh . . . God! What is this crime I have to share in.!" Viswalingam thought bitterly to himself. Every single moment they were here, felt like walking on hot coals. When he realized that she was planning to use the girl's love and innocence to manipulate her, for the first time, he felt a sudden rush of hatred towards Maheswari. He realized that he had been foolish to think of the woman as naïve, and to want to help her.

Amba must have realized that something was not right here too. When Maheswari said that people had been dispatched to kill him, Amba's legs began trembling. She had felt a stiffening in her hip. But she couldn't see a fraction of that fear in the mother who had delivered the news. Amba began to suspect that she had come with a sickle to cut out their relationship. Her eyes began to well up with tears. Oh God . . . don't let me cry, she prayed.

She had herself told him that she didn't deserve the life he had provided for her.

As far as she knew, the people from Sri Lanka were involved in something shady. There was a mystery around Rajan too. It was true that he was leaving it all behind. But there was still a mystery. His trips to Trivandrum for instance. Outwardly, he ran a travel agency. But he did something shady behind that as well. So, there could well be dangers surrounding him, as his mother said. But he mattered the most. If he needed to leave her behind, let him go. If that was the sacrifice she had to make, she would do it. She wasn't the fighting kind. Her life had been too good, just as she had feared.

Maheswari could see that she was recovering from the shock. "Now . . . the only way we can save him, is to send him overseas somewhere. Never mind what country it is. If he can get to a country where he is safe, and he can live without fearing for his life, that's enough for me."

She began playing it up a little. "Even if my child is out of my sight, I have to bear it and do what's best for him. Are you going to say, 'I need a husband, my child needs a father' and keep him here and let him be sacrificed? Or are you going to let him go, so that he can be safe, wherever he is? I need an answer now."

It was only then that Amba began to cry. Losing track of reality . . . losing all understanding of language . . . a silence fell on her like a stone. She knew now she had been cut out. There was no going back . . . not anymore.

She had at one time lived with the thought that they might be separated one day by his mother, or his sibling . . . by his relatives. It had finally come now.

Whether his mother was telling the truth or not, she had no choice but to agree. As far as she knew of their lives, she needn't assume it was a lie. Even if it were a lie, she didn't have the strength to fight it. She had been weakened at the core.

Seeing her still unmoving, Maheswari turned to Krishnan.

Krishnan called out to her. "Amba, we can't remain like this. What is your reply?"

Amba came back to reality. She looked at Viswalingam. She saw a fury in his eyes. It gave her a sense of peace. He was seething at the injustice being inflicted on her because he saw her as a woman, as someone deserving mercy. She turned calmly toward Maheswari. "Send him. As long as he's safe somewhere, that's enough for me. The child and I will survive somehow," she said.

She shed tears. They flowed like fire.

Contentment was written all over Maheswari's face.

"Then, you'll go back to your village in a day or two?" Krishnan interjected, not losing track of the reason they had come there.

She agreed.

It was only then that she seemed a little angry.

Maheswari's heart rejoiced that it all seemed to be working out beautifully. And then something seemed to diminish her before Amba. She felt embarrassed that Amba had gone along with her lie even without setting eyes on the pouch of money she had brought along to lure her or break her. She couldn't take the money back. Neither was she so stone-hearted as to take it back. She turned to look at the pouch that they had all forgotten. She took it from Viswalingam's hands and opened it out to show her the wads of money in there and left it on the small table in front of them.

"There's two hundred thousand rupees here. Keep this."

Amba shook her head furiously, refusing it.

Viswalingam insisted. "Don't turn it down. You need it to raise your child . . . to educate him. Think of it as fate. That's the only way you can bear this tragedy. You can go back to the village you were born in . . . live in a little house . . . with no difficulties. If you put it in the bank, you can live off the interest. Get some advice from some good people you know before you act."

He didn't stand there any longer but went out into the hall.

Maheswari said, "Viswalingam anna will come back the day after tomorrow. He'll send you off to your hometown. You can give him the keys. Your jewellery . . . clothes . . . whatever cooking utensils you need, take it all with you, okay?"

The child must have woken up.

Amba went in and brought the boy out.

"Won't he come back here at all?" she asked, looking at the child to stop herself from bursting into sobs.

"Who? Rajendran? It's dangerous for him to be going here and there now, isn't it? Don't worry. I'll tell him everything."

She went out.

Krishnan followed behind her.

Amba stood rooted to the spot.

She didn't even feel sad that their sweet life together, comfortable . . . peaceful . . . like a bubble, had come to an end. People are all the same at turning into liars when it suited them. The Maharashtran was the same as the Assamese. The Malayali was the same as the Punjabi. The Sri Lankan was the same as the Indian. That amma might have given birth to my husband. But she didn't consider that the child, even if it was born to me, was also born of her child! How could she close her eyes and leave after seeing this colour . . . this face . . . this nose? Even as she snatched back her son, at the last minute, his amma could have picked up his child . . . kissed him . . . and shown me before she left that it was only circumstances that brought us to this. It's enough for me to have his memory . . . enough to live on.'

Another knot of mystery came to her. Where was the link between her fate to bear a child to a Lankan Tamil, and his fate to come to India as a refugee?

Or was it that fate was the same everywhere every time?

Time murmured in the sounds of the wind.

50

Chennai, India

MAHESWARI FELT A GREAT sense of satisfaction at having accomplished her task. But her sense of satisfaction remained incomplete. She had to pass through another obstacle first.

A short while after she had returned to Chennai, washed, and sat down to eat, she heard someone shouting from next door: "Mala . . . phone . . . Canada phone!" She dropped the food from her hand, stood up in a hurry and ran to the bathroom to plunge her hand in a bucket of water to rinse it before rushing next door.

The news she heard plucked away her excitement.

At nine o'clock, she went out to the public call office and called Chandramohan.

"Amma . . . when did you come back? How was Bombay?" he asked animatedly.

She was not in a mood to chat. She half replied to him, and half laughed. "We came back just this morning. Thambi, I need to speak to you urgently."

He told her he was on his way out.

"Then . . . tomorrow morning?"

"I'll come for sure."

Before she hung up, she asked: "There was some talk that Suthan might accompany you when you come?"

"That's true. But Prabu asked him to come to Germany at the last minute, and he went there. Whether he comes here depends on the answer we give him."

Maheswari called Raji afterwards and asked her to come by with Kamala that afternoon.

When Raji arrived, she saw her mother's condition and asked: "What is it amma, you don't look right . . . ? Are you not well?"

"Nothing wrong with me . . . I'm fine . . . I'm just worried. I got a phone call from Viji this morning."

"What did she say?"

"Viji is going to need a caesarean. I have been worried ever since I heard it."

"These are small operations over there, akka, nothing to worry about," Kamala reassured her.

"That may be true. But I have been with her for the past twelve years, and to not be there at a time like this, when she's about to have an operation . . . that's what . . . ," Maheswari replied. Then she turned to Raji. "What's Rajendran doing?"

"He's at home. He's watching a film on the VCR.," she said. She felt she shouldn't hide the information and steeled herself to add that Rajan had been out drinking the previous few nights.

Maheswari shook her head but remained silent. After a while she told them what had happened in Mumbai, giving them a shortened version of events, and leaving out anything that could be upsetting. It seemed as if she was telling Raji that only her matters needed to be seen to. Raji felt a tremor in her chest.

There had been a cat that once gave birth to four kittens in their house on the island. Two of the kittens had gone missing somehow, in the first month, and only two remained. Then they were down to one kitten. It was Rajendran who had brought the cat home, when it was a kitten, saying it was a beautiful cat. Maheswari had shouted at him, "It looks like a female kitten, take it back and get rid of it." "No amma, it's a male kitten," Rajan had insisted. "If it's a female, get rid of it," Maheswari had said and left it at that. When the cat had kittens, she started again. But when was Rajendran ever going to listen to her? After telling him a hundred times and tiring of it, she put the mother cat and kitten into a bag and took them away herself. She took them as far as the marketplace so that they wouldn't return under any circumstances. When she saw her mother return without the cats, Raji had begun to cry. She had felt a physical anguish at the thought of the suffering cats. She was reminded of that incident now, seeing its parallel. Again, amma had "abducted" a mother and child and returned, unaffected by it.

Poobathy brought them some tea. Maheswari drank it and went upstairs to the balcony. Raji followed her, unbidden. Kamala stood up slowly.

The surroundings were beautiful. But neither was in the mood to appreciate it. The trees and buildings had been washed by the heavy rain the previous night and looked fresh and new. The breeze still held a dampness.

Maheswari began, "I have asked Chandramohan to come here tomorrow . . . "

"Amma . . . that . . . "

"You don't need to say anything. You had a week to think about it. There's nothing here to think about, anyway. Wasn't this the life you chased after? Does it make sense to turn it down now? Try to put aside your rudeness and stubbornness and try to think a little in your life from now on. It looks like Suthan is not the same as he was either. Going back to Suthan is the right thing for you to do."

"No, amma . . . "

"It's no use waiting for you to decide anymore. Okay, you go. I'll take care of my own fate now . . . "

Raji was startled by her determination. "No amma . . . tomor-row morning . . . "

"What about tomorrow morning? Tell me now."

"I'll be coming back here tomorrow. I'll tell you then."

Maheswari calmly peered through the spreading darkness and looked into her daughter's eyes. The fear of what her mother might do was clearly written there. She could wait one night. "Alright. You will give me an answer. And you will only give me a positive answer. Go."

She went downstairs.

Raji and Kamala didn't stay upstairs much longer.

It was nine-thirty by the time Raji got back home. She spread out her mat as soon as she got back and lay down. She didn't even eat. Seeing her state on the bus ride back, Kamala called her for dinner once, and left her alone when she didn't come.

Amma had clearly told her the answer she expected. She had forced the reply on her as she was leaving as well.

She had to go back in the morning and say what she had decided. She had thought through all of it. But her mother's rigid-ity made her fearful and forced her to rethink her own decisions.

"Yogesh, won't you come?" He wouldn't. She knew it. He was not hers anymore. It's what she had wanted. But she felt saddened at the thought that he wouldn't come back. He had been her legs, doing things she couldn't do herself. She needed him now to help her flee this place. She felt defeated, knowing it was impossible now.

She had always loved life. She had had beautiful dreams. In her mind, love was balanced by thoughtfulness and stayed within the bounds of tradition and propriety. Her sense of playfulness had still stayed in line with a way of life that brooked no discord. She had redeemed herself every time she fell from grace. That was something to be happy about. But was this a fall to be rescued from?

She felt that she needed some tea. She got up and made herself a cup and sat at the table with it, looking out through the window.

She liked this room. It reminded her of her room in their home on the island. It was about the same size. There were trees outside here too. And, occasionally, squirrels and parrots.

Her eyes teared up at the memory.

What did it really mean when they said, "the sky had spread out"? Didn't it mean that they had crossed a boundary? Not just that. But that the sky was the same colour everywhere. Fire burns the same anywhere. A breeze is pleasant anywhere. Water tasted the same anywhere. Rain falls the same. But the soil? Home?

Nagabooshani guarded her soil.

That island, surrounded by sea spray, where the seven rivers separated with resounding noise; Arasi had told her it was still the same. Some faces had gone, some faces had grown, some faces had arrived recently, that was all the change it had gone through. The land had not changed. Its fecundity had not changed.

"I came here in search of him. If he is no longer, what do I have here? Arasi has left Kachai. I have the island. The farm garden. The paddy plot. If I tend the garden I can survive. I'm just a burden on others if I stay here," Valambikai had said one day.

"I came to bring you back home too. What else do I have here?" Arasi had replied.

What drew them home?

Something within her drew her to the island too. But amma was behind her pulling her back.

"Nagabooshani Ammale!" she cried. "You . . . only you . . . you are the goddess who can save me."

In these times of distress and hopelessness, it was natural to lose faith in human beings.

Raji drank her tea and lay back down.

She fell asleep after a long time.

Yet, just moments after, she felt as though someone awoke her by whispering in her ear. "And who is there for me? I only have you. I eased your sense of uselessness, Raji. But I am a lonely man. I am a lonely man."

51

Chennai, India

COULD HER EYELIDS BE so heavy? Though she was awake, she could not open her eyes. She forced them open and turned towards the window to see the dark of the night still lingering in the morning.

Somewhere in that little town, a cock crowed.

She felt miserable when she remembered that she had to go to Anna Nagar.

She was going to refuse this. But she had to go there to do it. If she stayed away because she was afraid, amma wouldn't bother with a phone call. She would get into an auto and come here.

She resolved to go and had got herself dressed when dawn arose.

Kamala woke up and brought her some coffee she had made.

The light and the sounds disturbed Rajan's sleep as well. He had not gone out the previous night and must have gone to sleep sober. "Kamala akka, some coffee for me too," he asked.

As he sat on the sofa drinking his coffee, he turned to Raji. "What are you going to say to amma, akka?"

Could she say, "If amma wants to climb the Anna Nagar tower

and jump off, then let her; I'm not going to abide by this woman's wishes?" It was, in a way, what she was going to say. It didn't mean she had to tell him about it now.

She finished her coffee and stood up, "I'll say something and sort it out," she said. "There's a bus now, isn't there, akka?" she walked away without waiting for a reply.

As she got closer to Mala's house, Raji noticed an auto parked outside. Chandramohan had arrived so early in the morning! She had hoped to get there, deliver her answer, and leave before he arrived, and she felt panicked knowing that it wasn't possible anymore.

It was only once she passed through the gate that Raji realized the house was blanketed in silence. Arasi and Valambikai were here too. Had Chandramohan brought them with him, or had they sent an auto for them after he arrived? What was their plan? What was the strategy here? She couldn't figure it out.

Viswalingam was standing in the verandah, leaning on a pillar, facing indoors. He hadn't even noticed Raji walk up behind him.

Everyone was gathered there. Even the children seemed frightened and weren't rushing around getting ready for school. Chandramohan looked blank. It was shock.

Seeing Raji in the doorway, it was Arasi who came rushing to tell her the news: "Someone shot Prabu in Germany . . . in a restaurant."

"Aah!"

"He died on the spot. And Suthan was with him. He was also hit . . . "

Raji looked up into Arasi's face. Was there shock in her expression?

Arasi continued: "Though he was hit they said on the phone that he's not in any danger. It was midnight when he heard Chandramohan's news. He waited until dawn and just came to tell us. We got dressed immediately and came here."

Arasi and Raji went inside and sat down on the floor, leaning against the wall.

Valambikai's whimpers broke the unrelenting silence.

Maheswari sat down beside her and attempted to comfort her: "The police in Germany are not like the ones back home. They would have caught the shooters by now."

"When Chandramohan asked them, they said they don't know who the shooters are . . . !"

"So what? They'll catch them soon. Once they know who and what, they'll provide some security for Suthan as well. You don't need to worry about Suthan. Why are you crying?"

Chandramohan had said that there had been a target on Prabu. Why was Suthan targeted? Was he shot by accident because he was with Prabu? Was this done by the Movement? Or was it some internal conflict? Or was it a strategy by a rival power to create some kind of confusion? What should she believe?

It was Chandramohan who finally broke the silence. "I'm leaving for Bombay right now. I'm going to Germany on the first flight I get. Did you know that Prabu is my own uncle? My mother's thambi. The funeral rites will be over by the time I get there, I think. But it will be a comfort to maami and Ananthi if I go and visit them. I'll be back. I'm just not sure when. But I'll be back."

He stood up. He turned around and looked at each of them, as though saying a silent goodbye. It seemed as though his gaze rested longer on Raji. Then he walked out to the auto that was waiting at the entrance.

52

Chennai, India

ONCE THE SHOCK HAD dissipated, they all dispersed. Viswalingam went to the tea shop after seeing off Chandramohan. Valambikai, Saraswathi, and Siva were in the front yard. Mala and Arasi were on the balcony. Poobathy was on her own. Senan too. The two little ones were off by themselves. Only Raji and Maheswari sat in the room, each lost in their own thoughts.

Maheswari had become discouraged when she heard that Suthan hadn't come with Chandramohan. When she heard that Suthan would come down from Germany if they managed to get Raji's consent, her hopes took on life again. Though it wouldn't have been easy to get Raji to consent, she would have found a way to wring it out of her. They were to have heard Raji's answer that morning. Just then they were hit with the blow of Prabu's death. Suthan would survive. That was important. But with Suthan injured and Chandramohan rushing to Prabu's grieving household, Raji might drag this on for even longer.

Raji stood up. "I'm going home now, and I'll see you later, amma?" she said. "Are you going straight home?" Maheswari asked. "No. I'll go see Rajanayagam sir before I take the bus back," she replied.

Raji left around ten o'clock. She felt slightly feverish.

Once Raji went home and lay down, it took her two days to get up again. Maheswari and Arasi came to visit her. Raji had recovered somewhat and walked slowly. She was seated in the hall watching television.

Rajendran and Viswalingam had gone to Mumbai the previous day. Maheswari had told him to sell the house and the travel agency. Gajen took over the travel agency, but only paid him half of what it was worth. They asked Krishnan for his help in selling the house. Rajendran didn't go by the house at all. He stayed in a hotel and asked them to bring him the documents for signing. They sold the place in a hurry. So, they didn't get what the house was worth either. When they got back to Chennai, Rajan took the money to Maheswari, who said, "It will be difficult for you to stay here, I know. But you can visit frequently, can't you?"

"Goodbye, amma."

They only understood the reason for his goodbye much later.

By the third day the agent had dropped him off in Thailand.

The route to Canada went through there now.

Maheswari didn't plan to stay in Chennai for much longer. She was already worried about Viji having a cesarian.

It was Mala who had made the most effort to take care of her and act pleasantly toward her when she was in Chennai. Maheswari had delighted in her care and had even mentioned to a few people that Mala took care of her as if she were her own daughter. Sheila still sent money, but it was very irregular. The days when it arrived "ding" before the fifth of the month, were now gone. They had to call her once or twice before the money reached them eventually. But she did say that she was trying one more time to bring Siva over. Mala hoped to ask Maheswari for her help in speeding up the process even in some small part. But misfortune seemed to dog them in every effort. Prabu's death . . . Suthan being injured . . . none of this should have happened, she thought selfishly.

Saraswathi was a world unto herself, but few noticed. She had her dreams too. As soon as there was a light in Siva's life, she thought she must ask them to call Senan. There was a family from Navali who lived in Kulathur now. Their son was in Switzerland. He had got his papers. He had a good job, too. There was a man from Kalvayal who was doing some marriage brokering in Anna Nagar. She had spoken to him about Poobathy and even passed on her photo. When she went back and forth to the market, she would stop by and worship Mariyamman and pray for this one thing. Then . . . the remaining three children, one after the other. It would be a few years before they grew up.

She didn't remember the island with longing anymore. A stone house, water that came through a pipe, a bathroom connected to the house, metro water that smelled of chlorine, all these things made her forget the smell of her hut, the taste of well water, the sweetness of a breeze without the smell of engine smoke. She had even forgotten the sound of bombs. There were bombs here too. They exploded and shattered here too. But they weren't directed at her.

The change in where they lived had changed how they lived.

Time smiled and floated in the breeze.

It was the same for many of the Lankan Tamils who lived there.

It was no one's fault.

Life has a different sound in each ear.

Colombo, Sri Lanka

Thiravi stared at the paper, his mind going blank.

The rotting corpse of Sankarananda Thero, also known as the preaching bhikkhu, had been found floating in the Kelani River.

Thiravi's eyes glistened.

The burden of this grief was so great . . . he couldn't cry.

A line had been torn into history.

Notes to Book 4 and Book 5 of *Prison of Dreams*

Anula story: A story from the Sinhala *Mahavamsa*, which depicts the queen Anula of Anuradhapura in a salacious manner.

book, head change, getting an entry, exit: the smugglers' slang for passport, photo switch, entry and exit visas.

Ceylon: old (colonial} name for Sri Lanka until 1972. Many Tamils still use the name Ceylon rather than Sri Lanka, as they see latter as a symbol of the rise in Sinhala Buddhist fundamentalism.

SJV Chelvanayakam: A Tamil lawyer, politician, and Member of Parliament who found the Ilankai Tamil Arasu Katchi (otherwise known as the Federal Party) and the Tamil United Liberation Front. He was affectionately known as Thanthai Chelva (lit. Chelva, our father).

Dutugamunu: A Sinhala king (born between 100-200 BCE) who is said to have ended the Tamil domination of Anuradhapura by killing the king Ellalan.

Eelam/Tamil Eelam: The independent state that many rebel groups hoped to form.

IPKF: International Peace Keeping Force, sent by India to Sri Lanka to help maintain a ceasefire. They eventually commited atrocities and aided the further fragmentation of the Tamil Movements.

JR Jayawardene: the former president of Sri Lanka, belonging to the United National Party; he was president during the pogroms of 1983.

JVP: Janatha Vimukthi Peramuna (People's Liberation Front), a Communist party formed in 1965 by Rohana Wijeweera. The group conducted two armed insurgencies against the Government of Sri Lanka, in 1971 and in 1987-9, with the aim of creating a socialist state.

Kantha Puranas: also known as Skanda Puranas, referring to Murugan, the son of Siva and Parvati. It is a sacred text composed by Kachiyapper, a Tamil scholar of Sanskrit, and refers to cosmology, pilgrimages, and the nature of right and wrong.

LTTE: Liberation Tigers of Tamil Eelam, a rebel group founded by Velupillai Prabhakaran in 1976, to secure the independent state of Tamil Eelam in the north and east of Sri Lanka.

Movement: The word *Movement* originally referred to the Tamil struggle in general but went on to refer to the various rebel groups in the Tamil struggle. It eventually came to refer solely to the Liberation Tigers of Tamil Eelam, after they eliminated or disbanded the other groups.

Mawbima Surakimu Viyaparaya: Sinhala fundamentalist Buddhist organization.

Nainativu: Also known as Naga Nadu (lit. snake land/island) in Tamil, and Nagadipa in Sinhala, a home of the ancient tribe of Naga (snake worshipping) people indigenous to South India and Sri Lanka. It is one of the small islands forming a cluster near the Northern Peninsula of Jaffna. It is a site of great historical and mythical significance and is referred to in the ancient Tamil Sangam epics Kundalakesi and Manimekalai as Manipallavam.

Prabhakaran: Velupillai Prabhakaran, the founder and leader of the LTTE until his death in 2009.

Special Task Force: A tactical unit of the Sri Lankan Police devised for covert operations, they are responsible for a large number of extra-judicial disappearances and killings.

Tamil Rehabilitation Organization: A group founded in 1985 by Tamils who had fled the violence in the north and east of Sri Lanka.

Theepavali: Festival of lights, celebrated by Hindus in November. It carries different meanings for Hindus of different areas and is also criticized as a celebration of the suppression of indigenous tribes.

TULF: Tamil United Liberation Front, a political party formed by SJV Chelvanayakam in 1972.

Mattavilasa Prahasana (Sanskrit): "A Farce of Drunken Sport," a one-act satire written by the Pallava king Mahendravarman in Tamil Nadu, India.

Pathmanaba: A founder of the Tamil rebel group the Eelam People's Revolutionary Liberation Front (EPRLF) who was assassinated by the LTTE in 1990.

settlement schemes: shortly after independence, the Sri Lankan government began giving land to Sinhala farmers in the more fertile regions of the country. While a small number of Tamils and Muslims also benefitted from these schemes, they predominantly worked to change the demographics of traditionally Tamil-dense areas.

Dravida Kazhakam: a caste abolitionist social movement begun by Periyar that called for an independent nation called Dravida Nadu. It gave birth to the political group Dravida Munnetra Kazhakam and All India Anna Dravida Munnetra Kazhakam.

Periyar: E V Ramasamy, called Periyar and Thanthai Periyar, was a caste abolitionist and an advocate of the self-respect movement in Tamil Nadu.

Muslim expulsion: the forced eviction from the northern province of more than 72,000 Muslims by the LTTE in 1990.

"We rose up to live": a line from V I S Jayapalan's well-known Tamil poem *Uyirthezhuntha naatkal* (Resurrection Days), written just after the riots of 1983.

PTA: Prevention of Terrorism Act, a draconian legislation passed by the Government of Sri Lanka in 1979 that became a tool for arbitrary detention and persecution of minorities, protestors, insurgents, and rebels.

Sons of the Soil: Sinhalaye Mahasammatha Bhoomiputhra Pakshaya (The Great Consensus Party of the Sons of the Soil of Sinhala) was a Sinhala Buddhist Fundamentalist nationalist party formed in 1990.

Sinhala Bala Mandalaya: a Sinhala Buddhist Party formed in 1981.

Bhoomiputhra pakshaya: formerly the Sinhalaye Mahasammatha Bhoomiputhra Pakshaya, Motherland People's Party, a Sinhala Buddhist Political party formed in 1990.

Sangha: monastic order of Buddhism, which along with the Buddha and the dharma are the basic creed of Buddhism, the threefold refuge.

Madhyamika Buddhist: the Middle Way, a school of Mahayana Buddhism, founded by the Indian monk and philosopher Nagarjuna, which recognizes truth as existing on two planes: the everyday (quotidian reality) and the ultimate (emptiness).

Parinirvana: "nirvana after death"; as one who attains nirvana in life continues into nirvana after death, they are released from the cycles of rebirth.

Q branch: a wing of the CID of Tamil Nadu police, originally formed for surveillance of the Naxal Movement.

Glossary

aacchi: grandmother or elderly woman

ahimsa: the Buddhist precept of nonviolence

aiyya, appa: father

aiyya (Sinhala): older brother

acharu: a mix of raw fruit with salt and chillie powder

akka: older sister

amma: mother

anna, annan, annai (affectionately): older brother

asoka tree: (lit. without sorrow) an evergreen tree believed to promote happiness

asura: a demon

ayubowan: a formal Sinhala greeting

bhikkhu: Buddhist monk. Also "hamaduru"

billa: a demon or bogeyman

bo tree: a tree considered sacred in Buddhism because the Buddha is believed to have attained nirvana under it

Daathu: the tenth year in the Tamil calendar cycle of sixty years. In this instance it refers to the great famine of 1876 in Tamil Nadu, India, brought about by poor distribution of food and monocultures under the British rule

double: two riders on a bicycle or motorcycle. Sometimes a motorcyclist would ride with a gun-carrying pillion rider to carry out assassinations or to intimidate people

ganga: river

heli: helicopter

iluppai: madhuca longifolia, or butter tree, whose nuts are used for the extraction of an emollient oil, and flowers are used for making an alcoholic beverage

kanchi: water in which rice has been boiled, or a thin porridge of rice or other grain

Kanthapuranam: A Saiva religious epic featuring the god Skanda redeeming the celestial beings from demons

karaiyar: a Lankan Tamil caste of Tamil people from the north and east who are associated with fishing and seafaring

Kathirgamam/Kataragama: a town famous for its shrine considered sacred by Saivites, Buddhists, and indigenous tribes of Lanka, where Kandasamy Murugan/Skanda or Kataragama is worshipped

Kavadi: a burden carried during a ceremonial dance as an act of penance, asking for blessings

Kelani/Kalyani River: a river stretching from the Siri Pada mountain range to Colombo, it has both Sinhala and Tamil names

kiluvai: commiphora caudata, or hill mango (though its fruit are not similar to the mango)

koburam: an ornately carved and often painted tower that is part of the traditional Hindu temple design

korai grass: Cyperus rotundus, also known as nut grass

kotiyas: tigers, referring to the LTTE

Lankapuri: an ancient name for Sri Lanka from the Ramayana

maama: maternal uncle, or father-in-law

maame (Sinhala): uncle

maami: paternal aunt, or mother-in-law

maaveeran: a hero; in this context someone who dies in the Movement.

machan: male cousin, also slang for close friend

machaal: female cousin or sister-in-law

malaivembu: mountain neem or margosa tree of the mahogany family

Manthikai and Nayanmarkaddu: places known for holistic treatment centres and a hospital

maravali kilangu: cassava tubers

Mareesan: the rakshasa who takes the form of a deer to lure Rama away from his wife in the Ramayana

marutham: arjun tree

mavilanga tree: crateva religiosa, also known as the sacred garlic pear or temple plant

Menik/Manikka River: a river stretching from the Namunukula mountain range down to the Indian Ocean through Yala National Park. It has both Sinhala and Tamil names.

mulmurunga: also known as Indian the Coral tree or Kalyana Murungai (wedding murungai)

Mutraveli: Mutraveli Appa shrine in Jaffna

nanthiyavettai: tabernaemontana divaricata, also known as pinwheel flower

neytal: the coastal land referred to in ancient Tamil Sangam poetry

odiyal: tuber from the roots of the palmyrah tree

oththu or **ottu**: a double reed wind instrument that produces a low droning sound, it often accompanies the higher pitched nathaswaram

paalai: manilkara hexandra tree whose wood is dense and often used for furniture

paatti: grandmother

Panchangam: Hindu calendar and almanac

pansala: Buddhist monastery

Pillaiyaar: the Tamil name for Lord Ganesh

Saamathiyam: puberty ceremony

Sanghamitta: the daughter of the emperor Ashoka, who became a bhikkuni (Buddhist nun) and went to Lanka to spread Buddhism in the mid 200s BCE.

Sannathiyan, sannathi: a sanctum where one is meant to experience the nearness of the deity

seettu: a local cooperative buying system where members pool money and take turns withdrawing amounts to make larger purchases than they could make individually

sempu: a metal vessel for holding water

siddhas: the liberated souls (Sanskrit), or masters who have attained nirvana

Somasuntharam or **Somapala**: the former is a Tamil name, the latter is a Sinhalese name, so it implies that they couldn't confirm if Soma was Sinhala or Tamil

thaali: a necklace tied around the bride's neck during the wedding ceremony

thambi: younger brother

Thamilarasi: Tamil queen, or queen of Tamil

thangachi: younger sister

thattivaan: a truck with a large, sheltered carriage for transporting passengers.

theeva: derived from the word *theeviravaatham* which means "terrorism"

thero: senior Buddhist monk

thetha: Strychnos potatorum, also known as clearing nut tree

thevadiyal: whore

Thevakumaran: a name meaning "godly prince." *Thevar* means "gods"

undiyal: an informal money remittance system set up by community members

vaakai: lebbek tree

vanakkam: "hello" (lit. "salutations")

visvasam: faith

vembu: neem or margosa tree

verty: cloth tied around the waist, worn by men

Vesak: a festival celebrating the birth, death, and enlightenment of Buddha

vihara: Buddhist temple

The Translator

NEDRA RODRIGO was born in Sri Lanka and came to Canada during the civil war. She is a translator, poet, workshop organizer, and community capacity builder, currently serving on the Board of the Tamil Community Centre project. She is the founder of the Tamil Studies Symposium at the York Centre for Asian Research at York University and founder and host of the bilingual, inclusive literary event series, the Tam Fam Lit Jam.

Nedra's poetry and essays have been published in various anthologies. Her poetry translations have been published in *Human Rights and the Arts in Global Asia; Jaggery Lit; Words and Worlds; Still We Sing: Voices on Violence Against Women*. Her translation of the memoir *In the Shadow of a Sword*, was published by SAGE YODA Press, India (2020); and her draft translation of Kuna Kaviyazhakan's novel *The Forest that Took Poison* (Nanjunda Kaadu) was shortlisted for the inaugural Global Humanities Translation Prize.